DEADLY SAFARI

'*Deadly Safari* has everything anyone could want: suspense, real people as characters, and real, untamed Africa out there in the darkness.' Tony Hillerman

In exotic, romantic Kenya, it's suddenly open season on rich tourists when murder shatters their paradise . . .

About to embark on the safari of a lifetime are two wealthy businessmen, Boyce and Al, manufacturers of Wild and Free shampoo, with an ageing wife apiece. They are accompanied by Cliff and Lynn, ingratiating representatives of Wild and Free's advertising agency. And Candy, a tall, blonde, and beautiful model.

Two of them will soon be dead.

Faced with these extremely alarming developments, Jazz Jasper admits that her first run as an independent safari guide might also be her last. But every animal, even a desperate two-legged one, leaves a trail, and Jazz, hardly certain whether she is hunter or game, sets about trapping a remorseless and deadly human predator.

DEADLY SAFARI

KARIN McQUILLAN

**MACMILLAN
LONDON**

First published 1990 by St Martin's Press, Inc., New York

First published in Great Britain 1993 by Macmillan London Limited
a division of Pan Macmillan Publishers Limited
Cavaye Place London SW10 9PG
and Basingstoke

Associated companies throughout the world

ISBN 0–333–59950–0

1 3 5 7 9 8 6 4 2

A CIP catalogue record for this book is available from
the British Library

Printed by Mackays of Chatham, PLC, Chatham, Kent

To the wild animals of Africa
and the brave struggle
to save them from extinction

ACKNOWLEDGEMENTS

I want to thank the women in my writers' group, whose support and feedback enabled me to write this book; Alan Feldman and Arthur Edelstein, for their excellent instruction in the art and craft of writing; my enthusiastic first readers, Jean McCann and Karen Lewis; my editor, Jesse Cohen, for loving my book and helping me make it even better; my husband, John, fellow adventurer on safari and patient helper with the manuscript; my father, who taught me to love Africa; and my mother, who taught me to love mysteries.

1

I WATCHED BOYCE Darnell push his way out of his tent and stride up to the Land Rover. "Miss Jasper, the keys." His voice boomed across the clearing and echoed back from the rocky cliff opposite us.

I followed slowly, trying to keep the dread out of my face. Were we about to have another Boyce Darnell temper tantrum? Yesterday's was enough for the whole trip, as far as I was concerned. Boyce pulled open the door and climbed into the driver's seat.

I put my foot on the running board and looked up at Boyce. He held out his hand for the car keys.

"Chris Mbare keeps the keys, Mr. Darnell. It's his job to drive the game runs—"

"I'll drive tonight. I don't like being in the passenger seat, never have."

"I know what you mean." I kept my voice even. "Let me think what I can do." Nothing came to me. Jazz Jasper Safaris was going to have a short life unless I learned how to deal with demanding clients. I had to deflect him. "How's this: When we get back to the game lodge on Thursday, I'll arrange what they call a self-drive car for you."

"Self-drive?" Boyce glared. There were starbursts of broken red veins on his nose and cheeks, like tiny explosions of anger. "I have enough of that already. I'm in the mood to drive."

"Sorry," I said, "but the Land Rover is not for the guests' use." He was nothing but a big male baboon, I told myself, rampaging through a troop, teeth bared, throwing sticks, asserting his dominance. The smaller baboons ran, or cringed and gibbered. I'd be damned if I would let Boyce start me gibbering. I turned and moved a few paces away. It would be harder for him to come down from the driver's seat if I watched.

The Rover was parked at the edge of camp, where the dirt track we'd followed for several hours last night ended at the bottom of a slope. The campsite was my favorite in the Serengeti, and I'd purposefully chosen it as the grand finale for the tour. All around us were the grasslands of Masai Mara, broad, rolling, punctuated by rock outcrops and distant blue hills. We were enclosed in the arms of a stream bend that created a flat area where I had arranged the tents in a line. Tall gum trees, supported by the year-round water, provided shelter from the heat of the day. It was at this campsite, just a year ago, that I'd concocted my scheme to have my own safari company, and now here we were, about to finish the first trip. I could hardly believe my good fortune.

Things had worked out pretty well considering I'd come to Africa with nothing more in my head than a childhood fantasy of Mowgli the Jungle Boy. Jazz Jasper Safaris gave me a way to stay in Kenya as long as I wanted, my own boss, living on my own terms. The world of academia, of art history, of people, cities, and museums belonged to another lifetime. I missed my friends, but thinking about my past life made me feel schizophrenic, so I didn't think about it much. I'd come to Africa to run away, after splitting up with my husband, not to run toward anything; I'd ended up finding in the world of nature a beauty and peace that I'd never dreamed possible.

The camp was quiet and almost seemed deserted. At this hour, the rays of the sun streamed low through the eucalyptus branches. It was still hot, and the air vibrated with the high thrumming of insects. They were probably something pedestrian, like grasshoppers, but they added to the African

2

atmosphere. Grasshoppers back home never seemed this loud. Molezzi, waiter and general factotum, hummed as he emerged from the dining tent with the cups and saucers from afternoon tea. No one else was in sight. It didn't look as if I'd have a full car for the evening's game run.

This first tour group was hardly your typical batch of tourists, which was exactly what I wanted. Tourism is a very competitive business, and as a one-woman outfit, I figured my only chance was to run customized trips at prices the big guys couldn't afford to offer. The hard part was getting my name out. When an old friend tracked me down, Jazz Jasper Safaris was about to disappear without a trace unless I got a first customer, and fast.

Lynn and I hadn't talked in years, though I'd heard of her meteoric rise in the advertising business, and she'd undoubtedly heard of my, my whatever, my ending up in Kenya. It had been quite a surprise to hear her voice, tinny but clear, over the long-distance line from New York.

"Sorry to hear about you and Adam. It seems like everyone is either getting divorced or having a baby these days . . . or both. I called that tour group you were working for and they told me you were on your own now. I may have work for you. Can you organize a custom trip for seven people? Great! I've written a fabulous ad campaign set in Africa, for Wild and Free Shampoo, and Cliff Edwards, my boss—actually, he's president of the whole agency—decided to come along with the clients, give them a treat. When we were roommates did you ever think I'd be writing TV commercials? What a laugh. It's a small agency but top-notch. I got a Cleo for my Wild and Free series last year. Anyway, we plan two weeks for location scouting, deciding exactly where we'll film and setting things up for when the film crew arrives. We'll need to nail down our establishing shots: Kilimanjaro in the background, plains of antelopes, a cheetah hunting, monkeys swinging, you know, the Tarzan bit. I'll mail you a storyboard so you'll see what I have in mind. Did I tell you seven people? It'll be me, plus Cliff, and the model, Candy Svenson—she's gorgeous, wait till you see her—and

3

the two clients and their wives. We need a luxury tour. The Hemingway touch, you know? Okay! That's what I wanted to hear. Can you do it for us right after New Year's? Great! Okay, now let's talk money.''

I'd been floating ever since. Next month, the film crew would be over to shoot the commercials, and then, who knows? If I could establish a reputation with the New York advertising agencies, it could mean my financial worries were over.

Until yesterday, the trip had been going beautifully. Despite his prima donna complaints, even Boyce Darnell, half-partner of Wild and Free Shampoo, had been expansive. The animals were so wonderful, it was hard not to respond; and Darnell had clearly enjoyed flirting with the model, despite his wife's presence on the trip. Eleanor Darnell was too sweet to complain about anything, and the other partner and his wife were enthusiastic travelers.

I looked over my shoulder. Boyce had climbed out of the Land Rover and now marched toward me with a determined look. I could feel my whole body tighten up. Boyce had a knack for making people feel he controlled their destiny, but he didn't control mine. Just keep calm, I told myself.

Above Boyce, a martial eagle floated onto a jagged nest in one of the gum trees. Its gray back and white speckled breast melded into the background like one more dappled shadow. A second eagle soared down with something in its beak—a branch; they were building a nest.

I turned to Boyce with excitement and pointed. "Mr. Darnell, there are a pair of martial eagles—"

He glanced up but failed to spot the nest.

"Jazz, let me tell you something." His voice softened. "Wild and Free started small, like your outfit, but Al and I never thought small. We aimed for the top, and we got there by satisfying the customer. I'll give you another tip. I won't even charge for it. Don't be a stickler about rules."

I sighed inwardly. It was the first time I'd seen martials nesting. "Mr. Darnell, I'm sorry that you're disappointed. I'm sure you're a superb driver."

4

The eagles began to mate, the male balanced precariously on the female's back. He opened his wings wide for balance, exposing the white primaries. The female stretched out her neck, head low. It was a fantastic sight.

The male eagle dismounted and I turned to face Boyce's tight-mouthed look. He'd missed it all. I tried once again. "Please, let us take care of you." I might as well try to reason a banana away from a baboon. "You'll be free to watch the animals. I'm pretty confident we'll see the lioness hunt tonight."

"What makes you so sure?"

"Well, the Masai say she hasn't made a kill in several days. We know she has cubs to feed, so she'll be out there tonight, trying her best."

"What's this about lions?" Lynn called out. She walked quickly. Her black chin-length hair bounced and swung with each step. She looked as if she was rushing to an important business meeting, which, in a sense, was true. Ever since yesterday's scene at the swimming pool, she'd been working overtime on Boyce.

I smiled. I always pictured Lynn rushing. We'd once lived in a collective household with nine other people. In those days, Lynn had worn her hair to her waist, a shining black waterfall. Everyone read Zen and tuned into being instead of doing, but being was not Lynn's natural pace. She'd rush off to her meditation class, then rush down to the coffeehouse to hang out, and rush on to her feminist support group. She had too much energy to do things slowly.

"Oh, Boyce," she said, "I love that cowboy shirt. Get a load of those abalone buttons! Would you believe it, with all the luggage I brought, I've started to run out of clothes. Everything gets so dusty. Thank goodness I have a lot of khaki—"

"Jasper says she's finally going to produce a kill for us," interrupted Boyce.

"Great! Educational TV, eat your heart out. We'll get it live." Lynn answered. "I hope it's not too gory, though of course I want to see everything." She smiled at Boyce. "I don't think we can use a kill scene in the campaign, but it wouldn't feel right to leave Africa without seeing a lion hunt.''

''You don't think blood and shampoo mix, young woman?'' Boyce gave a barking laugh.

Lynn's smile stretched a little thinner.

Boyce threw an arm around her. ''Well, you're the writer. Wrote a damn good ad series. Good original concept. I liked it as soon as I heard it, and I still like it. Animals are in. Wild and Free Shampoo is as natural as anything.''

He breathed into Lynn's face. ''I was telling your friend here''—he nodded toward me—''that I don't think this Jazz Jasper Safaris of hers is worth a damn. When we come back to film the commercials, I want to use a bigger company.'' Boyce smirked. ''You tell Cliff after the game run. No, I'll tell him myself.''

Lynn lost her smile completely now. ''Mr. Darnell, I'm sorry to hear you're not happy.'' She glanced worriedly at me. I shrugged. ''Is it anything I can help you with?''

I could see her mind work. Cliff would not be pleased. Lynn had taken a risk when she suggested they use an unknown safari company run by an old friend. Cliff had trusted her. He'd even invited the clients along. I was grateful to her, and I didn't want it to blow up in Lynn's face any more than she did.

None of that meant Boyce could decide he'd drive my Land Rover.

Something else was going on. This had nothing to do with driving. Today Boyce was scapegoating me, yesterday it was Candy. Who would be fired next? Lynn?

I took a deep breath. Had Candy done something to set him off, or was she merely the first victim? Yesterday morning at Masai Mara Lodge, he'd turned on her without warning. We'd had a terrific early game run, seen a big herd of elephants bathing at a waterhole, and after breakfast most of us had gone down to the pool to sunbathe and swim ourselves. The pool was set in a tropical garden behind the lodge. An ultramarine kingfisher called in its harsh voice as it flashed overhead. I was lying on the lounge chairs with Lynn and her boss, Cliff, idly watching Candy do her mile laps, and melting in the sun.

Candy finished and climbed out of the water, as tall and lithe as a Watusi, but all in blond. She sat at the end of the diving board and dangled her legs over the edge as she shook the water from her hair. The various groups of tourists fell silent. A young man in Hawaiian swim trunks stared so hard he tripped over my lounge chair.

Suddenly, I heard Boyce Darnell's resonant voice from behind the hibiscus hedge.

"I don't know why Cliff hired that little tart. She's decorative, but it's the wrong look for Wild and Free. Not like Cliff. Terrible lapse in taste."

Candy's head snapped around. Her blue eyes narrowed. I looked at Cliff and Lynn. They were as startled as I was.

"Oh, Cliff, there you are. Dammit, I've been looking all over for you." Boyce strode into the pool area. His well-muscled chest, covered with curly gray hair, quivered slightly with each step. His wife, Eleanor, trailed behind him.

"Dear, I'll be here at the bar with the Harts," she told him in her high little voice. Eleanor's face was set, as usual, in a sweet, semi-anxious expression. She perched on a stool next to Madge Hart, the other partner's wife, and whispered an order to the barman.

Boyce didn't acknowledge Eleanor's defection. He marched to the foot of Cliff's lounge chair. "Why are you always lying around when I need you? You're supposed to be working for me, not working on your tan."

"Boyce, something seems to be troubling you." Cliff was smooth as water. He stood, showing off a flawless tan and bikini trunks the same color as his blond hair. It was hard to believe he was the same age as Boyce. "Let's go where we can have some privacy, and you tell me all about it."

Cliff moved toward a bench under a striped awning at the far end of the pool. He was master at diffusing confrontations, but this time Boyce was unstoppable. Although he followed Cliff to the bench and allowed himself to be served a cold drink, he spoke in a voice calculated to carry.

"I want to know why you invited that pinhead along, Cookie or Candy or whatever she calls herself."

"Surely you mean pinup?"

The attempt at humor was a miscalculation. Boyce's voice rose higher. "I want her out. Her looks are all wrong. She's not the type for shampoo. We need someone who looks clean, not like a trumped-up tart.'

The night before, Boyce had been plying Candy with champagne in the bar long after his wife had gone to bed. It seemed his big move on Candy had gone sour.

Candy sprang to her feet. She stalked the length of the pool, full of contained energy, like a lioness moving in for the kill. She stopped in front of Boyce. "You've got a lot of nerve, Mr. Darnell, but you don't know who you're messing with."

"I was not speaking to you, Cookie."

"I'm warning you." Candy's voice shook. "Don't you try to put me down in public or anywhere else. I'm not a cookie, and I don't crumble. You don't insult me and get away with it."

Boyce pretended she wasn't there. "As I was saying, Cliff, the whole idea we're trying to get across is quality. Nothing but the best. Get rid of her."

Afterward, Madge Hart had talked to Candy, and Al Hart had talked to Boyce, and it was agreed Candy would finish the location scouting trip with us but would not be hired for the job. Everyone had been acting very civilized since the fight, but now it seemed Boyce was itching for a showdown with me, too.

Lynn tried another smile, which Boyce didn't return. "Is there something you want? If you don't like the camp, we could—"

"Mr. Darnell is a bit unhappy right now because I won't let him drive on the game run." I looked toward the tents. No one would come to rescue me. I had to decide this on my own. "I can't take the chance. We'll cover some very rough

8

terrain tonight. You have to know how to handle your vehicle around the animals."

"You're darn right I'm unhappy."

"I'm sorry, I can't compromise on this. I don't think you understand, Mr. Darnell." My voice sounded calm; I hoped my face was equally bland. "We have animals here that can pick up that entire Land Rover with everyone in it and fling it into a tree."

I did my best at a conciliatory smile and marched off toward the tents, leaving Lynn to soothe his ruffled feathers.

A tittering sound came from near the cook tent. I headed that way. A few steps farther and I could see between the tents into the central work area, a circle of hard-beaten earth surrounded by the staff sleeping tents. The kitchen was a cluster of tables, a portable stove, and a kerosene refrigerator set under a canvas roof.

Ibrahima, the cook, a robust man with dark pockmarked skin, plunged out of his tent as he pulled on a pair of pants. A T-shirt saying VISIT DISNEY WORLD barely stretched across his belly. It was undoubtedly a gift he'd requested—off the back of a former tourist. Ibrahima's mobile features were twisted into a clown's mask of delighted anticipation.

None of the staff was watching Ibrahima's contortions. I noticed Molezzi bent over in suppressed laughter, focusing his attention on something in the guest's half of camp. The others, too, were craning their necks to peer past the dining tent. I turned to see what they were staring at.

Candy Svenson had emerged from her afternoon nap. She stood framed by the tent awning. A mane of tawny hair stood out wildly from her head. A yellow robe with enormous padded shoulders and bird tracks all over it hung open and revealed a skintight green satin nightgown underneath. She stepped forward and stretched languorously.

You would never accuse the woman of being shy; but why be shy when you looked like that?

Molezzi rushed past me with a steaming kettle and filled the canvas sink outside Candy's tent. Candy bent over and splashed her face with the heated water. Molezzi watched as if memorizing her, his triangular face serious and intent. I smiled to myself. If Candy was alone in the middle of the Sahara, men would pop up out of the dunes to ogle her. She straightened and patted her face carefully with the towel, then looked around for the first time.

"Oh, Jazz!" Candy waved and waited for me to come to her. She ignored the group of gaping men behind me. "Do you know who's going on the game run this evening?"

Despite the disingenuous tone, it was easy to guess the reason for her question. Since the ugly scene with Boyce, she had kept a low profile. I was surprised; I'd have predicted a series of minidramas starring Candy, with Madge Hart, the other partner's wife, in a supporting role. Maybe Madge's long talk with her after the fight had a big impact. Whatever the reason, staying in the background must have been quite a strain for Candy. The first half of the trip, she'd managed to be center stage at every opportunity. I thought of telling her I'd just been fired too, and thought better of it. Maybe my dismissal wasn't final, and telling Candy wouldn't do a bit of good. She wasn't the sympathetic type.

Candy tossed the damp face towel on one of the director's chairs. She picked up a hand mirror, applied red lipstick, and rolled her lips together to smooth it out. She threw the black and gold lipstick container onto the table, amid a jumble of other cosmetics.

"Eleanor isn't coming," I told her, "and neither is Cliff. So it'll be Boyce, the Harts, and Lynn. Do you want to come? Boyce is impatient to start."

I glanced into Candy's open tent. There was a metallic blue leotard on top of her unmade bed, along with glossy skin-colored tights, and a headphone cassette player. Not the usual outfit for a game run.

Candy pushed the pile of makeup around on the table, found her mascara wand, and, with a few swift strokes, turned her lashes from blond to navy blue. It made her sapphire eyes looker bluer, something I wouldn't have thought possible.

10

Candy spoke into the mirror. "No, I think I'll let this one pass. I haven't worked out since Nairobi, and it's beginning to show." She lowered the mirror and tried to catch a roll of flesh on her midriff, except there wasn't anything to catch.

"You look fantastic, Candy. What are you talking about? You don't have to worry about getting fat. You barely eat as it is."

"Yeah, thanks to my secret weapon—my good old diet pills. Otherwise, I have the appetite of a farm girl, which is what I'll look like if I don't watch it." She puffed out her cheeks to demonstrate.

"Right. You look as much like a farm girl as Mick Jagger. Well, be careful and pace yourself. It's not just the heat—we're a mile up here."

"Are you kidding?" Candy slipped off the oversize robe and tossed it over the other chair. Her bare arms were a pale golden color, muscled and slender. "I'm used to working out four hours a day. Those diet pills are much worse for you. They're basically legal speed. I only use them on the road." She pulled back the mosquito net, walked into the tent, and picked up the leotard. Its shiny fabric hung in limp folds. "I wish we could jog here—running with the lions, living free."

"Running from lions—not so much fun. You're better off sticking to exercise in the camp."

The Kenyans were going to love watching this. What would they make of aerobics? They'd probably think Candy was practicing a ritual dance for membership in some secret society. Maybe she was, come to think of it.

I retreated from the tent entrance. "I have to collect the rest of our crew and get going. We'll be back after dusk."

Candy didn't look up. "See ya. Oh, could you let down that tent flap for me?"

I unhooked the tent door so it fell closed, hiding Candy as she reached for the hem of her nightgown.

Eleanor Darnell was sitting in the shade of her tent veranda, bent over a pad of pink airmail stationery, with a glass of iced tea on the table in front of her. She was wearing a shirtwaist dress with tiny bouquets all over it, looking like escaped wallpaper from a little girl's room. Her hair was lacquered into a stiff blond confection, defying heat and dust. You'd swear the woman didn't sweat.

"Well, you look comfortable," I said. "Can I tear you away for a game run?"

Eleanor put down her pen. "Thanks, dear. I really must write to Wendy. I missed yesterday, and you know I've been trying to send her at least a postcard every day. The time has just been flying on this trip!" She gave her sweet, worried smile. "Do you think she'll get it before we're back?"

"Sorry, I doubt it." I shook my head. "One of the staff is going in for supplies tomorrow, and he'll mail it for you, but still, you've got to count on at least two weeks."

"Of course."

"This way, she'll be getting fun surprises even after you're home." Eleanor raised a rescuing impulse even in me; no wonder she and Madge Hart, that supreme rescuer, were old friends.

I look my leave of her and set off to gather the rest of the party.

Cliff was sunbathing in butter-colored swim trunks even skimpier than my bikini bottoms. He put down his drink, carefully rearranged the towel he was using as a pillow, and pointed his classic profile toward the sun.

"Game run, Cliff?"

"Darling, can't you see I'm busy with more important things?"

"Admit it, Cliff, even you are falling in love with Kenya."

"I decided long ago only to fall in love with myself. It's safer."

I moved so that my shadow fell over Cliff's face. He opened one blue eye. "Cliff, something's gotten into Boyce again. Now he's insisting he drive the game run. I had to tell him no, and he's quite peeved."

12

"Boyce Darnell is my antidote for optimism about the human race."

"He reminds me of a hyena. Do you know how they hunt? Bite off the victim's balls. The animal goes into shock and then the pack tears it to pieces."

"Darling, you come up with the most repulsive facts."

"Boyce is starting to get to me. It helps if I think of him as a new subspecies, complete with ecosystem."

"I've never been called an ecosystem before."

"Why do you work for him?"

"Money."

"He's impossible."

"Money makes him easier to tolerate."

"How have you managed to keep his account all these years?"

"Please . . . by pure genius." Cliff smoothed an eyebrow with his pinky.

I enjoyed Cliff's gay mannerism. I'd been avoiding Americans for two years, living like a cultural hermit, and it was fun to joke around with no fear of entangling alliances. Beneath his witticisms lay a cool cynicism that wouldn't have appealed to me in former days, but since my divorce, I'd changed.

Cliff lit up a cigarette and flicked out the match with a practiced flip of his wrist. "Besides, I'm fascinated by Boyce's power; you may not have seen much of it on this trip, but the man knows how to get what he wants. If he wants you, it can be very rewarding. If not . . . well, you saw him with Candy. I don't know what Al did to stop him from sending her right home."

I found Al Hart in front of his tent gulping down a cup of hot coffee and gesturing with a half-eaten dessert roll in his other hand. A garland of camera equipment and binoculars hung around his neck, comfortably supported by his ample belly. His back was to me and he was talking animatedly to his wife, who was still in the tent. Al was loud, vulgar, uneducated, and told stupid jokes, but I liked him. His

13

warmth was genuine, and so was his enjoyment of life. Al was Al, and that was it. He and Boyce Darnell made odd partners, but judging from the success of Wild and Free, they obviously worked well as a business team.

"Have you got the canteen?" called out Madge. "I'll pack an extra scarf in case anyone needs one." She poked her head through the tent door. She had an oversize Gucci scarf covered with bright butterflies and flowers tied under her chin. "Hi, Jazz, just about ready." She popped her head back in.

Al finished his roll in one gulp. "So, what ya' going to show us today? Baby Godzilla?" He laughed.

"Well you know how it is, Al. We've just got to go out there and see."

"Reminds me of sales." He patted the video pack. "I'm taking plenty of tape today. I want to show Joey what his Grampa and Granma are up to. I got some great shots of the elephants yesterday."

Madge came out of the tent. She wore dark sunglasses and had a pith helmet on top of her scarf. She looked like Golda Meir on a bad day. "Al, you've got everything but your hat and the video camera. It's still sitting on your bed."

Al dived back into the tent. Madge saw me looking at her. "I know, I know, but at least I won't get dusty." She looked at me sharply. "Is everything okay?"

"Boyce just fired me, but otherwise, things are great."

"Oh, that man." Madge shook her head.

Al emerged from the tent in a matching pith helmet, with a video camera in one hand.

"Al, did you hear what Jazz told me? He's fired her."

"Fired who?"

"Boyce fired Jazz."

Al looked disgusted.

"Can't you do something?" Madge asked him.

Al rubbed a hand over his face and thought a moment. "Okay, let's play it like this. Jazz, as far as I'm concerned— and I know Cliff would agree—you've been doing a great job."

Madge took a step forward and laid a hand on Al's arm. "I was just telling Al what a fabulous trip it's been. It's not easy to make travel look easy, especially in a Third World country. I mean, we're not visiting Yellowstone. I can tell the planning and organization, the checking and rechecking, that goes into a smooth trip. And you make it all so interesting, too. Your enthusiasm shows."

I started to stammer my thanks.

"Yeah, I agree with Madge. Absolutely. It's been one of the best trips we've ever been on, right babe?" Al smiled at Madge and then looked solemn and shook his head. "The thing with Boyce, which I can tell you've picked up on, is not to get into a head-on confrontation. He likes feeling he's king. King of the Beasts." Al laughed. "But the bottom line with him is what's good for business. So what we're going to do right now is nothing. We'll wait till the end of the trip and see how things stand. I already told Madge, I can't do much for Candy. As far as Wild and Free, she's out. Damn shame, too. For this thing, let's wait and see. I bet it blows over. If not, I'll talk to him."

He took Madge's arm and steered her toward the Land Rover. She bent her head toward his ear. I was only a few steps behind them and could hear every word.

"I think Boyce has been getting worse, don't you? I'm worried he's going to foul things up. What are we going to do about him?"

2

So FAR, IT looked as if Al had read his partner correctly. Boyce seemed to have put defeat behind him.
He sat in the front passenger seat cracking jokes with Chris
Mbare, the driver, who was behind the wheel, much to my
relief. They were both drinking Tusker beers straight from
the bottle, which didn't please me as much. I'd talk to Chris
about drinking and driving later. I wasn't about to correct
him in front of the others.

Chris Mbare was a stocky man, invariably dressed in dark
baggy pants, a brilliant white shirt, and impenetrable sunglasses. The dark glasses gave him a sinister air that was
misleading. He was the sweetest of men, a valuable attribute
for any driver, especially in Kenya, where few people—drivers or pedestrians—seemed to understand the basic rules of
the road, which could goad a saint to mayhem. Paved roads
in Africa were still a novelty. In Masai country, south of the
Rift Valley, you were lucky to have hard-packed dirt. Each
rainy season, the roads became quagmires, and when the
ground dried again, it was congealed into fantastic textures
of ruts and ridges. To avoid the axle breakers, every drive
became a game of chicken, as cars going in each direction
borrowed the oncoming lane whenever it looked smoother.
We had done the long legs of our trip by air, but if we wanted
to see animals, we had to go by car, often without the help
of any road at all. Mbare drove with skill, diplomacy, and

aplomb. Besides, he'd been in the business long enough to have a lot of favors owed him, in the form of good tips from the other drivers on where big game had been spotted recently. I was grateful to have him.

Lynn leaned against the Land Rover and looked dreamily into the treetops. Probably scheming how to reverse Boyce's decision to dump Jazz Jasper Safaris.

"Good afternoon, Jazz," Chris Mbare greeted me in his African British accent. Two gold-capped teeth glinted when he smiled. He gave me a meaningful nod. "Mr. Darnell likes our Kenyan beer very much. He says it is bad form to drink alone."

So Boyce had bullied him into drinking. Probably to get back at me for insisting Chris drive. It didn't surprise me that Boyce was vengeful.

"Hiya, folks, how's it going?" Al released Madge's arm. "Ready for action, Boyce?" Al aimed his video camera. "Turn the bottle around so we can see the label. That's okay, Lynn, you can be in the picture. Boyce likes pretty girls around him."

Boyce obliged, hamming it up. He leaned out of the Land Rover and waved the bottle at us. Lynn turned on a grin. Fun on safari.

"This is the life!" Al exclaimed. "How do you like our new hats?" He knocked a fist against the crown of his helmet. "Dr. Livingstone, I presume, eh, wot?" He laughed, delighted with his own humor.

"More like Tweedledum and Tweedledee," Boyce said.

Al laughed, but Madge darted Boyce a sharp look. She took her hat off and extended it toward us. "Lynn, do you want to try it on? They're great sun hats. At this altitude, you have to be careful, even with your dark hair. One size fits all."

"Don't tell me they already have you on commission?" asked Lynn. "Fast work." She held up her hands. "Toss it over here."

Madge tossed the pith helmet like a Frisbee. Lynn snatched it from the air and put it on her head. "Ooh, I love it."

Al handed Madge into the Land Rover. For a medium-sized woman, everything about Madge was large: large, round, and soft. Big brown eyes, a big nose, a big smile, a big bosom. Her skin looked soft, as if your fingers would sink in a little ways. I liked to see the way Al touched her, as now when he helped her up the high step with a hand on her elbow. It looked as if he enjoyed being near her.

"Let Al and me sit in the back." She maneuvered around the middle seat. "There's more leg room in the middle for you and Lynn."

Al handed Lynn up next and clambered after her.

"Okay. All aboard?" I swung up onto the Land Rover and stuck my head through the oversize sunroof so I could spot game in all directions. "Chris, let's try the other side of the stream, on that west-facing slope. You know the one I mean? Where we saw the topi earlier."

Topi are common, but they're one of my favorite antelope. To be honest, they're all favorites, depending on which one I'm watching at the moment. I love topi because they are improbable. They remind me of a book of made-up animals I loved as a child. They're the size of a moose, with cat's eyes, purple thighs, and yellow stockings. Their big round ears are striped inside. I'd never even heard of topi before coming to Kenya. Maybe that's why I liked them so much.

I grabbed onto the edge of the roof as Chris put the Land Rover into gear. We followed the line of trees along the creek, then climbed up a short hill and left the camp behind. Golden grasses extended endlessly before us, dotted here and there with thornbushes and flat-topped acacia trees. Off in the distance, smaller dots marked a herd of wildebeest. Way off, there was a rectangular brown patch—a Masai compound built of dried manure. It was the only sign of man.

I turned my face into the wind and enjoyed the breeze through my hair. The acrid smell of dust overlaid the herbal scent of grasses warm in the sun. I breathed in deeply.

Chris drove us to the edge of a tall rocky bank and stopped. "Hold on everyone!" he cautioned. "Jazz, you, too, better sit down."

I dropped into my seat and braced myself. "This is where we ford the stream, believe it or not."

"Madge, hold on tight," Al said. "This thing is going to buck like crazy."

"I'm fine, I'm fine. You make sure you have a hold of your equipment."

The Land Rover plunged downward at a thirty-degree angle, bouncing wildly over water-rounded rocks. We hit the bottom with a splash, plowed through the shallow stream, and rushed at the steep opposite bank.

I was tossed against Lynn, despite my grip on the seat back, then flung the other way. Boyce's jacket fell to the floor. A plastic pillbox in pharmacy amber slipped out of the pocket and rolled between our legs. I grabbed for it and missed. Lynn scooped it up with one hand, stuck it in her pocket, and grabbed for the seat back before she lost her balance. Boyce was too busy holding on to the dashboard to notice.

The engine roared as the four-wheel drive caught and held the loose sand and rock. We hauled slowly to the top. A giant thornbush overhung the track. As the Land Rover ground against it, twigs and thorns rained through the sunroof.

"Great, this is just terrific," fumed Boyce. "You call this a ford?" His face was pink with heat and bad temper.

Al helped Madge pick two-inch thorns out of her clothes and hair. "Where's your sense of adventure?" he asked his partner.

"Watch it, Al. I've just about had it, you hear me?"

"Mr. Darnell, straight ahead, this is our opening shot! What a beaut," Lynn cut in.

We entered a herd of gazelle. The animals moved a few steps away, then continued to graze, creating a tunnel through which we drove. We were surrounded by the long-necked elegant creatures, close enough to see their wet noses glisten and to admire the red-gold softness of their coats. A termite nest blocked the way: a four-foot mound of red earth with lumpy turrets, like a sand castle that had caught a wave. A

19

male gazelle with black lyre-shaped horns perched on the top and surveyed the females.

"Quality above the common herd. What do you think?" Lynn asked.

"Hey, Chris, hold it. I want to get a picture of this."

Chris Mbare stopped the car. Al raised his video camera and panned across the herd. The male gazelle jumped nimbly from the termite mound and followed one of the females. He stretched his neck full length to sniff under her tail and curled his lip like a wine connoisseur.

"He's testing to see if she's in estrus," I explained. "In heat."

"Yuch." Lynn giggled.

The male gazelle tapped the female's flank several times with a foreleg and mounted.

"I love it." Al was busy with his zoom lens. "Did you get that foreplay?"

"Need to take lessons?" Boyce asked.

Boyce had not been nasty like this earlier in the trip. A complainer, yes, but he also knew how to make people like pleasing him. I'd been assuming it was something with Candy that had brought on this bad humor, since she'd been the first target. Now I wondered whether it was something between him and Al. I hoped he'd get over it and finish the trip in good spirits.

"These darn animals won't stop doing it," Lynn said. "How are we going to get any usable footage?"

"Why should they be any different?" Al turned off the camera and sat back in the seat. He put a hand on Madge's knee.

"Walt Disney never showed it like this," Lynn answered.

"Kid, if you think Walt Disney showed it like it is, you're in trouble. This is nature. Life, death, sex, the works."

We drove for another half hour, stopping regularly so that I could scan the rolling terrain. It was nearing six o'clock, the hour when the equatorial sun turns into a big red ball and falls behind the horizon. The edge between day and night was sharp, not like the gentle prolonged dusk I'd known growing up in North America. It was the hour of the hunt.

I relaxed my eyes as my friend Striker had taught me and used my peripheral vision to spot movement. Striker was my best friend in Kenya, an American conservationist working with all the passion of his being to save African wildlife from extinction. He'd taught me most of what I knew about finding animals in the bush. There were plenty of grazing animals in sight, but no lion. I was fighting the pressure to produce a hunt. Only the lioness could do that. Being there when it happened took as much luck as skill. That was part of the wonder.

Boyce leaned back in his seat and folded his arms across his chest. "Getting dark," he announced. F45669

In the end, it was the zebra who gave it away.

There was a family group at the top of a rise: five sister mares, three with foals, a couple of young males, and their current stallion. I studied them through the binoculars. They munched peacefully, tails whisking away flies.

The binoculars were one of my prized possessions, a splurge of a surprise gift from Striker when I launched Jazz Jasper Safaris. The first time I used them had been a revelation, a new realm of seeing. Their lenses gave my eyes the distance vision of a hawk and the night vision of an owl.

One foal kicked up its hind legs and ran a few feet, then looked back at its playmate. The third foal was younger and stuck close to its mother's side. The mother was barrel-chested and stocky, a powerhouse of an animal. The baby was built more like an Arabian. It had long delicate legs, a muzzle so soft-looking I longed to stroke it, and a crisp diamond in black and white between its wide eyes.

"More zebra. Big deal," Boyce said.

"Watch the stallion," I told the group softly. The stallion was not happy. His head was up and he stared into the grass about three hundred feet to the right of the Land Rover. He took a few mincing steps and snorted.

"This could be it." I used the binoculars to follow the stallion's gaze. At first, I couldn't see a thing. Then there

21

was a hint of movement. Then nothing. Then movement again. It was the flick of a tail. Shifting the glasses, I made out the rounded shape of an ear. "There's the lioness."

"Okay, we're in business," Lynn exclaimed.

Within seconds, everyone had their binoculars aimed at the lioness's broken silhouette. She crept forward, invisible to the zebras farther up the slope. Her head was low to the ground, her body taut. Her haunches swung from side to side with suppressed eagerness. She was like an arrow trembling in a fully drawn bow. Every line was lovely, energetic, and deadly.

The stallion sensed the lioness's presence. He pranced a dozen steps to the right, then to the left. The other zebras turned to face the same way, a comical row of big round ears swiveling back and forth. The foal edged closer to its mother.

"Chris, move up another hundred feet," ordered Boyce.

Chris didn't move. I leaned forward and explained: "We don't want to interrupt them."

The stallion emitted a piercing two-note alarm call. He'd decided it was time to act. Would the herd move off to the right, to safety? Or to the left, past the lioness? It was a moment of fate. I held my breath.

He chose the left.

The lioness flattened to the ground and moved forward, tail flicking, and disappeared in the grass. The stallion dropped back, urging the alpha mare forward with a nip to the flank. Maybe he could pull it off.

"She blew it," said Boyce in disgust. "Why'd she let them pass?"

Then the zebras exploded. The stallion reared up on his hind legs with a short high scream that raised the hackles on my neck. The mare with the littlest baby zigzagged abruptly. The lioness raced after her, body low to the ground, feet flying. The rest of the zebras disappeared over the crown of the hill. The mare swerved in an attempt to rejoin the group.

It was a mistake. The foal lagged a few steps behind, and with a swift turn, the lioness cut it off from its mother. The foal wailed with distress and headed toward the Land Rover. The sound was almost human.

I could hardly breathe. I wanted the baby to escape with all my might, while I loved the lioness equally for her powerful grace. The foal zigged and zagged, ever closer to us. The lioness cut each turn even more quickly. The distance between them narrowed to a few feet.

"She's got him, she's got him!" Boyce pounded on the dashboard.

He was wrong. The mother zebra was right behind the lioness. The three animals whooshed past the Land Rover.

The zebra stretched out her neck. The stiff mane looked like the bristling helmet of a centurion. She ran straight at the lioness and reared up to strike a blow with her front hoof. The lioness twisted away and turned to face her attacker.

The foal swiftly dashed to its mother's side. The mare faced off the lioness. The lioness snarled and lunged. She raked the zebra with swift claws. Blood spurted from the mare's flank. The mare screamed. The foal bleated over and over.

"Oh, I can't look!" Madge said.

Boyce shouted encouragement to the lioness, as if he were watching the Super Bowl in overtime.

A dull thunder emerged from the falling night and grew louder. The family herd surged over the crest of the hill and bore down toward the trio below.

"Beautiful," Al exclaimed from behind his camera.

The herd swirled around the Land Rover in a blur of moving stripes and dust and the smell of horse sweat. They surrounded the hunted mare and her foal and kept on running. The injured mare and foal were gone—hidden in the center of the herd.

The lioness was alone. She watched their dust disappear, her tail twitching, her sides heaving as she regained her breath. She looked disgusted. Without a backward glance at her human audience, she disappeared into the grass.

I sank down into my seat. "Whew—"

"That was terrific!" Al exclaimed. He and Madge and

Lynn babbled excitedly about the hunt. "Well, Boycie, what do you say, hot stuff or what?"

Boyce sat silently and stared straight ahead through the windshield. He was probably fuming because the baby zebra got away. In the mood he was in, he'd think of some way to blame it on Jazz Jasper Safaris.

I swiveled to face the Harts. "Al, did you get that on film? That's only the second time I've seen a hunt. We lucked out." My heart was still pounding.

"Boyce, are you all right?" Madge asked. Still no answer.

"Mr. Darnell?" Lynn sounded worried. She reached forward and gave his shoulder a little shake.

Without a sound, Boyce slumped sideways and slipped to the floor.

3

I SWUNG MY legs over the open side of the
Land Rover, jumped to the ground, pulled open the front
door, and bent over Boyce. He had slipped into the narrow
space between the seat and the dashboard. His mouth hung
open and he breathed noisily through yellowed teeth. I leaned
over to see his face. He looked at me dully and closed his
eyes. His skin was pale and beaded with sweat. I touched his
cheek with the back of my fingertips: clammy.

I looked up and met Mbare's eyes. His pupils were black
holes, like a dark vortex. I wondered whether I looked that
scared myself. Al crowded behind me.

"Let me see him," Madge said.

I relinquished my place to her. She leaned forward and
listened. "He's not completely out, but his color scares me."

"He doesn't look good," I agreed. "Let's get him
stretched out on the middle seat."

With Mbare on his legs, Al helped me support his shoulders and we somehow managed to maneuver Boyce onto the
long middle seat. His body sagged heavily and it was hard
not to bump him against things. Boyce's eyelids flickered
open and he mumbled. We placed him on his back.

"He doesn't look comfortable," Madge said. "I'll sit in
the middle with him." She cradled Boyce's head on her lap.
"He shouldn't be lying flat, anyway."

"Let's get back in the Land Rover. That lioness may still be around," I said.

Lynn squeezed into the back with Al. I returned to my usual place in front, next to Mbare, twisting around to watch Boyce.

Al reached over the seat and took Boyce's hand. It hung heavily in his grasp.

"Take it easy, Boyce," Al said. "You're going to be okay."

"I have his heart medicine," Lynn said. She patted the pillbox in her pocket.

"What are you doing with his pills?" Madge asked her.

"They fell out of his pocket when we were fording the stream."

"They won't help now. They're for hypertension," Madge said. "It won't do anything for a heart attack." Her voice shook. "He couldn't swallow a pill now, anyway."

Heart attack. She'd given words to everyone's fear.

"At least he's semiconscious," I said. "Let's get back to camp, pronto. I'll radio for a plane and a medic."

Mbare had the Land Rover in gear and we rumbled back over the rough track. Flattened grass marked the way we had come. No one spoke. It was a black night. The headlights reflected the eyes of invisible animals. Hyena's eyes were at knee height, giraffe's higher up. They hung in the dark like tiny red lanterns.

Abruptly, there was a tan flash of a bushbuck in the headlights. I saw its furry coat and startled eyes and it was gone as Mbare swung the Land Rover hard to the right and we bounced off the track and into long grass. Boyce rolled heavily, and Madge clutched him around the chest. The grass swished against the headlights, sucking at us like the tide. It was a relief when Mbare pulled the Land Rover back onto the beaten trail.

The rock hyraxes started their nightly singing. They shrieked and moaned like the sound track of a horror movie. I gripped the dashboard. The Land Rover seemed to rush over the ground at enormous speed, but at the same time I felt we were getting nowhere, trapped in a nightmare.

At last, the kerosene lights at the camp showed dimly ahead. Another hundred yards and we could see the tent's shadows cast against the trees. A big bonfire blazed in front of the dining tent. There was Cliff's slim silhouette surrounded by flames. He stood, drink in hand, unaware of what the Rover was bearing down upon him. Cliff had produced Boyce's advertising since they were both young men. Please don't let him die, I prayed silently.

Mbare drove right up to Boyce's tent. Once more, Mbare took his feet, Al and I took his shoulders, and we moved him carefully into the tent. Was it my imagination that he felt heavier? Eleanor and Cliff came running.

"What's happened?" Eleanor cried, her voice shrill with alarm. "Is Boyce hurt?"

She brushed past us and into the tent without a pause. Cliff was right after her, his drink still in his hand.

"Was it the lion?" asked Candy.

I left the others to explain. I ran to the staff area, where the service van was parked, and radioed Masai Mara Lodge— thirty kilometers away—to send a flying doctor. They were terribly sorry but it was impossible to land near the camp at night. I quickly calculated. It would take at least two hours to drive to the lodge. Perhaps it was safer to let him rest and wait till morning for a plane. Damnation. I heard running footsteps and turned, to see Madge appear out of the darkness.

She gripped the van door as if she needed support. "He's stopped breathing!"

My heart started to pound. I ran to Boyce's tent, going over in my mind the steps of CPR. It was aeons since I'd taken that first-aid course. The bonfire burned alone. Everyone was gathered in front of Boyce's tent.

Cliff had pulled Eleanor Darnell out of the tent. He had an arm awkwardly around her. Eleanor looked smaller than ever, frozen with fear. Lynn and Candy stood nearby. Lynn was telling Candy the story of Boyce's collapse in an overly loud voice. It already sounded like old news.

I raced past them and pushed into the tent. Al was bent over Boyce, giving him mouth-to-mouth resuscitation. Someone had hung a kerosene lamp from the ridge pole. It cast a great hunched shadow over the bed.

"While you're doing that, I'll work on his chest," I volunteered. I thumped Boyce over the heart, as I'd been taught, and then placed one hand over the other with my arms straight. I pumped rhythmically, timing it with my own breathing. Push, relax. Push, relax. I willed the life and strength to flow through my arms into the inert body beneath me.

Hope died slowly. I couldn't bring myself to admit defeat. Boyce had been a jerk, but he had been vitally alive. This seemed so wrong. Someone in the prime of life shouldn't snuff out, not like that. It didn't make sense. Poor Eleanor. Four kids, the youngest one still at home. My eyes filled with tears. The abalone buttons on Boyce's shirt glinted in the lamplight. My arms tired. Push, relax. Push, relax.

We continued on, long past the point of no hope. It was finally Al who called a halt. He tested for breath, listened cheek to chest for a heartbeat. Then he reached for the blanket and pulled it up over Boyce's face.

We joined the group outside. "He's gone," Al said simply. His shoulders began to shake, and he cried, one hand hiding his face. Madge threw her arms around him, crying a little also.

I went over to Eleanor. I wanted to hug her, but she went stiff, so I patted her arm instead. "I don't think he felt much pain. He slipped under and never came out of it."

Eleanor looked up at me with lost eyes magnified by tears.

"What am I going to do?" She fumbled for a tissue in her pocket and blew her nose. "I should never have let him come on this trip, not with his heart. But you know how he was. He would never listen." She turned to Cliff, sniffing and dabbing her eyes. "How do we get home? What about Boyce?"

"We'll call your sister, and she can call the funeral parlor to take care of Boyce when we arrive. How's that?'' Cliff ran a nervous hand through his straight blond hair. He was doing his best, but Cliff's forte was keeping things smooth. There weren't any witticisms suitable for sudden death.

Madge came up and offered Eleanor a clean tissue. ''You'd better lie down before you fall down,'' she told her. ''We'll deal with getting home and whatever has to be done. Don't worry about a thing. We'll fly back with you.'' Madge folded Eleanor into her arms and led her away.

By nine, I had finished all the arrangements I could make from camp: a doctor to issue the death certificate, a funeral parlor to handle shipping the body, new hotel and plane reservations. I was almost sorry when I ran out of things to do. Eleanor had dinner on a tray in her tent. The others picked at a solemn meal and regrouped around the fire. It was a nightly ritual to build a blazing circle in the open, next to the dining tent. Evenings were chilly, thanks to the altitude, but not cold enough to need a fire for warmth. The fire gave the camp a focus at night. You looked at the leaping flames and turned your back on the dark and the noises.

I didn't feel like being social, but neither did I want to go lie down and be depressed. Might as well face death in the traditional manner: join the circle of firelight to keep away thoughts of the long night awaiting us all. The hyraxes had started up again, as loud as if they were screeching in my ears. Usually I loved their strange sounds, but not tonight. I was too close to wailing myself.

Cliff pulled me into the group. ''You look tired, darling. Drink, death, and taxes are the only certainties, and drink comes first. Molezzi!'' he called, and turned back to me. ''Cognac?''

Molezzi brought my cognac and I gingerly took a sip. The fumes felt funny in my nose.

''I hate it when people drop dead, don't you?'' Cliff said. He swirled the cognac against the sides of the glass. ''It's the only thing that makes me insecure. I'm sure it's bad for my health.''

Cliff was back in form; impossible to tell what he was really thinking. I looked around for Lynn. There she was, in a dark cotton suit, talking with Al and Madge on the other side of the fire. I hoped for her sake that the series wasn't scrapped. Even if Boyce was dead, Wild and Free Shampoo lived on and still needed commercials. Who owned the company now? Eleanor and the Harts? That wasn't a polite question to ask tonight.

Candy had changed into a long black dress that merged into the night. Its material followed the lines of her body, making her look like Jane Avril from a Toulouse-Lautrec poster. Her blond hair gleamed in the firelight, a nimbus around her pale face. A heavy gold chain and bright red lipstick provided the only details.

She turned to Cliff and gestured with her half-empty glass. "So what does this mean for the job?" she asked. "Are we all going back to the States? There's really no need for me and Lynn to go back—"

Cliff waved a long, manicured hand. "Darling, I can't think straight right now. Do you realize how long I've known Eleanor? Since high school. Boyce was my first client."

"Yeah, I know the whole story," Candy said. "Madge told me about trying to fix you and Eleanor up your junior year. Adorable. I was just wondering if this is going to affect the shooting schedule. You know I have a job in the Caribbean in February. You promised me we'd be done shooting here in four weeks. I don't want to fly home and then turn around and come right back."

This seemed a bit crass even for Candy. It sounded as if she automatically assumed that she was back in the commercials now that Boyce was gone. I studied her face. She was pouting, but it lacked conviction. It looked more like an invitation to admire her full lower lip than like genuine petulance. Ah, I got it. Candy was no longer in hiding and needed to be the center of attention, even if it meant throwing a scene. It was pretty hard to compete for attention with a corpse. I took another sip at my drink. Time to wander over to Lynn and the Harts.

30

Eleanor chose that moment to join us. She, too, had put on black, a dress with flared skirt and ruffles at neck and wrist. She paused and blinked at the fire. Lynn came over and greeted her somewhat effusively, but Eleanor ignored Lynn and spoke to Cliff.

"Someone put the lantern out in Boyce's tent. That's not right. . . ." She looked up at him helplessly, a femme fatale of another generation, another style.

Lynn leaned toward me. "I still have Boyce's pills," she said softly. "I don't know what to do with them. It feels creepy to throw them away."

Candy had overheard. "What's creepy?"

"I was telling Jazz I have Boyce's heart medicine."

"Oh." Candy seemed disappointed. Not creepy enough.

"I guess I'll just keep them for now," Lynn said.

I pushed a log forward with my foot and the fire burst into a brighter flame. I hadn't lost my ex-husband Adam to death, but I could guess some of what Eleanor must be feeling. The first few days, it seemed unreal; she'd be in a kind of emotional cocoon. Hopefully, she'd be home before the magnitude of her loss struck.

Molezzi appeared at Candy's elbow and offered her a fresh cognac. He bore off her empty glass without noticing anyone else, and I had to call him back. Candy was oblivious to his homage. She offered her hand to Eleanor. Eleanor looked surprised and touched fingers with her briefly.

"This must be terribly hard on you," Candy said. "Boyce worshiped you, in his own way." She put two hands around her glass and held it to her bosom in a theatrical gesture. "I hope you know that." Eleanor stared, clearly at a loss for words. Candy continued. "I'm sorry if I made things worse for you."

Eleanor stiffened. "You never understood my husband very well. I didn't notice you had the slightest effect on Boyce or on me." She looked to Cliff for rescue.

"Boyce was a big personality. We'll all miss him," Cliff cut in, and he raised his glass in a salute. "At least Boyce went out in style."

A hyrax shrieked in the distance.

"About the shooting schedule," Candy began.

"Could one of the servants . . . the light," Eleanor said.

Cliff ran a hand through his hair. "Molezzi!" he called. "We'll get that lamp lit for you right away." He turned to Candy. "Let me get back to you on that, okay?"

Candy gave him a tight-lipped smile and started to tell Eleanor her scheduling worries.

Al cut in. "The job is going to go ahead on schedule. It's only this vacation that's canceled." Candy opened her mouth to speak, and Al held up a stubby but commanding hand. "As far as I'm concerned, Cliff can hire whoever he wants, if that's what's giving you ants in the pants. Okay? Now, enough already. What's the matter with you, pestering Eleanor about this?"

"Look"—Candy raised her voice—"I work for my living, and I've got to know what I'm doing. I can't afford to fool around with my schedule. Do you know what rents are like in Manhattan these days?"

Lynn, ever the peacemaker, said, "I know how Candy feels. We're all shaken up. It makes you very nervous about everything."

"Can I help you?" Cliff asked someone behind me.

I turned to see who he was talking to. A slim, muscular black man holding a tall spear stood at the edge of the firelight. He was naked except for a rough ocher cape and bright red cloth draped around his hips. The whites of his eyes stood out sharply against his dark skin.

"*Jambo! Habari gani?*" he greeted us, and hummed.

He stepped forward into the light. Now I could see the fine bone structure typical of the Masai: the long narrow face, the high cheekbones, the aquiline nose. His jewelry glimmered in the firelight, elaborate beadwork encircling brow and neck and waist. His earlobes had inch-long slits decorated with beads and silver. He wore his hair, which started high up on his brow, in dozens of shoulder-length braids coated with animal fat and ocher. Despite the strong

32

smell of goat fat, he looked like a Greek god, complete with toga.

"Jambo!" I replied. *"Mzuri sana."* I shook his hand. His palm was hard and calloused.

"What does he want?" Madge asked.

"He's Masai, probably from that village down the valley. Either he's paying us a visit out of curiosity or he might have something to sell." I almost asked whether they'd like me to arrange a visit to the village, but then I remembered. They weren't tourists anymore. Boyce's death had transformed us all into mourners.

"Jambo," Al and Madge chorused.

Cliff stuck out a hand.

"Look at those cheekbones," Candy said. She stood next to him as if to measure his height. The Masai give such an impression of stature, it's disorienting to realize they're the size of ordinary mortals.

Lynn kept her distance on the other side of the bonfire. Eleanor moved a few steps off, out of the light, and Lynn called to her to come join her.

Jambo and a handful of memorized phrases were about the extent of my Swahili. I resolved for the hundredth time to learn more. Meanwhile, where was Chris Mbare?

As if reading my thoughts, Chris came over, wiping his mouth with the back of his hand. The arrival had evidently interrupted his supper. Chris was Kikuyu, shorter, rounder, more expressive than the Masai visitor. The Kikuyu were farmers, the Masai nomadic herders. Where the Kikuyu had embraced Western influence and eventually pushed out the British to take over the country themselves, the Masai had remained aloof. They were one of the few tribes in Africa that remained tenaciously loyal to their own ways.

I wondered whether looking so elegant made them look down on everyone else. It probably had more to do with being nomads, with the fierceness they cultivated instead of crops. Young Masai men were raised to kill a lion single-handed when they came of age, though of course that was illegal now.

Chris Mbare and the stranger greeted each other back and forth, the standard formula rattled off in a rapid rhythm, punctuated by humming. Then they had a short, spare interchange. Chris turned to me and explained the Masai had a spear to sell. He'd asked an astronomical price, but if anyone was interested, Chris would bargain for them. Eleanor murmured something about needing a sweater and went off to her tent. I hoped this wasn't offending her; should I have sent the man away?

Al was definitely interested. He took the spear and struck a pose.

"Hey, Madge, what do you think? Joey will go crazy over this."

Joey was a much-beloved grandson we'd heard a lot about on the trip. Al had already bought him a safari outfit, a skin drum, a set of carved wooden animals, and a T-shirt saying I CLIMBED MOUNT KILIMANJARO.

"Don't you think it's a little dangerous?" Madge eyed the sharp point.

"He's thirteen. He knows better than to do something stupid."

"How will we get it on the plane?"

"They'll crate it up for us at the hotel."

It was impossible for Madge to withstand Al's enthusiasm. He looked as excited as a kid himself, holding the seven-foot spear. It was an impressive weapon. There was a short segment in the middle in pale wood incised with dark lines. Above it slanted a long sharp blade; below it, there was a metal shaft that narrowed to a point, looking almost as dangerous.

"Okay, okay, but if anything happens, I warned you."

Mbare acted as middleman. The bargaining was lively, but money eventually changed hands. The Masai thrust the pointed shaft into the ground. The spearhead quivered like a released spring while he disappeared back into the night.

4

WHEN I AWOKE the next morning, the wails of the hyraxes had given way to bird song, but my spirits were leaden. The events of the night before rushed in on me: our long search for the lioness, the hunt, Boyce's still, crumpled body in the front seat of the Land Rover. I stared at the tent roof and replayed the nightmarish drive back to camp, Al pulling the cover over Boyce's face. I clutched the blankets tighter over my shoulders. If we hadn't found the lion, would Boyce be alive today? Ridiculous thought. No one killed Boyce, not me, not the hunt. Boyce's heart killed him.

Today was going to be a stinker. I didn't want to go back to Nairobi. I didn't want to face Eleanor's grief. I didn't want Boyce to be dead. I didn't want my first trip to be messed up. I didn't want to be feeling sorry for myself. I burrowed into the warm hollow of the mattress and closed my eyes.

Short melodic lines shifted and repeated as two birds sang a duet. "Weee-ooo, weee-ooo," called another. "It's dawn. Here I am." If Striker were here, he would know who was speaking, like the fairy-tale prince who understood the language of the birds. The ravens gave him the key and he won back his kingdom or the princess or something.

This was great. I flipped over on my stomach and hugged the pillow. I reminded myself I didn't believe in princes anymore. My princess days were dead and gone, as dead as Boyce Darnell. I caught myself slipping into bitterness about my ex-husband, Adam. I turned onto my back again, brushed the hair away from my eyes. I hadn't thought of him in weeks, maybe a couple of months. I was definitely getting better. Boyce's death was dredging up my own losses. Why did it have to happen? I stared at the canvas roof bulging softly above me. If I couldn't fill in a client before my next job, I'd see whether Striker was willing to put up with me at Mt. Kenya for a week.

As I said, Striker was my one close friend in Kenya. He was a free spirit, an American writer who had made the lower slopes of Mt. Kenya his home for the last ten years. That is, when he wasn't on safari. He spent as much time among the animals as any of the scientists, and wrote fiery articles about the need to take action now. At the rate things were going, within a generation people would only know the big mammals in zoos. Nature preserves were no protection against poaching for the Japanese ivory trade. It looked like the elephants only had about a decade till extinction, and once they went, the savannah grasslands would fill in and eventually all the other animals, from impala to lions, would be lost, too. This was the decade of decision, according to Striker—and all the other experts. He fought back through his work, as if threatened with imprisonment himself—which in a way was true, for all of us, when you think of what the world will feel like when we've killed off everything else.

I admired Striker and learned about Kenya from him whenever I could. He was something of a loner and could be prickly at times, but that didn't bother me. I needed time to myself as much as he did.

We'd met shortly after I arrived in Nairobi. He'd rescued me from a job as a cocktail hostess at the Grand Palace—a job I'd been very happy to land one week off the plane—and helped me get the tour-leader position at Seven Seas. It gave me the chance to see a lot of the country and learn the tour business. Jazz Jasper Safaris would never have happened otherwise.

Meanwhile, between my Seven Seas tours, Striker and I went off by ourselves on some memorable trips: We'd watched leopards hunt at night on Mt. Kenya, seen hippos fight on the shores of Lake Victoria, witnessed two million flamingos turn the sky pink above Lake Nakuru. The pair of nesting martials I had spotted yesterday was a small thing, but Striker would have loved seeing them.

Striker and I had hit it off from our first meeting together, that night at the Grand Palace. He walked into the cocktail lounge with his usual relaxed gait, wide-brimmed hat in his hands, and gaped at the lavish decor, the way people did after a long stay out in the bush. He didn't notice when I walked up and stood at his shoulder.

"Hard to believe it's the same planet?" I asked

The country-bumpkin illusion disappeared as soon as he looked at me with those fiercely intelligent green-brown eyes.

"Ah, the person I've come to see," he said. "I heard there was a new American in town, wanting to get involved with conservation, and I thought I'd come by and say hello." He held out a strong, tanned hand. "Dan Striker. My friends usually shorten it to Striker."

He invited me to join him for a drink later. When I got off work, I slipped into the booth opposite him and we had one of those conversatons in which you meet a stranger and talk on and on for hours, bouncing stories and ideas off one another. By the end of the evening we were friends. It was "like at first sight," as Striker put it. I was undoubtedly the only single white woman in Kenya who hadn't made a pass at him, and, at least at first, he'd been just as happy to be turned down. Lately, things had been getting a bit tense between us, but I was hoping that would blow over.

Fortified with that cheering thought, I managed to get out of bed. The straw mat on the floor was cold and I curled my feet onto their edges. I pulled jeans, thick socks, and a heavy cotton sweater from my suitcase and quickly dressed. I yanked at the zipper on the tent's mosquito netting and it stuck on the fabric. After wrestling with it for ten minutes and working myself back into a foul humor, I finally gave up, zipped open the bottom, and crawled out on my belly. The whole day was going to be like this, I could tell.

As soon as I got outside, my mood lightened. A soft dawn

light suffused the sky. The sun wasn't actually up yet. Molezzi had the fire going and a small wisp of gray smoke rose skyward with the bird song. He had filled my camp basin with hot water and I gratefully splashed my face. The pitcher on my little table had been refilled, too. I poured out a glass of water and brushed my teeth standing in front of the tent. Maybe things wouldn't be that bad, or at least I could make the best of them. The others had stayed up late, talking and drinking. Still, if I went for some tea, I might get caught by an early riser. I'd have tea later. I needed to get myself in order first.

I got my binoculars from the night table by my bed and headed for the stream. Within moments, I was out of sight of the camp, snaking through the bushes on a little path that led down to the water. The stream was shallow and fast running where it narrowed after passing under the bluff.

I walked slowly along the sandy bank and looked for tracks. Something had passed by, probably an antelope of some sort. The only track I always recognized was the elephant. This was not a source of great pride. Their footprints were the size and shape of a dinner plate—a dinner plate with a rippled texture and eight hundred pounds pressing it into the earth. Not to mention the swathe of broken tree limbs and uprooted trees, or the piles of giant turds. When elephants had passed by, I could tell.

The sun had risen and a shaft of light penetrated into the hollow, as in a Rembrandt painting. A swallowlike bird with a cream head swooped through the light on green iridescent wings. A yellow bishop landed on a bush and puffed out its shoulder patch.

Yellow bishops reminded me of redwing blackbirds, the first bird I'd learned, not counting sparrows and pigeons. That was back in the days when Lynn and I lived together. With our other roommates, we spent most of two summers building a cabin up in Vermont farm country. We'd cook up a big breakfast on the wood stove, work all day, climb the hill to watch the sun set, then sit outside and talk and watch the stars revolve till late into the night. I wondered whether

Lynn carried vivid memories of that era, too. If so, they didn't show. I'd have to ask her.

I sat on a rock and studied the yellow bishop through my binoculars. It emitted a series of cheeps and twittering calls. I could see its throat swell and tremble as it sang. A tiny turquoise bird landed near my feet and pecked at an invisible seed. It was as brilliant and finely detailed as a Fabergé jewel. Striker had taught me that one on our first trip together: the red-cheeked cordon-bleu. Satisfied, I rose to head back to camp.

The bushes behind me formed a complex wall of foliage and shade. Out of the corner of my eye, a pattern jumped out at me. Motionless on the bank stood two Masai. My heart lurched. They'd finger-painted pink mud on their legs in abstract designs. The body paint broke up their outline as effectively as camouflage. They wore russet capes knotted at one shoulder and short leather skirts. One of them carried a bow slung over one shoulder, and a broadsword at his waist. The other one gripped a modern, heavy-looking rifle. How long had they been watching me? We said *jambo* without smiling. They continued to stare at me. When they disappeared, the bushes didn't even stir.

The one with the rifle had looked familiar. I bent my head, searching for the memory. I recalled it and scowled. He was a poacher. Everyone knew it. Last year, he was rumored to have murdered a park guard, another Masai, but nothing could be proved. There was a virtual war going on between poachers and park rangers. The poachers were winning. There were so few rhino left, soon the park could assign a guard to each one, and a cage while they were at it. Elephants would be the next to go: Three-quarters had been wiped out in the last decade.

I stared into the bushes where the two poachers had vanished. There was absolutely nothing to fear as long as I didn't have a horn on my nose or ivory tusks. Nonetheless, I hurried back to camp. Suddenly the idea of hot tea in the dining tent was very appealing.

* * *

Al, Madge, and Cliff were already at breakfast. The three of them sat at one end of the long dining table, like the Mad Hatter's tea party. A buffet was set up against one wall, with big urns of coffee and tea and covered dishes of eggs and toast, bacon, and sausages on warmers. The British empire might be gone, but the hearty English breakfast remained.

Al was bent over a plate piled with scrambled eggs and crisp bacon, eating quickly. Madge stood at his shoulder and refilled his coffee from a silver pot while she talked.

"I found her next to Boyce's body, crying her eyes out," Madge said. She pushed the creamer over toward Al with one hand. With the other, she raised the coffeepot aloft, offering to serve me. I shook my head, no thanks. Madge sat next to Al and sopped up the remains of a fried egg with a corner of her toast.

Cliff wasn't eating. He balanced his chair on its two back legs and drank a cup of black coffee. "I had trouble sleeping, too. I can't believe the bastard is gone," he said. "It leaves a real hole in my life. He made everyone else seem so pleasant by comparison."

Cliff's sleeplessness didn't show. He wore a white raw silk suit and pale yellow shirt, which set off his tan. He looked so much younger than Al and Madge, but I gathered from what Candy had said last night that he, Eleanor, and Madge were in high school together. I realized with a start that Cliff dyed his hair. The advertising business.

"I hope I go as fast when it's my turn," Al said. "Hey, honey, how about a bit more eggs and another sausage." He held his plate out to Madge, who got up and served him.

"You're on the right track," Cliff said. "I'd call that a suicide breakfast."

"Aw, you can't believe everything those experts tell you," Al answered. He tucked into his breakfast, undeterred.

I poured myself a cup of dark Kenyan tea, added milk, and slipped into the seat next to Cliff.

"I was just telling the others, I got up to go to the bathroom in the middle of the night—" Madge said.

"What do you expect?" Al cut her off, taking his refilled

plate. "Of course she's all upset. You'd be all upset, too. We'll get her home fast as we can."

"I'll check if she's awake. Maybe she'd like her breakfast in bed," Madge said, and she bustled off.

"Have you seen Lynn yet?" asked Cliff.

"I left camp before anyone was up. Took a walk along the stream. The only people I saw were two Masai dressed in fingerpaint and leather skirts."

Cliff wanted to hear all about them. "The Masai are terribly photogenic," he commented. He gestured with his coffee cup. "It's not just their good bone structure. It's that superior aloofness, like the British aristocracy but good-looking and without the stiffness. Utterly superb. I'd like to see a shot of one striding along with his herds for our series."

"Not with those getups they wear," said Al. "Too much leg showing." He laughed roundly.

"We'll take some footage. You can make up your mind when you see the rushes. It fits right in with the Wild and Free theme. Wait till you see it."

Cliff the creative adman, reducing everything to a commodity. I sipped my tea and didn't say anything. Maybe I'd be better off with regular tourists who would ooh and aah over the animals and leave it at that. But no, the more publicity the animals got, even in a shampoo commercial, the better for their survival. If only they showed the commercials here in Kenya and got the people to associate their parks with slick Western fun. One week with Cliff and Lynn, and it was rubbing off on me.

Madge returned and poured another round of coffee. "I peeked in and she's sleeping like a baby. I'm glad she's catching up; it's hard to sleep at night after something like this. It takes a long time to get back to yourself."

Candy came into breakfast dressed in her green nightgown and yellow Merlin the Magician robe, yawning ostentatiously. I noticed she'd managed to put on a full set of makeup.

"Did you guys leave any for me? I'm as hungry as a lion," she said. As she went down the length of the buffet, Molezzi miraculously appeared and lifted the covers off each dish for her inspection. She sat down with a plate loaded high with eggs and sausage and a second plate with slices of fresh pineapple and papaya. Molezzi poured her a cup of coffee.

"Sure you got enough to eat?" Cliff asked her.

"My appetite is wicked this morning." Candy speared a sausage with her fork and delicately bit off one end. "It's going to take me hours to pack. My tent is a complete slag heap. I can't find anything. The new pillbox I bought in Nairobi is missing."

"If it isn't Little Miss Sunshine. We're all in bad moods, darling. Do you want to hear about mine?" Cliff asked.

"I can't find the spear I bought last night, either," Al interrupted.

"Molezzi probably put it away for you," I said. "Do you want it?"

Al waved a stubby hand. "Nah, he can keep it with the drum he's holding for us. The tent's crowded as it is."

Candy continued to eat, calmly and steadily. "I'm glad we're going back to the lodge on our way home. I'll be able to swim this afternoon."

"Don't pick on her," Madge said to Cliff. "It's good she's eating. It's going to be a long day."

An hour later, I was instructing Ibrahima about packing up the camp, when Cliff approached me again to ask whether I'd seen Lynn. He wanted to talk over the new job schedule with her. Most mornings she'd been among the early risers.

Lynn's tent was zippered shut, I pointed out. It had been a tough night and she might have had trouble sleeping. Better let her sleep in, at least as long as Eleanor was still asleep, too. There wasn't a big rush to get anywhere since the plane to Nairobi didn't leave till evening.

Cliff looked worried. "Lynn is up at seven every day of the year."

"Oh, come on, Cliff. Let the poor woman rest. You've got the jitters, like all of us."

So it wasn't until late morning that I went over to Lynn's tent and called her name softly. No answer. I called louder.

Still no answer. Maybe Lynn had gotten up early, while I was taking my walk, and wandered off on her own. No, she wouldn't be so stupid. I had warned the group over and over about how dangerous the animals were.

I brushed the worried image out of my mind impatiently and quietly pulled open the tent flap. There was a buzzing of flies to which I didn't react at first. It was dim in the tent. I unzipped the inner layer of mosquito netting and pushed my head through. One of the camp beds was neatly made, with Lynn's suitcase stowed under it. The other bed was a rumpled mountain. Lynn's arm poked out from under the gray blanket. She'd managed to keep her long nails all through the trip. Unchipped red nail polish—what a girl.

"Lynn." I took a step inside the tent. My foot squelched on the wet floor. I looked down: wet and dark, with flies buzzing in it. "Lynn."

I was at my friend's side, but I couldn't understand what I was seeing. Something was wrong. Lynn's throat looked weird. There were blood and flies everywhere. I bent closer to see, the flies buzzed up, and I recoiled as if I'd been struck. There was a jagged hole in Lynn's throat where her windpipe should have been. Her skin hung in tattered flaps, gooey with blood.

I closed my eyes, unable to face what was in front of me. "No!" I yelled. "No!" My voice came out as a strangled croak.

The next thing I knew, I was out of the tent. I bent double, my stomach in a spasm. My stomach heaved and my breakfast made a nasty splash on the ground. I retched again and again, my throat burning, my mouth full of the horrible taste, my eyes hot and wet.

Cliff came out of his tent next door. "Jazz! What is it?"

It was like a gruesome replay of last night.

"Don't go in there." I had another fit of retching. "It's horrible. Someone's killed her."

Cliff made for the tent door and I caught at his arm. "Listen to me. No one should go in there. We've got to get the police."

5

CLIFF OFFERED ME a large white handkerchief. I spat on the ground and wiped my mouth.

Cliff's face was taut with shock and dread. "Are you sure? Did you check if she's breathing?"

I shook my head wearily. "Cliff, believe me, there's not a chance she's alive. You don't want to look. There's a lot of blood."

"I think I'd better check."

"Stop," I hissed at him as he reached for the tent door. "Do you want to mess up any clues? The police need to see it undisturbed. Please, don't make me fight with you."

Cliff ran a hand over his forehead. "You're right. I'm not thinking. This is unbelievable. Listen, get yourself a drink of water, and radio the cops. I'll hang around and make sure no one goes near the tent."

I agreed and set off, concentrating on placing one foot in front of the other. My body felt too heavy to move. Despite the brilliant sunshine, I had the sensation of darkness in front of my eyes. It couldn't be true. I flinched at the memory of buzzing, blood-gorged flies. It couldn't be true.

I found myself in front of my own tent. Cliff's handkerchief, now dirty, was clenched in my fist. I threw it on the mat, splashed water on my face, which helped somewhat, and rinsed my mouth out over and over. The taste of bile lingered in my throat. I cast a surreptitious glance around the clearing. No one had noticed the commotion. Al sat in front of his tent, putting film in his camera, a pile of luggage neatly set out beside him. Madge was walking down the line of tents, her back to me, carrying a tray with a teapot and cup. She must be going to rouse Eleanor. Eleanor was presumably asleep, maybe too depressed to move. Candy wasn't in sight.

I had to tell the police. I pulled myself over to the staff area, where the service van was parked. It was the site of industrious activity. The men had packed up most of the kitchen equipment and the ground was scattered with crates and chests. Two men were busy striking the tents. Ibrahima was at his worktable, cutting sandwiches with a big knife. Molezzi and Ngueye sat in the shade and shouted advice to those working. Their laughter seemed very loud.

I climbed into the van, not bothering to shut the door, and began to fiddle with the radio. Ngueye, the assistant cook, a square fellow with tribal scars on his temples, called out some joking comment to me, which I didn't catch.

"Shut up, you fool," Ibrahima told him. "Can't you see something is wrong?"

"You might as well listen," I told them. My face moved stiffly, like a wooden marionette.

Instead of radioing the police directly, I radioed Striker. I wanted his advice on how to deal with the Kenyan system. One thing I'd learned in my two years here was to take my ignorance about Kenya for granted. I didn't want this case politicized; I wanted Lynn's murderer caught. Should I call the police myself or tell the embassy first? The first steps I took might affect the outcome.

Striker listened to my tense explanation. "Lynn, killed? This is unbelievable." He paused. "Look, would you like me to contact the police? I'd say they're the right place to start, and I know of a good detective on the force in Nairobi, an Inspector Omondi. I'll call him and be right over."

Right over? Mt. Kenya was on the other side of the country.

"Thanks for making the call, that's a big help, but there's

no need to come. I'd prefer you didn't. It would be distracting, and there's going to be a lot to do here."

"Are you sure? I'd feel better being there, with a killer on the loose."

"It's funny, I haven't had time to be afraid."

"Why do you have to act so tough?"

"I'm not acting tough, dammit; I'm just trying to do my job. Please, don't start in on me now, okay?"

"Okay, I get the message. Listen, if you change your mind, or want to talk things over, I'm here. Anything I can do . . ."

"Thanks. I'll come cry on your shoulder after it's over."

"That's a deal. I'm sure you'll handle everything just fine."

I felt a bit better when I signed off. It would have been nice to have Striker come. Why did I say no? I told myself it was just as well: He was busy finishing an exposé on the ivory trade, racing toward the deadline, and it wasn't as if I needed someone to be here.

Molezzi and the others had gathered around the van door. It was the first time I'd ever seen Ibrahima with a long face. He gazed at me with sympathy.

"Big trouble, Miss," he said.

Tears started to my eyes. I wished I was good at being tough. I didn't want to bawl in front of the staff. I paused until I could trust my voice, then asked Ibrahima to assign two of the men to relieve Cliff. They were to watch Lynn's tent and make sure no one went in. No one.

I met Al as I passed the dining tent, and I told him about Lynn.

"Her throat cut," Al said. He sank into one of the chairs around the ashes of the campfire, cradled a fist in his other palm, and was silent for a moment. He shook his head. "Who would kill a nice girl like Lynn? We're in the goddamn middle of nowhere." He looked up abruptly. "Was she raped?"

"I don't think so, Al. I don't know."

Al drummed on his leg. "Good thing I'm getting Madge out of here this afternoon. First Boyce, and now Lynn. This place is jinxed."

If Al thought he'd still be flying out of Masai Mara this evening, he was kidding himself, but I didn't feel like arguing over it. I changed the subject and sent Al off to rustle up drinks before lunch. Once everyone heard the news, they'd need them. While he was busy with that, I roused myself to one more effort. I wanted to tell Madge the news about Lynn myself.

I was starting to think, not just feel. First Boyce, and now Lynn. Was Lynn killed because of Boyce? The laws of chance dictate that coincidences exist, even bizarre coincidences. Was it a coincidence or not? Even worse to think about, Was it someone in the camp who killed Lynn? It could be any of them, guests or staff.

I thought over Al's reaction to the news. He'd seemed genuinely shocked. The murderer, of course, would have rehearsed a convincing reaction. Still, with the exception of Candy, no one was a professional actor, and it would take a lot of talent to portray a natural reaction. Or maybe it wouldn't; I wasn't much of a liar myself, so I tended to overestimate how hard it was to lie convincingly. In any case, people had to be told. Even if I couldn't read guilt in somebody's face, I wanted to see each person's reaction myself.

As soon as Al disappeared toward the staff tents, I searched out Madge. As I might have guessed, she was in Eleanor's tent, rapidly gathering toilet things from the bedside table and stowing them in an overnight bag. Eleanor's clothing was already neatly packed in an open suitcase. Madge moved without hesitation, each movement decisive and efficient.

Eleanor sat outside, out of the way, holding a cup of tea halfway to her lips, as if she'd forgotten what she was doing in midact. There was a plate on the table next to her with remnants of toast. She wore a khaki shirtwaist with a black scarf, and looked bloodless under her tan. She'd put on too much hair spray and her hair looked gummed together. I hated to tell her about Lynn. This whole thing was a worse nightmare for her than it was for me. I'd lost a friend from the past; she'd lost a husband. As I hesitated, the two women looked up. It was too late now.

47

"Madge, could I talk with you for a second?" I beckoned with my head, signaling a short walk without Eleanor. Madge gave me a piercing look, stowed away what she was holding, and came out to join me.

"I think Al was trying to find you," Eleanor said. Her hand had a slight tremor. "He's around somewhere." She looked about the camp without focusing on it. "Will we be leaving soon?"

"Sweetie, I'll be back in a minute," Madge told Eleanor. Lowering her voice, she asked me, "Are you okay? You look awful. What happened?"

The sun was near its zenith and there wasn't much shade, even with the trees. The birds were silent now, but the air was loud with the monotonous shrilling of insects. A cicada pierced the air above our heads like a violinist gone mad, the same note vibrating over and over.

Madge looked strange in drab clothes instead of her usual brash prints and bright colors. Her soft baggy face was furrowed. Was it the strain of taking care of Eleanor? Or did Madge know what I was about to say?

We paused beside the peeling green-gray trunk of a gum tree and I leaned against it for support. I told her in a few words that I'd found Lynn dead. Repeating it didn't make it any easier to say. Madge fished a crumpled tissue out of her pocket and started to cry, quietly so Eleanor wouldn't hear. My eyes filled with tears, too.

"I don't understand," said Madge. She dabbed at her eyes. "I must be smudging my mascara something terrible. I'm going to look as bad as you." She laughed through her tears.

I tore strips off the bark I had peeled from the tree. I might as well pluck petals from a daisy, she's guilty, she's not. I couldn't judge anything from this conversation.

"Was Lynn having an affair with Boyce?" Madge interrupted my thoughts.

I felt a flare of anger, and squelched it. Those questions and even worse would have to be asked. "I couldn't tell you. Lynn and I were roommates a long time ago. She wouldn't

48

necessarily have told me.'' A wave of fatigue came over me. I needed to get cleaned up and lie down.

"Well, you saw Boyce. He was always after a pretty girl. Not above bribing people with hints about business favors, either.''

Madge was a sharp woman. She'd picked up on Lynn's ambition and how that might have made her vulnerable to Boyce. Still, I couldn't see Lynn following that old sexist script. Yes, Lynn wanted to get ahead, but it was because she wanted to prove her talent and ability. Sleeping with your client just proved you were a patsy. Or was that my own naïve idealism? The thought of Lynn using sex with Boyce to advance her career was extremely distasteful. I'd had enough of this conversation.

I threw the strip of bark onto the ground and started back toward Eleanor's tent. "I guess you should mention your ideas to the police,'' I said. We cut between the tents. "There's Al and Cliff with Eleanor. I wonder if they've told her.''

"Are you kidding? Men? They'll have left it to us,'' Madge said.

Sure enough, when we reached the others, Al said, "We were waiting for you two.'' He cast a meaningful look toward Eleanor.

Madge gave me a complicit smile, which I ignored. I don't like it when women patronize men, any more than the reverse. I offered her a beer from the tray on the table and poured one for each of us, tilting the glasses carefully so they wouldn't foam over. The bottles were nice and cool.

"Well, ladies,'' Al said, then stopped.

Eleanor had put on lipstick and some blusher, but it only made her pale skin look sickly.

"How are you feeling?'' I asked her.

"Eleanor's doing great,'' Al said.

"I'm all right, thank you. It's getting hot, isn't it?'' She attempted a smile. "I was just wondering . . .''

"Yes?''

Eleanor fidgeted with the scarf around her throat. "I was

just telling Cliff and Al. I am a bit concerned about getting to the lodge. You know, with Boyce and the heat . . .''

Eleanor had to be told about Lynn. The police wouldn't be here till afternoon. To try and avoid upsetting her would only make things worse later. And of course she was right. We did have to get both bodies out of here or it would be horrible.

Cliff rubbed a thumb across the moisture condensed on his glass. "Have something cold to drink, darling. You need to fortify yourself." It looked as if he was drinking Scotch on the rocks, and not his first, to judge from his glassy eyes.

"You're all taking such good care of me," Eleanor said. "I don't know what I'd do without you."

I looked at Cliff. He took another swig of his Scotch.

"Well, as to your concern about time," I told Eleanor, "we're expecting a plane from Nairobi. I'm not sure exactly when they'll arrive. You know African time. We'll be able to fly Boyce out of here and have all that taken care of."

"Thank you. That's all I wanted to know." She smoothed her skirt. "That sounds fine."

"Wait a second. I'm glad you're sitting down." Wasn't that the standard hint that something terrible was about to befall you?

Eleanor perched on the edge of the chair, looking like an attentive pupil but with a hint of dismay in her eyes. Somehow I babbled out that Lynn had passed away. I despise euphemisms but it was hard to say the word *dead* to Eleanor.

Eleanor's jaw started to tremble. She twisted her hands together, then pressed one hand against her lips as if to stop anything from coming out.

Madge sat next to her and murmured, "Be brave. We'll help you." She patted Eleanor's knee. "This has nothing to do with Boyce."

There was Madge, fixing things up, trying to minimize the whiff of scandal that she thought she could smell.

"I'll be all right. Don't worry about me." Eleanor got unsteadily to her feet. She stood wringing her hands but at least she'd gotten her jaw under control. "So we'll be leaving

50

as soon as the plane arrives? Will they take us all the way to Nairobi?''

"That's not up to me. I'm afraid we had to call the police. To investigate.''

"Oh, I see. A police plane. Yes.'' Eleanor nodded up and down rapidly. "So they're not going back right away? Maybe we should drive Boyce out to the lodge now instead of waiting for them.''

"Let's wait till they arrive, at least,'' Cliff said. He swished his ice around in his glass and took a last swallow. "If they can fly him to Nairobi, that would be the quickest.''

I looked at my watch. "Does anyone know if Candy's in her tent? I want to tell her, too . . . I assume you haven't told her?''

Cliff and Al said they hadn't seen her since the discovery of Lynn's body.

Candy wasn't in her tent, nor in the dining tent. I started to worry.

Molezzi appeared, balancing an enormous tray of plates and sandwiches on one upraised arm. His muscles bulged beneath his T-shirt. I noticed the leather thong across his chest that held his magic charms. I could use some magic myself. If something had happened to Candy, I didn't know what I would do.

Molezzi was able to help me. Yes, he'd seen Candy; she had come by the staff area asking for cigarettes not too long ago. He thought she was smoking down at the fallen tree. Feeling foolish and relieved, I found Candy at the far end of camp. The splashing of the stream was more audible here.

Candy sat on the log with her long legs stretched out in front of her. She wore a slinky white dress and a Masai necklace she'd picked up at the Masai Mara Lodge. The necklace was a broad stiff disk, a flat version of the ruffs worn by Dutch burghers in seventeenth-century portraits. Instead of linen, it was made of tiny beads in broad bands of pure color, red and blue and orange and yellow.

The exotic effect was somewhat ruined by the earphones

51

of her portable cassette player. I could hear a tiny sound, as of Liliputian music, when Candy pulled them down around her neck. It must have been on full blast. She clicked the machine off.

"Have a seat." She had a little pile of cigarettes next to her. She picked one up, lit it, and coughed. "These crummy Kenyan cigarettes are too strong."

I hadn't seen Candy smoke before on the trip. I resisted the impulse to bum a cigarette. It was five years since I'd smoked, but at times it was still a temptation.

"Are we leaving soon?" asked Candy.

"I don't know. We have to wait for the police." I told her about Lynn.

"Hey, you want to sit down?" Candy indicated the expanse of log stretching away from her. We sat in silence for a moment. Candy took a long drag and exhaled the smoke through her nose. "I wondered why those two guys were hanging around her tent playing cards." Candy threw her cigarette to the ground half-finished. "Ugh, these taste awful."

She picked up another cigarette, tapped its end to dislodge loose flakes of tobacco, and stuck it between her lips. She struck the match so hard, its head broke off. On the second try, she got the cigarette lit.

"Lynn was okay. I liked her." She took short puffs without inhaling. "But why the police? She wasn't attacked or anything, was she?"

"It might be that."

Candy crossed and uncrossed her legs. "This trip is turning into a total disaster." She glanced at me appraisingly. "You look like a wreck. You better get yourself cleaned up, or the cops are going to think you did it."

I felt a bite of irrational fear. "What are you talking about?"

"Look at your shoes. You've been walking in blood."

6

I LEFT CANDY, slipped behind the tents, and
made my way to the staff area. The trees' shadows had re-
tracted to small irregular patches around their trunks, brim-
ming with reflected light, no refuge at all. I needed to reach
Striker and confirm that his Inspector Omondi would, in fact,
be flying out. I shouldn't have told Eleanor there'd be a plane
coming until I knew for sure. Damn.

The staff sat in a circle on a straw mat under the kitchen
awning. They were dipping into a big common bowl of stew
and rice from which rose a pungent spicy aroma. They used
tablespoons instead of their fingers, and instead of a calabash, the bowl was an enamel washbasin imported from
Hong Kong, but otherwise it was a traditional scene. Ibrahima stood up when I approached, but I waved him back and
went straight to the van.

It was stifling, even with all its windows open and its little
blob of shade. The plastic seat cover burned my thighs. I
reached around the steering wheel and unhooked the mouth-
piece. It took Striker awhile to answer my call. He should
be home in the heat of the day. Even the animals holed up,
or lay gasping in scraps of shade. By the time I heard his
voice, I was ready to scream. This was bad. I was starting
to lose it.

At least his news was good. He'd reached the head of
homicide, and they'd assigned Inspector Omondi to the case

and put a plane at his disposal. He and an assistant should arrive by midafternoon, four at the latest.

"Thanks a million," I told him with relief. "I'll keep in touch and let you know how things go. Now, please don't worry about me."

"Who, me? Why should I worry? Just because the woman I love insists on dealing with a murder by herself?"

I decided to ignore "the woman I love" bit. I didn't have the energy to fight about our relationship at this moment. My personal world seemed very far away. It was going to take all I had to get through the next few hours and days.

"I'm not by myself. There are a lot of people here."

"That didn't help Lynn."

"It happened in the middle of the night," I said. "She must have been killed before she could cry out."

"That makes it better?"

"Cut it out, I'm feeling guilty enough as it is."

"Guilty? What could you have done? I'm trying to scare you, not make you feel guilty."

"You want to scare me? Striker, I don't need this."

"I think you should be a little scared, don't you?"

"No, I don't. Being scared doesn't make you any safer. Besides, I don't think I'm in danger."

"Bad things only happen to other people?"

"Why are you picking a fight with me?"

"You goddamn idiot, I'm worried about you! I love you."

I closed my eyes. My stomach contracted. He'd never said those words straight out. They echoed and re-echoed in my skull. The teasing references to love that Striker had begun recently, I could fend off. These words scared me. This was the one threat that could get around my armor, my nice, warm, safe armor, the cozy burrow I had lived in since fleeing the States. I wanted nothing to do with it.

"I'm sorry, Striker. I'm very tense. You're my good buddy and I love you, too."

I knew that wasn't the way he meant it, and he knew that I knew, and that I wasn't willing to hear it. As I said, we'd always had great communication. We signed off amicably.

54

My stomach knotted up tighter at the thought of joining the group for lunch. I'd done what I could for the moment. I wasn't going to sit there choking down food and peering at everyone to see who acted like a killer. I could take some time for myself now, before the police arrived.

I gave Ibrahima and Molezzi instructions to keep Lynn's tent under guard, and took off. I circled behind the staff tents, pushed through the bushes that bordered the stream, and came out on a narrow beaten path. It led to a place where rocks blocked the current and formed a shallow pool. I wondered if the men came down here to cool off in the heat of the day, or maybe to fish. The air smelled damp and rich with decaying leaves. I splashed across in my running shoes, hoping to rinse them off. The mud seemed clean after what I'd stepped through in Lynn's tent.

The high point of the bluff towered above me, so close I couldn't see the jagged top. The cliff face was a crumbly surface of weathered rock streaked with ocher and rust. Stunted trees had managed to find a purchase here and there. It didn't look that hard to climb.

I scrambled up the tumble of boulders at the base of the cliff. I was moving fast, not paying attention to what I was doing. A small boulder rolled beneath my foot and I fell. My palm was scratched and oozed blood. I spit on it and wiped off most of the blood and dirt on my jeans.

The cliff leaned outward at the bottom, blocking my ascent. I walked along until I spotted a ledge above me. It had been years since I'd done chin-ups, but I managed to pull myself up and sort of flop forward on my belly. Loose pebbles knocked off by my steps clattered onto the rocks below. I picked up a fist-sized rock and aimed at the pool. I threw another and another. One hit a rock and splintered into a dozen pieces. "Damn," I muttered through clenched teeth. I wanted to shout but I was too close to camp. "Damn, damn, damn, damn."

The fit passed. It seemed easier to go up than to retrace my steps. The ledge narrowed and I began to grab on with fingers and my rubber-soled toes, until it got too narrow even

55

for that. Impasse. I rested against the rock. A point poked into my shoulder blade but I ignored it. I'd climbed from the shade into the sun; I was above the treetops. From here, I could see the entire camp. The people looked like little figurines. I didn't want to see what they were doing. I closed my eyes for a moment. Red stars exploded inside my eyelids.

I turned back to the rock face. There were enough pro-- jections to offer toeholds. Less than an inch was all rock· climbers needed. I looked over my shoulder. I wasn't a rock: climber. This was crazy. I looked at the top of the cliff. If wanted to get up there. I just wouldn't look down.

I tested a knob in the cliff face above my head. It seemed solid. I pulled harder. It still didn't crumble. I gripped it with my fingers and managed to launch myself up. Piece of cake. My fingers were trembling with the strain but they didn't feel weak. In fact, I'd never realized how strong they were.

I scouted around blindly with my left foot until I got a good purchase. Next a new hold for my right arm. Slowly and deliberately as a mime, I managed to climb toward a split in the rock face. The effort exhausted me. I leaned my cheek against the cliff. The stone was hot. Flakes of dirt stuck to my damp skin and I could feel sweat trickling down my sides and between my breasts. The sun was a palpable force that pushed against me, blinding me and weighing me down.

What did I think I was doing? This was the stupidest stunt I'd ever pulled. Now I was stuck. I had to keep going; there was no way I could back down this thing. I studied the crevice through slitted eyes. How the hell was I going to get inside it? I had an image of falling through space like a rag doll, end over end, mouth open in a soundless scream. There was a certain appeal in the image—not a good sign.

I began to climb again, proceeding more by feel than by sight. I wedged my foot onto a bit of rock. With a scratching sound, it broke loose and my knee scraped against the cliff. I clung there with one leg dangling in air. The image of falling became stunningly real.

I panicked. My pulse pounded through my arteries like

waves against a dike, threatening to wash me away. I could feel the tears welling up. This was not the time and place to get hysterical. I gripped the cliff face and forbade myself to fall apart. You're all right, you can make it, I chanted like a mantra. I concentrated on taking one deep slow breath after another. Calmer, but heart still pounding, I continued my crablike progress upward.

At last, I could peer into the cleft. It was about four feet deep, widening rapidly at the top. The far end was filled with debris, fallen rocks, leaves, and dead branches. A hyrax, looking like a giant guinea pig, stood on a boulder and scolded me, then disappeared into a hole. Good, that meant no snakes.

I climbed down to the fallen rock. It was a relief to be going down, to have two narrow walls enclosing me. If I fell now, I'd be wedged into the cleft and they'd find me eventually. I smiled at the image of myself stuck in midair. It was the first time I'd smiled since finding Lynn and it made me want to cry.

So that's what I did. I picked a good flat boulder in the shade, sat down, and cried. Memories of Lynn flashed through my mind: Lynn rushing into the kitchen with two bags of groceries clutched in her arms, Lynn sunbathing naked in a Vermont field, her long hair glimmering around her like a blackbird's wing, Lynn meditating, cross-legged, on the plant-room floor, Lynn taking longer showers than anybody, singing loudly when you pounded on the bathroom door. She'd had a lousy voice and always got the lyrics mixed up.

I gave way to deep, wretching sobs. My mind was blank, full of shapeless misery, which every now and then congealed into a vivid image, which in turn dissolved into blankness. After a while, I started crying about Adam, the point where all tears lead. He'd told me over dinner at our favorite restaurant. He was having an affair with a student and she'd gotten pregnant. They were having the baby, he told me. My fork was poised over a luscious shrimp scampi. On automatic, I speared the shrimp, realized I couldn't swallow it because my throat had closed off, and balanced the fork on the plate's rim. It seemed terribly important not to get butter and garlic sauce on the thick white tablecloth, but the overloaded fork slipped off and rolled. I dipped my napkin in my water glass and rubbed at the greasy stain. "Did you hear me?" Adam asked in a testy voice. I looked at him and shook my head in disbelief. "I'm divorcing you. I'm going to marry Elise," he told me. "I'm sorry." I heard a loud voice yell, "You fuckin' bastard." Faces turned all over the restaurant, pink blobs with staring eyes, and my plate of shrimp scampi hit Adam midchest.

I groaned aloud at the memory. Death, even murder, seemed clean by comparison. Adam's shabby betrayal had ripped out all my love for him, like ripping out my heart, so what was left to guide me through the loss? I was left tiptoeing around a black hole that became the new center of gravity in my universe. No wonder I'd fled the continent. Could enough dawns and sunsets, enough zebras courting and elephants playing in mud holes, enough eagles and ostrichs fill up that hole?

After a long while, my tears were used up. I groped around in my pockets and found a tissue, with which I cleaned my face as best I could. I felt better. Time to get back. The others would be wondering where I was. No more rock-climbing stunts, either.

I scrambled out of the cleft and found myself on the lip of the bluff. Bushes grew in patches almost to the edge. Treetops hid the stream at my feet, but I could glimpse an elbow of water farther off. I could see a few of the tents, the little canvas shower stall, the burnt circle of the campfire, the fallen log where the clearing narrowed. The martial eagle floated below me and disappeared into the trees. It was like the miniature world in the background of Early Renaissance paintings, every detail clear.

Eleanor came out of Cliff's tent, her shadow a dark blob under her feet. I hoped she wasn't pressuring him to drive Boyce's body out before the police arrived. In her passive way, Eleanor could be quite single-minded, not that I blamed her for wanting to get the body out of a sweltering tent. I scanned the sky. No sign of the police plane, just the usual circle of vultures floating effortlessly on the thermals, waiting for something to die.

I blinked in the glare. I'd follow the top of the bluff west. It sloped rapidly toward the road into camp, a half mile at most. It was going to be a hot walk.

7

"WHAT THE HELL happened to you?" Al spotted me across the camp. "Ibrahima said you went for a walk, but it's been"—he looked at his watch—"almost two hours. We didn't want to lose you, too, kid. Madge's been worried sick." He took my arm and cradled it protectively against his white-shirted belly.

I laughed weakly and freed myself from his hand. "I'm filthy, don't touch me." My arm left a rusty smear of dirt across his shirt. "I'm sorry you were worrying. I'm fine. My walk turned out a little more adventurous than I'd planned, but I'm fine."

The sun beat down like a fist. I kept straight on toward my tent. Al drew his heavy brows together with concern as he trotted along with me. I knew I was a sight: shoes black with mud from the stream, hands scraped from my rock climbing, face streaky with sweat and tears and coated with red dust. Al called Madge and she joined us as we reached my tent. I poured myself water and, still grasping the carafe by its neck, flopped down in a chair. I gulped down all the water and refilled the glass. Water was the most wonderful thing in the world. I was filled with gratitude to be alive.

"Listen, would one of you do me a favor and ask Molezzi to get me water for a shower? It feels so good to sit down, I don't want to move for a second."

"Did someone attack you?" Madge asked.

"No, I tripped, it's nothing. Is everyone taking a siesta?"

Madge took off her pith helmet and waved it in front of her face like a fan. "Have Molezzi bring some sandwiches, too," she told Al. He set off. "I bet you haven't eaten anything today, have you?"

I realized with surprise that she was right. I was starving.

When I'd run from the camp, I'd wanted to blot everything out, to escape from everyone and everything—from Lynn's death, the tour, Striker, my own history. Climbing that cliff had changed something for me. I'd never been so scared nor so brave in my life. I wasn't going to run from this murder. I was going to do all I could to help the police find the killer. If they couldn't, I realized almost with surprise, I'd do it myself.

Madge watched me drink a quart of water and eat two ham and cheese sandwiches before she allowed Al to drag her back to their tent and leave me to my shower.

The canvas shower stall had a changing booth with a wooden bench, on which I deposited my towels and clean clothes. I slipped out of what I was wearing and left it in a dusty pile on the ground. I inspected my naked body. Aside from the dirt, I had a minor scratch on one knee and a scraped hand. My fingernails were the worst: torn, scratched-up, and filthy. Filthy could be taken care of, and I wore my nails short anyway, so torn didn't show much. I flexed my right biceps. My arms felt strained from the rock climbing. I was damn lucky I'd survived the morning intact. I stepped onto the wooden shower pallet.

I pulled the chain and lifted my face up to the flow of tepid water streaming through the bucket's perforated holes. Ahhh. That was good. The slotted wooden pallet cleverly kept my feet out of the mud I was creating. I groped for the shampoo and measured a small amount onto my palm. So what had I learned, if anything, from people's reactions when I told them Lynn was dead? Al thought it was rape; Madge thought it was a sex scandal; Cliff had hit the bottle; Eleanor was out of it; and Candy accused me of having blood on my hands, or, rather, my shoes. Well, not accused exactly; observed. I spread the shampoo on my wet hair and worked up a good lather.

Both the Harts immediately came up with an explanation that excluded them from suspicion. I rubbed my scalp vigorously. Was that a sign they'd concocted these theories in advance? It didn't seem so weird to come up with a neat explanation. It showed they were smart, or kept thinking under stress. Unlike some people. I reached for the cord to let down more water. My own reaction seemed more bizarre—oh, I went and climbed a cliff and cried about my divorce.

I held my head under the spray, turning this way and that to get all the lather. As for Cliff slugging back the Scotch, that was hardly a sign of guilt. In some ethnic groups, you were supposed to drink when people died. Who was I to judge what form to freak out in? I tested my hair with my fingers. It squeaked. The same went for Candy's bumming those cigarettes. Boyce's death and the atmosphere in camp were enough to make her nervous. Your honor, the murderess smoked cigarettes for the first time on the trip. It was ridiculous.

I soaped my body and watched the soap turn brown with dirt, using the water sparingly now. One long last rinse until the water ran out, then I stepped into the canvas dressing room and toweled off. Maybe I had picked up a clue without noticing it. If one of them had committed murder, there had to be a sign. It was like tracking: Not every animal was going to leave an elephant trail, but eventually it would step in mud, or catch some hair on a branch, or leave a scat. If you were patient and kept your eyes open, you could figure out what had passed by.

I drew on my jeans and khaki shirt and slipped sandals on my feet. My hair dripped onto my shirt, leaving wet streaks. I wrapped a second towel around my head, turban style, and made my way back to my tent.

There was a pad on my night table under a pile of books. I dug it out and sat at the card table in front of the tent. I wrote down four headings: suspects, motives, means, and opportunity. I felt the fool making a list, playing a detective out of mystery stories, but I couldn't bear to sit and wait for the police without doing something.

I tapped my pen against my lips. Suspects. I put down everyone in the group, the staff, the Masai who'd sold Al the spear and the two I saw at dawn, then a question-mark category. I looked up at the sound of footsteps.

There was Cliff, approaching with a highball in hand. Every blond hair was lined up in place, his chinos might have been newly ironed, even his lime green polo shirt looked crisp and cool. He peered at my paper, pulling it halfway around so he could read it. "Do my eyes deceive me? You're solving the murder." He pulled up a chair next to me. "How perfectly thrilling. And you have us all down. Am I at the top of your list?"

"Want to help? I'm up to motives."

I doodled a skull and crossbones on the margin of the page. Cliff's mockery was a welcome leavening to my heavy mood.

"What drives man to murder?" Cliff asked rhetorically in his light voice. "Greed . . . was Lynn standing in the way of someone and a lot of money?" I wrote it down as he spoke. "Passion," Cliff continued. "A secret affair with Boyce? Or with one of the other men."

"Meaning Al?" I looked skeptical.

"We're brainstorming, right? You put it down and we'll pick out the best ideas at the end. Don't cramp my creative flow."

I wrote down lovers: Boyce, Al, Cliff, staff.

Cliff read what I had written. "Every list must be complete. I'm sensing an obsessive streak in you that I hadn't suspected, darling."

"Fear," I said. "Who'd be scared of Lynn?"

"Aha." Cliff clapped his hands. "Here it is: Lynn was blackmailing Boyce. He'd had enough and was going to expose her. She killed him with a hat pin through the top of his skull. Eleanor discovered this and murdered Lynn in revenge."

"Very imaginative. You missed your calling doing ad campaigns."

63

"Not at all, darling. They're entirely made up. Well, I think we've covered motive." He checked the next heading on my paper. "Let's see what we can do with means."

This seemed more promising. "Find the weapon," I printed in block letters. "Who had access to a knife?"

"I would say everyone," Cliff pointed out.

He was right. The kitchen area was rarely deserted, but the knives weren't exactly under lock and key, either. Hell, it might even be a steak knife pocketed at the dining table. Horrible thought. I pictured the Masai sword I'd seen the man wearing that morning, then quickly pushed the image from my mind.

I looked over the sheet. "Our list of motives is completely nebulous."

"We won't discover the motive until we find the murderer. First we need concrete evidence."

"How about blood, is that concrete enough?"

There'd been a lot of blood. It wasn't so easy to clean up or get rid of bloody clothes when you lived in a tent. For the first time, I felt a surge of hope. I wrote "Blood" and under it: "clothes, shoes, footprints," and, as an afterthought, "traces—skin, nails."

A small sound made me look up. I'd been concentrating so hard, I hadn't noticed Eleanor approach us. I hurriedly put the pad down and drew my binoculars over it. Her hair wasn't as lacquered together and she seemed to have better color in her face. Her stride looked steadier also.

"Were you able to nap?" I asked her.

"I did lie down for a little while. Am I interrupting something?"

"Stay, stay." Cliff gestured. "Let's get you a drink." He lifted his empty glass with his cigarette in hand. "Looks like I need a refill myself."

"An ice tea would be lovely." Eleanor sank heavily into a chair. "I'm worried about this heat."

Above the cicada's loud shrill, I could hear the buzzing of an airplane. The police had arrived.

8

I JUMPED TO my feet and knocked against the camp table. Water pitcher, binoculars, pens, and pad went flying. I lunged forward and caught the binoculars in midair, enjoyed an all too brief sense of triumph, overbalanced, flailed wildly, and ended up on the ground myself. The pitcher lay unbroken next to me in a puddle of water. At least I'd missed the puddle.

"Damn." I got to my feet.

"Oh, heavens." Eleanor bent to help me gather the things scattered about.

The list of suspects was an inky smear on a wet page. Big deal. I crumpled it up and threw the wad of paper into the tent, to join my dirty clothes already on the floor. It wasn't worth much except as a mental exercise, anyway.

"Do you have something to mop this up with?" Eleanor asked.

"Other than my handkerchief," said Cliff, poking at the now-sodden mess on the mat floor.

"Sorry, Cliff. I'll wash that before I return it. Don't worry about the water. It will soak through the mat and disappear. One of the advantages of camping out."

The humming of the airplane engine grew louder. I walked to the center of the clearing and looked up. A bush plane appeared in the gap of trees overhead.

65

"I'll go pick them up." I got my car keys and a hat and headed for the Land Rover. "Be back in a few minutes."

"Mind if I join you?" Cliff asked. "Wait a second, I'll get a hat, too."

"I'll be in my tent," said Eleanor. "I hope they get this over with quickly and let us go home."

Al came out of his tent in a T-shirt and pants. "That the police?"

"I assume so. Cliff and I are driving over to the landing field." I jingled the keys.

"Okay. I'll get Madge up, too. We'll be ready by the time you get back."

Cliff returned wearing a white Panama hat. He climbed into the passenger seat without hesitation. Was it only last night that Boyce had been sitting in that very seat?

I put the Land Rover into gear and drove out of camp. How amazing and beautiful that hunt had been. It was one of the most memorable experiences I'd had in Kenya. In Kenya? In my entire life. I'd never forget the fierce grace of that lioness, the courage of the mother zebra, or the thrill of the zebra band thundering over the hill to the rescue. Hard to believe how suddenly and how totally everything could change.

"I hope these guys know what they're doing," Cliff said.

"Amen."

"It shouldn't be too hard. There are only six of us to choose from." He gave a mirthless laugh. "What a six-pack."

"Six?"

"You have to remember to count yourself, too. The police will."

Cliff fished a roll of breath mints out of his pocket and offered it to me. "Want one?"

I shook my head. So Cliff was assuming it was one of the group.

"Do you have any guesses?" I asked him.

"No, I'm leaving that to the professionals."

We lapsed into silence and bumped along in the heat. I

66

concentrated on driving through the long grass. We flushed a helmeted guinea fowl. It burst from under the tires like a small black bomb and whirred away on stubby wings.

I pulled up to the edge of the landing strip and turned off the engine. *Landing strip* was a glorified name for what was simply a two-thousand-foot stretch of fairly flat land, thorn-bushes hacked off with machetes, marked by empty oil drums. I was stunned by the roar of the descending plane. After a few days out here in the wild, I'd forgotten how noisy man-made things were.

A dozen Cape buffalo grazed in the dry grass or stolidly chewed their cuds. Their hides were a dull brown. Massive horns grew from the middle of their heads in two swells separated in a part, a regular barbershop quartet, except the horns swept upward into scimitar points. Next to the hippo, they were the biggest killer of humans. If I'd met a buffalo on my walk home at midday, I'd probably be dead.

The plane buzzed the field once to chase off the animals. The buffalo grudgingly gave way. A warthog ran off, squeal-ing, its tufted tail held high in the air. One buffalo passed by the Land Rover and gave us an aggressive stare but kept on going.

The plane circled and came in for a landing: one bump, a second, the scream of the engine as it taxied to a halt, then sudden silence. The propeller on its pointy nose stopped at the horizontal, giving the jaunty impression of a mustachioed Frenchman. My ears were still buzzing. It looked enormous compared to the two-person planes I was used to seeing land without benefit of tarmac. A door in the side flipped open and two figures emerged and came toward us. A third figure began unloading luggage and cases of equipment from the rear of the plane.

Cliff and I went to meet them. The man in front moved faster than any African I had seen. The way he fluidly darted forward reminded me of a red squirrel—cheerful but pur-poseful. He wore a gray tropical suit and a soft cotton shirt open at the collar.

His companion was twice his girth: some fat but mostly

muscle. He lengthened his stride in a halfhearted effort to keep up, but the space between the two men steadily grew wider.

A broad smile creased the face of the first man and he reached out his arm for a handshake when he was still twenty feet from us. "Inspector Omondi," he sang out. "And you must be Jazz Jasper, that my new friend Striker spoke so highly of." By now, he was upon us. He shook my hand, pumping it energetically up and down while he anchored my elbow with his other hand, and he said, "Very, very pleased to meet you."

The inspector's skin was warm and silky. He kept my hand in his and studied my face with interest. "You are young to be running your own safari company. Kenyan women, too, are smart businesswomen. Very good." He pumped my hand once again. "It is very good of you to give your energy to our country."

He turned to Cliff. "What a fine hat," he said as he shook Cliff's hand. "You must be careful of our equatorial sun." He patted the top of his own spongy black hair and laughed. "You are not well protected as we are."

"Cliff Edwards. Pleased to meet you, Inspector."

"And this is my invaluable assistant, Sergeant Kakombe." Omondi whirled around and tugged at his companion, who had just come up to us. Kakombe greeted Cliff and me with a slight nod. He dwarfed all of us. His wrists were the size of my arms, each thigh as wide as my hips. His nose and lips were emphatic, as if carved with a sculptor's knife. His eyes were appraising and not all that friendly. Striker would be relieved if he could see who they'd sent us.

Inspector Omondi waved his long elegant hands as he talked. "Don't let us worry you," he said, and pointed to the pile of baggage swiftly accumulating under the plane. "We are not planning on spending a month on this case. I have exactly three days before I must be back in Nairobi to testify in an important trial, so we must be quick."

"Three days?" I was dumbfounded. Three days didn't seem much time to solve a murder. What a favor they'd done us. This was the usual African bullshit of never wanting to say no. Why hadn't they told Striker that his Inspector Omondi had no time for us?

Omondi was looking over the luggage. "Yes. Sergeant Kakombe, I'm afraid, must bring this shocking amount of equipment." He turned to us. "That is why we look like a nine-month safari expedition." When he smiled, his whole face lit up with good humor. "Photography. We must document everything most carefully in situ, as the Latins would say."

"Don't worry, we have some extra tents we can put you up in," I told him, swiftly calculating how to make good on this promise. "We are very glad to see you."

Omondi bundled us into the Land Rover. "We have a lot to do here. And not much time. Pull right there, next to the baggage, I think."

The pilot was a young man, only in his twenties, who seemed very proud of himself, his uniform, and his plane. I wondered how many hours of flying experience were required for his job. I prefer pilots who are distinguished rather than excited, with some gray around the temples. This fellow looked as if he didn't shave yet.

Omondi continued to talk as the pilot and Kakombe loaded the Land Rover. "I want to inspect the bodies. Then our pilot here can fly them back to Nairobi this evening, for the doctor to see." He nodded for emphasis. "The autopsies, the lab work, and so forth. It would have been better for the police surgeon to come along, but he is a sadly overworked man, and you are far away here. So Sergeant Kakombe and I will do what we can. Yes, I think that will all work out quite nicely."

I found myself nodding up and down in unison with Omondi. He got into the passenger seat next to me, Cliff and Kakombe sat behind, and I turned the Rover toward camp. We left the pilot propped against the wheel on the shady side of the plane, his hat low over his eyes, looking out over the empty landscape.

The sky ahead of us was a clear deep blue, the color of

morning glories. A single thunderhead floated above the eastern horizon. It billowed up in alabaster domes of blinding white. I remembered an afternoon in Granada, years before, spent floating dreamily through the Alhambra: filigreed white stucco, intricate blue tiles, splashing pools. I brought my eyes back to earth. Heat waves danced above the double line of crushed grass we'd made on the trip from camp. The cloud might as well be a mirage. The likelihood of rain was zero at this time of year. There was no escape from the heat but to wait for nightfall.

Omondi swiveled in his seat so that he faced us all at an angle. "Striker tells me we have two bodies here. A middle-aged man who seems to have had a heart attack, and a young woman who seems to have met a violent end. A strange coincidence."

Omondi didn't wait for the formalities of introduction before starting work. There were only a couple of hours of daylight left, he explained as we pulled into camp, and it was most important that they examine the murder scene and dispatch the bodies to Nairobi. He meant business, today, not tomorrow.

"You are thinking, Most un-African," he told me, his eyes bright. "Sergeant, if you would get your camera, we will leave the unpacking till afterward."

"Yes, sir." Kakombe's voice was a soft bass that emerged from deep in his chest.

We all climbed out of the Land Rover and waited while Kakombe sorted through the bags and extracted what he needed. The camera looked miniature in his fist.

"I can have my men unload your things and set up tents for you, if that's all right."

"Fine, by all means. So sorry to put you to all this trouble. Yes, when it comes to murder," Omondi continued, "I am a man in a hurry." He thought a moment. "Although, when it is necessary, I can be very, very slow. Slow like the crocodile waiting patiently where the antelope come down to drink." His right hand lunged forward and he snapped his fingers closed like a crocodile's mouth. Cliff jumped. "If you please, show me the scene of the crime." Without waiting, Omondi led the way toward the tents. We hurried after him.

Cliff pointed out Lynn's tent. "Here you are, Inspector. No one has gone near it since this morning, when Jazz went in to wake Lynn. These two fellows have made sure of that."

I stood a few paces back. Omondi spoke in Swahili to the men playing cards in front of the tent and dismissed them. He zipped open the door and looked inside for a long while in silence, then stepped aside to let Kakombe take some photos from the entrance. When they pulled the tent flaps up to let in more light, I left. I didn't want to see inside that place again.

I told Ibrahima the bad news about unpacking everything. "We're going to be here at least one night, maybe more."

"It's all right, Jazz. I'll take care of it." He nodded gravely, then turned around and made some crack in Swahili that got the men laughing to their feet.

"Molezzi, I think it's time for cocktails."

"It is already done." He smiled a little cat's smile. "Would you like a gin and tonic for yourself?"

Drink in hand, I went to the dining tent. Al, Madge, and Eleanor were sitting in front, around the ashes of last night's campfire.

"So those are the African policemen, huh?" asked Al. "They look like a comedy team. Is the squirt the guy in charge?"

Madge hushed him and he patted her rounded knee.

I sipped my drink instead of answering. The sun was low enough to cast broad shadows over the clearing, there was a slight breeze, and the stream made a liquid sound. They were all false cues: It was still hot.

"Are they going to fly us back to Nairobi?" asked Madge.

"Inspector Omondi said something about spending a night or two here," I said.

"Oh, no. Oh, no." Al shook his head emphatically. "There is no way we are staying here. No way."

71

"Now, Al," Madge started.

"Don't 'Now, Al' me. I'm not having you—and Eleanor—or Jazz for that matter—sleeping where there's a killer on the loose. You can't lock the door on a tent."

Cliff joined us in time to hear Al's last sentence. "So you think we have a serial killer on our hands? Let's wait and see what the inspector has to say before we panic and run, shall we?" He took out a cigarette and lit up. He spotted Molezzi across the clearing and signaled to him with a hoisted arm. "Scotch and soda," he called out.

"Who's in a panic? I just don't want—" Al said.

"Shh, you're making Eleanor nervous," Madge cut him off. "Honestly, Al, I'm not the least bit worried. I think Lynn must have taken her own life."

She glanced at Eleanor, as if uneasy about the implication that there was something between Lynn and Boyce, but Eleanor wasn't thinking along those lines.

"I'm not nervous for myself, either," Eleanor said. "As long as they take care of Boyce."

Everyone, I noticed, cast surreptitious glances toward Lynn's tent. I couldn't help doing it myself. The two policemen were inside, and there was nothing to see.

Candy joined us. She wore the slinky white dress and beaded Masai ruff. She sank into a chair, stretched out her legs, and brushed her hair away from her forehead. "Whew, it's still hot. Cliff, can I bum a cigarette from you?" Cliff tapped out a filter tip, which she delicately extracted from the pack. "Oh, good. These won't make me dizzy." She lit up, drew deeply on the cigarette, and exhaled a puff of smoke through her nose.

"I didn't know you smoked," Madge said.

"Oh." Candy waved her hand. "I'm an on-again–off-again smoker."

"Candy pretends she doesn't really smoke by never buying cigarettes herself," said Cliff.

Molezzi appeared with Cliff's Scotch and a white wine for Candy. How had he sensed her arrival? Shock waves?

Omondi and Kakombe emerged from the tent. We all

stared, even Candy. Kakombe squatted and examined the ground carefully, slowly covering the entire area. At one spot, he lay full-length on his belly, cheek to the ground. Omondi bent down next to him. Kakombe switched the lens on his camera and took some close-up shots of the ground. They seemed to trace the signs a short way, then returned to the first spot, measured it, and took a sample of the dirt. Then they disappeared behind the tent for a long time.

Kakombe reappeared and approached us in an unhurried gait. He seemed to cover the ground in a few strides. "Miss Jasper, would you come with me, please?"

His deep voice was honey-smooth but he looked at me coldly through heavy-lidded eyes that seemed to proclaim guilty until proven innocent. I returned the cold stare. I wondered what Omondi wanted. I took a big gulp from my drink, put in on the ground under my chair where it wouldn't be kicked, and followed Kakombe. My mouth felt dry.

He led me to Lynn's tent. I stared at the dark stain of sweat between his shoulder blades. I was afraid of what he was leading me to see. We circled behind it, staying clear of the area he'd photographed in front of the door, where I guessed they'd found footprints. I had the distinctly unhappy thought that any bloody footprints there were probably mine.

Omondi stood about three feet out from the tent wall. There was something small and dark on the ground by his feet. I stared at it nervously, then saw it was a pair of blue jeans.

"Look at this." Omondi indicated the jeans with his foot.

I looked where he pointed, then my eyes were caught by the back of the tent. It had been cut. There was a three-foot vertical slit down the center. The canvas lips luffed in the breeze.

"You can walk right up," Omondi told me. "Unfortunately, the ground is very hard-packed; there are no footprints."

"Did you find prints on the other side?" My voice sounded strained.

Omondi looked at me and gave a kind smile. "Yes, probably yours, no doubt."

"That's just what I was going to say. I did get blood on my running shoes when I went in this morning."

He looked down at my sandals. "We'll have to see those shoes in a little while." He tapped his toe on the ground next to the jeans. "The reason I called you over was to ask you if these belong to Lynn."

I walked next to him. He was a comforting presence. Designer jeans, prefaded. I nodded, then added a small "Yes." My voice came out sounding normal, so I tried a longer sentence. "At least, they look like the pants she wore on our game run last night. Candy wears jeans, too."

Omondi held a hand up to Kakombe as a stop sign. "We will ask Candy later." He reached down and picked up the jeans with his fingertips. "This is very interesting," Omondi said, "In there"—he nodded toward the tent—"it is swimming with blood. But look." He turned the jeans backward and forward. "There is not a drop of blood on these pants. There is no blood out here at all."

9

OMONDI ANNOUNCED HE was now ready to meet the others. We joined the group in front of the dining tent, Omondi bounding ahead of me. I gestured him toward a free chair, sat down, and rescued my drink.

"What can I offer you?" Cliff asked.

Omondi pulled his chair around so he could see everyone and he smiled. "A Tusker would be most welcome."

Cliff gave the order to Molezzi, while Omondi looked around the group with curiosity. I barely noticed. I was distracted, puzzling over the cut tent, the pair of pants dropped outside, the absence of blood. It was hard to put together a picture of the previous night's events. And I'd imagined there would be a bloody trail leading right to the murderer.

Cliff leapt to his feet and began the introductions. Omondi held Eleanor's hand in his and patted it as he offered his condolences. She explained her concern about flying Boyce's remains back home as soon as possible.

"Do not worry, madam," he added. "We will get your husband's body on the plane to Nairobi before dark, and if all goes as expected, we will be able to follow soon after. As I explained to Jazz and Cliff, I hope to finish here in three days at the latest." He gave her hand a last pat and released it.

Al pushed his chair back and stood. Omondi was about my height, which made him a couple of inches taller than

Al, but they were two opposite body types. Al thrust forward his square hand and pumped Omondi's long elegant one. "Hi. Al Hart. And this is my wife, Madge."

Omondi and Madge shook hands.

"Nice to meet you, Inspector." Without her usual animation, her heavy features seemed drooping, weary. "Three days sounds like an awfully long time. This has been a terrible ordeal, especially for Eleanor and Jazz."

Al ran a hand over the freckled top of his head. "Everyone is yelling me down, but I'll tell you, I'm not happy about having all these ladies here with a killer on the loose. I think we should fly them out tonight."

Omondi nodded gravely. "I am glad to see you are thinking of everyone's safety. It is the unsuspecting antelope that is caught by the leopard."

"I make some antelope, Inspector." Al patted his paunch. "I'm not as fast as I used to be, and what about when we're asleep in our beds? As I told them a few minutes ago, it's not like you can lock the door."

"Mr. Hart, if there is any reason to suspect another attack, we will take you all out of here. At the moment, please, do not alarm yourself. I have never heard of a group of people being killed off one by one, except in the inestimable British mystery novel. Tell me, are you a fan of Agatha Christie?"

Cliff threw back his head and laughed.

Al smiled thinly. "You don't want to fly the women out tonight, that's your decision. Me and Madge and Eleanor are booked on a Nairobi–New York flight tomorrow that I plan on keeping, if I got to drive to Nairobi myself."

Madge patted his arm, whether in encouragement or to calm him down, I couldn't tell.

Omondi smiled. "You are setting me an even harder task than my superiors. They gave me three nights to do my investigation; you are giving me one night."

"Your investigation has nothing to do with us," Al said. He jabbed at the air with a pointed finger. "That's your job. My job is taking care of Madge and Eleanor."

"I'm afraid it may not be possible for you to leave so

soon," Omondi said. "You need an exit visa to leave the country."

Could they withhold exit visas? I couldn't tell whether Omondi's diplomatic phrasing was meant to avoid a shouting match or to hide the fact the police didn't have the power to keep anyone here.

"I want to go home, too," Candy said.

"Hey, wait a second, everybody," I said. "Give the man a chance. I'm sure we all want Lynn's killer caught. The more we cooperate, the faster it will go."

Al sat down again, but his hands were fists, poised uneasily on his broad thighs. "They find evidence that allows them to keep me here, I'll stay."

Madge looked at Omondi sympathetically. "Al, you're giving the inspector the wrong impression. I think we can agree to catch the next flight, don't you? When is it, Friday? That will give them their three days."

"I said what I think," Al said. He looked at Madge and abruptly added, "But do it your way."

"Can you stand staying till the next flight, at the end of the week?" Madge asked Eleanor.

"Please don't worry about me," Eleanor said in her sweet voice. "It sounds like we don't have much choice, anyway. As long as we get Boyce to the funeral parlor . . . I guess we'll have the funeral Sunday, then? That should work out."

"Fine, I'll change the reservations," I said. Even though she'd been maneuvered into acquiescence, I felt grateful toward Eleanor. She had more right than anyone to insist on leaving. I studied the lemon wedge sunk to the bottom of my glass. The ice cubes had melted, and I gulped down the last inch of watery gin and tonic. I was angry at Al, although I could understand his point of view. He didn't feel loyalty to Lynn the way I did. Or was his reason less innocent? The killer wouldn't care to hang around until the investigation was concluded.

"I appreciate your cooperation." Omondi leaned forward. If he was annoyed or suspicious, he was too professional to let it show. "Now let me get who's who clear in my mind." He turned to Al. "You were Mr. Darnell's partner?"

"I'm in charge of marketing and sales for Wild and Free Shampoo. Started the company with Boyce more than thirty years ago."

Omondi offered his condolences to the Harts also and asked some questions about the shampoo business.

Candy was next. She folded her long legs under her and rose for her introduction. Cliff's head came up to her brow and she towered over Omondi.

Omondi's face lit up. "You are regal as a goddess," he told her. "Few women can wear the jewelry of the Masai so proudly."

Candy smiled and went on about the beauty of the Masai. "Two of them visited camp last night. Incredibly thin, but in great shape, you know? They look like they're ten feet tall."

At first I thought Candy, with typical insensitivity, was gratuitously insulting Omondi about his height. Then I wondered whether she wanted to let him know without being obvious about it that outsiders had been around. I found it hard to read Candy sometimes. It was easy to be distracted by her looks.

Molezzi arrived with Omondi's beer and a fresh Scotch for Cliff.

"Beer," Omondi said, "has been very important in African history. It was with beer that the Pharaohs nourished their people. Without beer, we would not have the pyramids, and world civilization would be much the poorer."

"What a concept for a beer ad," Cliff said. "Pyramids make a great visual. 'Man does not live by bread alone.' "

Omondi took a sip and then returned to Candy's comments. He questioned her closely about the Masai's visit, and I helped fill in details.

"So he sold you a spear?" he asked Al. "May I see it, please?"

Al made a face. "Don't tell me it has anything to do with

the murder," he said. "I couldn't find it this morning. Jazz, did you remember to ask Molezzi about it?"

I admitted I'd forgotten. Kakombe came over and Omondi gave him orders in Swahili. Kakombe's eyes flicked rapidly over Candy and he sauntered to the staff area.

"Where had you put the spear?" Omondi asked Al.

Al looked shamefaced. "To tell you the truth, I didn't put it anywhere." He looked at Madge for corroboration. "We were hanging around the campfire drinking till about midnight, I guess, and the spear was right there," He pointed to a spot about six feet past the blackened stones that marked the campfire. "I went to bed and left it."

"Didn't you notice it was gone in the morning?" Candy butted in.

Madge looked at her sorrowfully.

"Yes, Candy, I think I mentioned that at breakfast." Al interlaced his fingers and stretched them until the knuckles cracked. "I figured one of the camp servants had put it away. They're always putting things away for you, doing your laundry without being asked," he told Omondi.

Molezzi was fetched and practically stood at formal attention while he answered Omondi's questions. I noticed that after the first question, his eyes strayed to Candy and stayed there. It detracted from his air of reliability. No, he had not taken the spear. Yes, he had seen it last night when he cleared up after the drinking party. No, it was not by the campfire in the morning when he had brought out breakfast.

Omondi sent Kakombe back to the staff area once again. When he returned, his eyes raked over the group with a flat, unfriendly stare. "I questioned the entire staff, sir," he told Omondi. "No one recollects seeing the spear this morning. It seems to have disappeared during the night."

"I think we've identified the murder weapon," said Omondi.

"Damn." Al cracked his knuckles again.

Madge reached over and took one of his hands. "Honey, it's not your fault. There was no way you could have known."

"How creepy," said Candy. "Does anyone have a cigarette?"

Molezzi darted over to her and fished an open pack out of his pocket. He shook it so three or four cigarettes were extended outward. "Please, take as many as you wish, Miss."

"The next order of business," said Omondi, "is to find that spear. May we borrow your car and driver for a moment?"

I gave my consent, mystified. Kakombe was dispatched to the staff area once again. A few minutes later, he and Mbare climbed into the staff van and headed out of camp with a roar.

"Here in Africa"—Omondi waved his hand in a broad gesture—"we have a tradition for the solving of crime. It is called the palaver. Everyone in the village, the victim's family, the accused and his family, relatives from the surrounding villages, everyone comes and sits under the tree in the middle of the village. Everyone gets a chance to talk. From the top man to the small man, everyone says what they know and what they think. After much talk, maybe for several days, they discover the truth. Often the problem lies not in the present but in the previous generation, or even the one before. Sometimes it is necessary to call in a special sorcerer to do a little magic and identify the witch or the unhappy ghost. It is an effective system."

"You and Sergeant Kakombe, the sorcerer and his apprentice," said Cliff.

"Ha, I like that." Omondi laughed. "But I promise you, we will not sacrifice any goats. We will all sit down together, and you will each one tell the story as you see it. The group will see the truth comes out." He nodded emphatically. "But first, we will do a bit more investigating in the Western fashion. The West wants facts. Science, not magic! Physical clues, not human verities. If you will be patient, I would like to search through all the tents first." He looked at the big gold watch on his slender wrist. "There is barely time before the sun goes down. We shall see what we shall find. And then, we shall have the palaver."

10

Omondi slapped his thigh and started down the line of tents. "Next, I will look at Boyce's tent. Please show me which one it is."

I showed Omondi to Boyce's tent and tried not to imagine what he was doing inside. Cicadas shrilled loudly in the late-afternoon heat. A lizard darted across the ground. Its scales were the copper-gray color of the fallen gum leaves, and as it scampered into the leaf litter, I lost it from view. A small breeze created a whispering stir above us.

Omondi stuck his head out of the tent and asked me to fetch Eleanor. The two of us waited outside until Omondi finished.

She fidgeted with the black scarf around her neck. "I'm so glad we didn't bring Wendy on this trip. I'd thought of it, but I didn't want her to miss that much school. She has a wonderful teacher this year who's doing such marvelous things with them."

I was glad to see her making an effort to act normal, but wasn't quite up to that level of pretense myself. Luckily, at that moment Omondi slipped out of the tent. He had what looked like a telegram in his hand.

"Ah, Mrs. Darnell, just a few questions." He handed her the slip of paper. "Can you explain this to me?"

Eleanor looked at the piece of yellow paper. "I'd better get my reading glasses." She bustled off to her tent and returned with a pair of frosted pink half-glasses. She fit them on her nose. "Let's see. Boyce was always telexing home . . . keeping his finger on the pulse of the business. He was such a thorough person!"

She pursed her lips as she read slowly and deliberately. I felt like whisking the paper out of her hands.

She finished it at last. "It's from his stockbroker. You should ask Al; he understands these things." She studied the paper again, then took off the glasses. "Boyce liked to follow the price of Wild and Free stock." She handed the telegram back to Omondi. "Down seventeen and three-quarters. That sounds like quite a bit. Do you think the company's in trouble?" She looked at us wide-eyed. "I wonder if Al knows. Boyce may not have wanted to tell him and spoil the vacation."

I tried to keep disbelief out of my face. The Boyce I'd met didn't mind spoiling things for people. Why pretend otherwise to Omondi? So as not to speak ill of the dead? Or did Eleanor see only an ideal version of her husband? In any case, she was probably right about the telegram. Al had given no indication he knew about the stock, and Al's emotions were usually right out there. If Boyce had told Al, we'd all have heard about it. But so what? How could this have any bearing on Lynn's death? Unless the company was in big trouble, and somehow she'd found out about it and—and what? I couldn't make that thought go anywhere.

Omondi took back the telegram, folded it, and put it in his pocket. "I will ask Al later. Thank you for your help. Do not say anything for now, please."

I watched him search Cliff's tent and start on Candy's. It was amusing to see how people stamped their individuality on their sleeping quarters in only forty-eight hours. Cliff's white silk suit hung faultlessly from a hanger hooked over the ridgepole. A leather toiletry bag sat on the night table, zipped up and aligned with the corner. A crisp-looking best-seller was aligned with the other corner. His suitcase was open on the unused cot, socks rolled up, a stack of bikini briefs and undershirts next to them, a pile of laundered shirts

82

with paper rings around them on the other side. Omondi gave everything a thorough going-over. He found nothing.

Candy's tent looked like a backstage dressing room. Every surface was piled with clothing, as if she had been unable to decide what to wear and had dumped out her suitcases in an indecisive panic. Or was this normal for her? There was a tangle of swimsuits and leotards, the green nightgown and yellow robe, silk underwear, the black dress she'd worn last night, sundresses in bright colors, slacks and shorts and skimpy tops, cleverly cut evening dresses, a romantic sun hat with a wide brim and a ribbon, a safari suit with miniskirt and padded shoulders, not to mention the pile of shoes and sandals under the bed. No wonder she'd needed four large suitcases. Omondi methodically worked through the jungle of clothes, leaving it exactly as he had found it. Again, nothing.

Omondi was undismayed. "That leaves your tent and—"

The end of his sentence was interrupted by shouting and laughter. Cliff and Al got to their feet.

"Do you hear that?" Madge called out.

We turned toward the sound. Twenty Masai filed into the camp.

There were elders, mature men with their heads shaved. There were the warriors with ochered curls, swords tucked into their waistbands. Adolescent boys, dusty from their hard work as herdsmen, hung together in a group. There were women, heads shaved bald, dressed in red cloth and leather and beads, some with babies tied to their backs. Children ran back and forth shouting.

The Masai stopped at the far end of the clearing and stared. At this hour of the day, their shadows stretched out tall and skinny before them.

"I didn't expect Kakombe to bring so many." Omondi laughed. "It looks like the whole kraal came. Very good, they shall help us. Please excuse me for one moment." He walked across the clearing and joined Kakombe and the Masai, while I went back to the group.

"He called them here on purpose?" Eleanor asked.

"You know, I never thought I'd say this, but on them, bald looks good," Al said.

"It's the bone structure," Cliff said. He threw his cigarette on the ground. I reached over with my foot and crushed it. "Sorry, darling. Was I sullying your pristine air? Shall I put the butt in my pocket? You don't seem to have provided ashtrays." He took out a fresh cigarette and lit up.

"You shouldn't smoke them back to back like that. Give your lungs a break," Madge told him. "What are you, up to two packs a day? It's the worst thing you can do to your heart."

"I'll share my health secret with you, gratis: no heart." He thumped on his chest, making a hollow sound. "That way, I can smoke as much as I like." Cliff blew a smoke ring.

Across from us, Omondi spoke at some length in Swahili, with many arm gestures, making circles in different directions around the camp. There was a loud discussion among several of the men and women. A young man stepped forward and talked with Omondi. I couldn't be sure, but he looked like our visitor of the night before, the one who had sold Al the spear. I scanned the men in the group. I didn't noticed the poacher I'd seen that morning.

Omondi returned. He waved his arms toward the Masai. "These families have kindly consented to help us look for the spear. I think we will find out if it's the murder weapon shortly."

The Masai dispersed in small groups, with much laughter and shouting back and forth.

My tent was next in line. Omondi hefted my binoculars as he looked over the odds and ends on my table. He moved to the doorway and scanned the tent interior. My dirty clothes were on the floor; the wadded-up list of murder ideas had ended up under the bed. I was embarrassed by the mess but resisted the impulse to apologize. Omondi was not conducting a good-housekeeping inspection. He fished out the crumpled paper, smoothed the creases, and read it over. I waited for him to tease me, but he didn't say a word. He put the paper down on one of the cots.

"I—"

He held up his hand. "It is self-explanatory. You naturally want to know who has killed your friend. I also find it useful to write lists."

He glanced over my night table and read the titles of the small pile of books I had by my bed—a field guide for birds, another for mammals, George Schaller's book on lions, *Among the Elephants* by Hamilton, and a couple of mysteries. I didn't like my things being examined, and turned my back to the tent.

"Sergeant!" Omondi called sharply. "Please take these clothes and label them. Handle them carefully. There is some blood."

I whirled around to face him. Omondi looked at me without smiling. I moved aside to let Kakombe into the tent.

"Is this all you want, sir?" his deep voice rumbled. He lifted the bundle of clothes in one lump. "What about these tennis shoes?"

"Yes, take those also. Measure them against the prints in front of the murder tent, and take a sample of the dried blood on them."

Kakombe brushed past me as if I wasn't there.

"I cut my knee this morning."

"Yes?" Omondi glanced down at my knee, which was hidden by my jeans. "How did that happen?"

"I was pretty upset when I found Lynn." I picked my binoculars off the table and fiddled with the strap. "First I called Striker and he said he'd try to get you assigned to the job. Then I had to tell everyone here."

Omondi nodded.

"So after I checked back with Striker and he said you were on the way, I asked a couple of the staff to guard the tent, and I left camp."

"You left camp."

I wondered how much was necessary to explain. I didn't feel like exposing my psyche to the police's scrutiny. On the

85

other hand, if I was vague, the whole thing would sound suspicious. The last thing I needed was to sidetrack the investigation by becoming the prime suspect myself.

"I needed to be my myself." Surely anyone would understand that. Any American would, but maybe not an African. I thought of a Kenyan family I'd visited in the city recently. When I'd entered their compound, the mother was sitting on a small mat with a relative and at least five children, maybe more. Everyone was intertwined, arms, legs, sides, backs, all touching despite the heat. They simply enjoyed sitting that close to one another, in a jumble. Going off alone was strange to an African.

I tried again. "I needed to cry and didn't want an audience. So I ducked down a path behind the cooking area. It led to the stream where it passes under the bluff." I pointed to the north end of the camp where the rock face was visible through the trees.

"And that's when you scratched your knee."

"I ended up climbing the bluff. That's where I did it, I think."

"Why did you climb the bluff?" Omondi's voice held genuine curiosity more than suspicion. At least, I hoped it did.

I sighed and put down the binoculars. "I was in a strange state. Numb but wanting to smash something at the same time. I didn't really think about it. I saw the cliff and decided to go up it." My eyes filled with tears. "Maybe I wanted to smash myself."

"Do you feel responsible for your friend's death?" Omondi asked me gently.

The man was good. I pulled out a chair and sat down. Omondi sat, too, and leaned toward me. I could feel the tug to talk on and on, explain, confide, confess. Would the murderer feel the same?

I fought the impulse and looked at him coldly. "No, of course not. I just needed to get out my feelings somehow; physical exertion helps."

"And then what?"

"Then nothing. I got to the top, had a good cry in private, and I walked down the long way." I waved my arm in a big arc to indicate my return route.

"Did you see anyone? Did anyone see you?"

"Inspector, what is so interesting about my taking a walk?"

Omondi patted my arm. "Jazz, be calm, be calm. I ask many questions. I don't worry too much, is this a good question, is this a useless question. I ask everything. The truth comes out."

I looked toward the top of the bluff. "The only creature I saw up there was a hyrax. When I got back to camp, I spoke to Al and Madge, who'd been all worried about me. I got out of those filthy clothes, showered, and waited for you. Actually, Cliff and I worked on that list together while we waited."

The martial eagle was back. It floated into the treetops like a dark shadow. There was a flash of white from its outstretched wings as it landed on its nest, then the glimmer of its pale breast. I couldn't see the second bird, but the light was too dim to be sure. I resisted the impulse to study the nest through my binoculars.

"You like birds," Omondi commented.

He didn't miss a thing. I could see why Striker had wanted him on this case. I said, "Yes, I love birds. Speaking of which, I took a walk earlier this morning, just at dawn, a bit downstream from here. I noticed two Masai watching me from the top of the bank. One of them I recognized; I don't remember his name, but you can ask Striker about him. A lot of people around here think he murdered a park ranger last year."

"Yes, I know the case. Poaching is no game around here," Omondi said.

I tried to smile but I was too worried. "Inspector, I want to find who killed my friend. Let me know how I can help. If you need a sample of my blood to test against my clothes, fine. I want to cooperate with you fully."

"Thank you. The more cooperation we have, the faster this will go." Omondi stood up.

"I was thinking that bloody clothes would be the key, but so far, the only bloody clothes are mine."

"Yes, blood is an important clue, here. Blood and no blood."

Eleanor took Omondi to search her tent, and I rejoined the group in front of the dead campfire. Our efforts at conversation were pathetic. Omondi was still with Eleanor when the Masai started to sing. First voices from one side of the camp, then from another, until we were surrounded. One group would sing a few phrases and another would answer. I automatically began to sway to the rhythm, then caught myself and stopped.

"Hey, Molezzi, what are they singing?" asked Al.

Molezzi was arranging the long narrow logs in a sunburst pattern for the evening campfire. He sat back on his heels. "I don't know. It is in their own language. Probably about finding the spear. Or about their cattle." He reached forward and arranged a bit of kindling. "Those Masai, they love their cattle like women."

"Better than loving their women like cattle." Al laughed. "He was telling me his father has two wives. That right, Molezzi? The Kikuyu can have as many wives as they can afford."

"Not so different from us," Cliff said.

The circle of voices contracted and grew closer.

Candy got to her feet and started to pace back and forth. "Their singing gives me the creeps. I feel like they're closing in on us."

I could feel the back of my neck getting tenser with each passing minute. Omondi and Kakombe emerged from Eleanor's tent and moved toward the next one.

"The last one. It must be the Harts'," Omondi sang out.

"Not so fast." Al surged to his feet. His balance was a little off, his eyes shiny with drink. "I never said you could look in our tent." He marched over to Omondi.

Omondi became glacially proper. "Is there some problem?"

"I don't like people pawing through my things, okay? You want to look in my private possessions, you get a warrant."

Madge followed Al and patted his arm. "C'mon, honey. You're being unreasonable. Inspector Omondi has looked in everyone else's tent. Do you want him to think we're hiding something?"

Al shook her off. "Kenya is like England and America, right? Innocent until proven guilty. I don't have to prove I'm not hiding anything. I don't like being treated like a goddamn criminal."

"Sir, I assure you—"

"Assurances, my—"

"Inspector, maybe tomorrow," Madge cut in loudly, and practically pushed Al into their tent.

"What does he think we've got in here? Another body?" The heavy canvas flap fell shut and muffled Madge's rejoinder.

Omondi beat a tactical retreat and followed Eleanor over to join us.

"The heat is getting on everyone's nerves," she told him. "You mustn't mind Al."

Omondi smiled. "I think he is not used to drinking at this altitude. It goes right to the head." He pointed to his temple.

"How long will it take you to get a warrant," I asked, "if Al really won't let you look in his tent?"

Omondi gave me an amused glance. "Do not worry, I think we have the power behind the throne on our side." I must have looked skeptical, because he added, "If Madge doesn't change his mind, I can have a warrant out here tomorrow." He shook a finger at me. "You are listening to the tick tick tick of the second hand, until you are as tightly wound as the watch spring. It is not good. You will crack before the race with the clock is over."

Omondi's attitude didn't reassure me. Africans don't live by the clock and have no respect for it. Omondi couldn't understand the meaning of a deadline to someone like Al.

Unless we found incriminating evidence to hold him, Al would be on Friday's flight to New York.

"If they don't stop singing, I'm going to scream," said Candy, and flung herself back into her seat. "It's making me crazy."

The Masai sounded close, at the perimeter of the clearing. There wasn't much daylight left. My stomach tightened.

Masai began to appear among the bushes. First a tall youth, then several women, a middle-aged man. Slowly, all of them stepped into the clearing. An elder came forward and spoke in Swahili. He gestured to the north, the west, the south, the east. I didn't need Swahili to understand the words.

They hadn't found the spear.

11

Two kerosene lamps cast a warm glow over the circle of faces around the long table. Tiny flames were reflected in the silverware and glasses. Molezzi stood discreetly by, ready to come forward with more food and drink. Dinner was rather late, since Omondi and Kakombe had questioned the staff and searched their tents in the midst of Ibrahima's cooking. Despite it all, the staff upheld the British tradition of civilized dining no matter the circumstance, be it camping in the bush or murder. I listlessly picked up and put down my fork. I wasn't in a congratulatory mood. Omondi seemed to be enjoying himself, and Kakombe seemed to be enjoying the food, but the rest of us were barely holding on.

The pilot had flown off at dusk, with Boyce and Lynn in police body bags, and my dirty clothes. Omondi said the forensic pathologists owed him a favor and promised to do the autopsy tonight. Still, I was discouraged by the search party's failure. How could a seven-foot spear disappear? If the Masai hadn't been able to find it hidden in the brush around camp, it must be far away, or else back in the Masai kraal, cleaned up and indistinguishable from its fellows. Omondi was convinced that a Masai would never commit this crime, that it had no place in the Masai universe. I tended to agree with him, but then, he'd also been convinced they would find the spear. He might move fast, but he hadn't gotten anywhere.

I took a small bite of the skimpy serving I'd accepted. We'd never find it. No bloody clothes, no tracks but mine, no murder weapon. What chance was there of finding the murderer?

The conversation went in little rushes with long lapses in between. In one of the pauses, I could hear the tap, tap, tap of a talking beetle, telegraphing for a mate. The peepers joined in with an exuberant chorus. Their little lives went on as if nothing had happened, while for us, time seemed to be as stuck as a rusty lock.

"Inspector, do you live in Nairobi?" asked Eleanor.

"Yes, the country is too quiet for me. I like the bustling crowds." He shook his head with a smile. "Oh, Nairobi. They keep me busy there."

"Do you come from a large family?" In the lamplight, Eleanor's skin tone looked less sickly than it had all day. She had put on her black dress again, with the ruffles at neck and wrist. It was more suitable for a party than a funeral, and yet each time I looked at her, it reminded me she was a widow, and my heart felt heavy.

"Very large." Omondi gestured broadly. "We are a strong family."

"How many are you?" Eleanor asked.

"About two hundred."

Al burst out laughing.

"Family dinners must be a bitch," said Cliff.

"We had a wedding last month. A big party. But I do not see my family as often as I would like. My mother and most of my aunts and uncles are farmers," said Omondi, "to the north, in tea country."

"Do they have wild animals there, too?" Madge asked. Wisps of hair had escaped from her French knot and there were dark pouches under her eyes.

"Ah no, not for some time now." Omondi put down his knife and fork and leaned forward. "The animals, you see, are very destructive." He made picking motions with his hands, like monkeys ravaging a field. "First the British came. They killed all the game they could find, for sport. Oo-ee, they liked to hunt, those British. Always killing something." He shook his head.

"There's no hunting allowed now, is there?" Madge asked. "Hasn't Kenya set aside more parks than any country in the world?"

"The big problem is that there is no more wild land. There are not even enough farms to go around. It is bad, because we need the animals to raise our most important cash crop—tourists." He laughed. This was obviously a favorite joke.

Eleanor managed a smile. A morose silence fell again. This conversation depressed me as much as Lynn's death. No hunting? What was poaching, then? Since the 1970s, most of Kenya's elephants had been killed. Everyone loves elephants, yet people keep buying ivory jewelry and trinkets, as if there was no connection. I felt like crying.

When the dishes were cleared away and coffee served, Omondi leaned forward with his elbows on the table. "My children, I know you are tired. I can see." He pointed to his right eye. "You are dispirited. Do not let this be. Let only the murderer be discontent, for we are on his trail. Together, let us sniff out his spoor."

He led us back and forth over the events of the entire tour, especially the previous day, culminating in Boyce's heart attack and the purchase of the spear. I could guess why he was focusing on Boyce. If the two deaths were unrelated, then it was conceivable that Lynn had been murdered by a stray psychopath who'd found the spear, killed her at random, and wandered back into the night. If Lynn died because of Boyce's heart attack, the killer was among us.

"This is a big waste of time," Al said. "We're not getting anywhere, sitting around and gassing."

"Maybe we should try sacrificing a goat, Inspector," Cliff said in his light voice. "At least you get to eat it afterward."

I let Molezzi pour me some hot coffee. He gave me a sympathetic smile. I cradled the cup and struggled not to give way to pessimism.

"I am listening, I am learning," Omondi answered. "Tell me again, who was on the last game run?" He signaled Molezzi for more coffee, added three teaspoons of sugar, and stirred vigorously.

"Chris Mbare and Boyce were in the front seats, then Lynn and myself in the middle, and the Harts were in the backseat," I told him.

Omondi asked the three who weren't on the game run why they hadn't gone and what they did instead. It was as if he'd switched perspective in looking at an Escher print: Suddenly, the staircase that looked so solid was seen to be hanging in space, oddly twisting upon itself. Cliff explained he was sunbathing, Eleanor writing letters, Candy doing aerobics, but Omondi persisted in questioning their excuses: Had they missed other game runs? No? Then why miss this one, especially when there was hope of seeing a lion hunt?

I was in a dilemma. No one was telling him about the fight between Candy and Boyce, and I certainly didn't want to win an unpopularity contest by bringing it up. My livelihood depended on pleasing these people. Should I wait and tell Omondi privately? We had no time. If I waited, he'd have to question everyone again tomorrow, wasting precious hours.

I sat up straighter. "I wonder if anyone else had the feeling I did, that something had upset Boyce and he wasn't acting like himself the last few days?" I met Omondi's eyes across the table, and the warm directness of his gaze jolted me.

Eleanor tried to deny what I'd said, but I think Candy realized her fight with Boyce was going to come out and she'd be better off telling it herself. We were hanging out at the lodge swimming pool, she told Omondi, when Boyce burst through the hibiscus hedge, grabbed Cliff, and started insulting Candy in a loud voice in front of everyone.

"Insulting you?" Omondi sounded amazed.

"He wanted me out of the series, said I didn't have the looks for Wild and Free. Can you believe that?" Candy pouted, showing her full lips to advantage.

"What was wrong with your looks?" asked Omondi.

"He said Candy looked like a tart. You know, a prostitute," I added, as if translating for Omondi. If that didn't uncork Candy, nothing would. She'd been so furious at Boyce when he said that, she might have killed him then and there. Startled by my own thought, I dropped the teaspoon loudly into the saucer, and the whole table jumped at the clatter.

"A tart," repeated Omondi.

"I don't like to speak ill of the dead," Candy said. She tossed back her hair. "But Mr. Darnell was a certain type. Just because he owned the company, or because we stayed up late flirting, and I let him buy me champagne, didn't mean he owned me, you know what I mean? I earn my own way. I didn't owe him any favors."

"You are saying that Mr. Darnell fired you rudely because you spurned his advances?" Omondi asked.

Candy nodded and looked down sorrowfully into her lap. The picture of injured innocence.

Eleanor said, "Really," in a shocked voice.

"Sorry, Eleanor. I wasn't planning on advertising this, but I don't want anyone getting the wrong idea about me." She turned toward Omondi. "Sure, I was mad at him for calling me names. I told him not to mess with me, and then I walked away."

There was a long silence. Candy looked around the table angrily. "It's not like I'm going to kill some old fart because he fires me."

"No one thinks you did," Cliff cut in. "It was a very normal sort of interchange—for Boyce, not for you, Candy," he added quickly.

Omondi asked, "What was normal?"

Cliff signaled Molezzi for a cognac. "I was devoted to Boyce, of course, but we all know he had his little ways. Personally, I found his temper tantrums rather endearing. It wasn't just Candy. He got mad at Jazz yesterday and wanted me to change safari companies once this trip was over."

Omondi turned to Madge. "You've been quiet, Mrs. Hart. What do you think?"

"About Boyce's behavior lately?" Madge raised her dark eyebrows. "I guess I'd have to agree with Cliff. We were all pretty used to Boyce. Jazz and Candy are not the first people he ever fired. This trip was actually better than most.''

Madge was lying, and I wondered why. I had clearly overheard her say to Al that Boyce was getting worse.

"He once fired you, too, didn't he, Madge?" Candy said. Madge looked annoyed.

"She told me, after Boyce was so mean, that he'd done the same thing to her, too," Candy explained. "You know, to cheer me up, that I wasn't the only one he'd ever trashed.''

"Tell me about being fired," Omondi prompted Madge.

Al leaned forward, elbows on the table. "When we started the company, Madge was our bookkeeper. We're talking thirty years ago, right? Once we had our first daughter, Boyce didn't feel Madge could give the job her whole attention. It was more of a mutual decision. But hell, that's a long time ago.''

"That's not what Madge told me," Candy said. "She said Boyce accused her of doctoring the books, because there was some little discrepancy, and pushed her out. That if they could have afforded it, Al would have sold out right then and there.'' She faced angry looks from both the Harts. "Well, we're supposed to be telling the whole truth, here, right? I don't want the inspector to think I'm the only one who wasn't a Boyce Darnell fan.''

Madge tightened her jaw and stared hard at Candy. "Are you calling Al a liar? After all we've done for you? I'd think twice before I ran off at the mouth like that if I were you, Candy.''

Candy was stunned into a momentary silence by this new aggressive version of Madge, then she muttered, "I didn't mean anything bad.''

Madge's face relaxed. "I know you didn't, but you're giving the inspector a false impression. I didn't tell you that stuff so you could broadcast it.'' She looked like herself again. "It sounds a lot worse than it was at the time, Inspector. What I told Candy was a bit of women's talk, to calm her down about Boyce, not take it so personally.''

"You yourself didn't take it personally when Mr. Darnell accused you of embezzling?" Omondi asked.

Madge shook her head. "It wasn't like that. There was never any question of embezzling. What Al said is true: I wanted to devote myself full-time to my children, and the company finances had outgrown me. Boyce didn't do it in a very nice way, but he was right; I had messed up the books. Once we all calmed down, it was a completely mutual decision. Bad feelings pass, and it's not the end of the world. That's the whole point I was trying to get across to Candy." She glanced over at Candy, who was pouting again. "I may have overemphasized my career ambitions, to show I understood her position—not that I'd call bookkeeping a career."

"Boyce didn't realize how deeply young people like Candy can be wounded by cutting remarks," Eleanor added. "I'm always telling my girls that. It was a terrible strain running a big company like Wild and Free, and sometimes he'd lash out without meaning to."

Omondi was starting to uncover some strange little secrets. I looked around the table and wondered if we'd heard the whole story. It made me see Madge in a new way. I couldn't have coexisted peacefully with Boyce after a nasty accusation like cooking the books. Madge had sacrificed her personal feelings with an almost ruthless practicality. Had she really forgiven Boyce, or was she hiding her anger behind a polite veneer all these years?

Omondi turned to Al. "Was it usual for both partners to travel together?"

Al leaned back so that his stomach bulged against his polo shirt. "Boyce and I thought the wives might like this trip. Seemed like a good idea at the time."

"Did the four of you socialize together a great deal?"

"The wives were good friends since way back when. They actually introduced Boyce and me. The four of us used to do more together, then the kids came along, the company got bigger. You know how it is. We don't hang out in the same crowd, but it's always nice to see Eleanor."

"Perhaps you can explain this telegram to me?" Omondi

97

reached into his pocket, drew out the yellow paper, and handed it to Al. "I found it among Boyce's things."

Al looked down at the telegram and a blank look came over his face. He sat taller in his seat, looking stiff and strange. If he was trying to hide a reaction, he was doing a poor job.

"What is it?" Madge leaned over his shoulder and quickly scanned the sheet. "When did Boyce get this? Al!" She darted a look at Eleanor.

"This worries you, Mrs. Hart?" Omondi asked.

Al threw the telegram down on the table. "I had a sizable loan out, Inspector, that's been on Madge's mind. Madge is a bit more conservative about investments than I am. Luckily, I paid if off before we left."

Madge looked down into her lap as she folded and unfolded her hands. I didn't believe Al and, judging from her reaction, neither did Madge.

Al slapped the telegram. "It looks like Boyce checked up on Wild and Free stock and that it took a little plunge. Gave me a shock there for a minute. Ha ha! It's really nothing to worry about, the whole market's been volatile lately."

I looked from Al to Omondi and back. Would Omondi accuse Al of lying?

Omondi picked up the telegram, folded it, and put it in his pocket. "Yes, before dinner Cliff was explaining to me about the extraordinary bull market you had been enjoying. I liked that . . . the bulls and the bears. Odd to see such a plunge against the current."

Al patted his paunch as if seeking reassurance in its solidity. "Yeah, well, when you've been around us long as I have, you learn not to get excited over every little upturn and downturn, you know what I mean?"

I would try asking Madge later, but somehow I doubted she would tell me what it was about. Maybe Cliff would know. My mind started to race. Was Wild and Free in big trouble? What were the Harts up to? Had business-smart Lynn discovered something that made her a threat to them?

"I wonder if Boyce took the bad news harder than you are,

Al?'' I said. ''Could this telegram have added to the strain on his heart?''

Madge frowned in concentration. ''That reminds me: A few hours before we left the lodge to come here, I saw Boyce coming out of the phone booth. He looked stunned. Sick. Maybe he'd just heard about the stocks.'' Her eyes were focused on that moment two days before. ''I asked if he was alright, and he didn't even answer, he kept right on walking, in a funny, jerky way.'' She shook her head as if to clear it of that image. ''The next time I saw him, he seemed his normal self, and I didn't bother mentioning it. He didn't like being fussed over.''

''Was that before or after the fight with Candy?'' Omondi asked her.

''Oh, definitely after, maybe three, four hours.''

Al picked up the telex and read the heading. ''That wasn't in reaction to this telex. He got it last week, when we passed through Nairobi. Unless things have gotten even worse. Damn. I better get to a phone myself.''

Omondi could probably trace Boyce's call. I wanted to check up on this stock business. A vision of Wall Street rose in my mind, Trinity Church dwarfed by the dark canyons of skyscrapers. Susan Greenburg: I had a stockbroker friend in New York who could find out for me. I'd have to get to the lodge tomorrow and call her; this was too complicated to explain in a telegram.

The group was silent, everyone preoccupied with their own thoughts. Omondi held his cup in midair as he spoke. ''Did anyone see or hear anything last night?'' He let the pause lengthen. ''Everyone slept soundly through the night?''

Eleanor fiddled with her ruffles and then raised a tentative hand, like a schoolchild. ''I may have heard something, but I'm not sure.''

''Tell us what happened,'' Omondi said in a soft voice. He replaced his cup with a delicate clink.

Eleanor opened her eyes wide. ''I lay down, but I, I couldn't sleep. I kept thinking of Boyce, lying there by himself. It didn't seem right. I wanted to make sure the lamp

99

was still burning in his tent. So I slipped over for a minute. To sort of keep him company." She tried a wobbly smile and caught her lower lip with her teeth.

"What time was that?"

Eleanor shook her head and shrugged.

"I'd guess somewhere around two-thirty, three A.M.," Madge said.

"Ah, were you there, too? Also unable to sleep?"

Madge looked a bit embarrassed. "No, I slept, but I had to get up to go to the bathroom. I usually do, around that time of night. I thought I heard someone in Boyce's tent and I went to check."

"By yourself?" Omondi asked. "Without waking your husband?"

"It sounded like Eleanor. You know, muffled crying. I helped calm her down and saw her back into bed, then I did my business."

"Did you notice Lynn's tent?"

Madge's voice dropped. "No, and I did glance around the camp. It was dark, and I felt a little nervous. The frogs were making a racket, and those hyrax were screeching, but that was all. I fell asleep pretty fast. I was exhausted."

Omondi gestured toward Eleanor. "Now tell us, when did you hear the noise?"

"After I was back in bed. I have no idea how long afterward. I was lying there quietly, trying not to think, and I heard a tiny little noise not far from my tent. I was scared for a second, but nothing else happened, and I told myself not to be so jumpy."

"What did the noise sound like?"

"I'm not sure." Eleanor looked worried, as if the teacher might scold her. "It was a sharp little sound. Not an animal call."

"Did you think it was a footstep?"

"I couldn't tell. Maybe a kicked pebble? Or a blowing leaf? Couldn't a leaf make a sound like that?" Eleanor's voice got tense. "Do you really think it was a footstep?"

"Don't start imagining things," Al told her. "It doesn't

matter if you heard a leaf or a pebble or a herd of elephants, anyway. We don't think a ghost killed her, so somebody walked around last night.''

Omondi rested his arms on the table, making a tent of his fingers. ''Thank you, Mrs. Darnell. Did anybody else hear anything? No? Let's go over again how each person came to be on this trip. Who decided who would come along?''

Cliff held his glass of cognac up to the light and squinted at the dark amber liquor. ''Maybe I can fill you in on some of those details. Let's see . . . Lynn completed the storyboard in September.'' He sipped and rolled the cognac on his tongue. ''We took it to Boyce and Al and got the go-ahead for a series of thirty-second spots. It was a natural. Everyone loved it. Wild and Free Shampoo and big game in Africa. We decided to come over with the writer—that was Lynn—do the location scouting, and hammer out the details right on the spot. I planned to hire a local assistant director and find out what kind of local crew might be available, then bring over the core film crew I like to work with from New York.''

''Very interesting.'' Omondi leaned forward, his eyes shining in the lamplight. ''So you will be using local film-makers, as well. We have many talented people.''

I scowled into my coffee. This is a murder investigation, I wanted to snap at him, not a chamber of commerce meeting. There's no time to waste. Omondi shot me an amused look, teasing and reassuring at the same time. It seemed to say, This is Omondi the wily charmer at work, have a little faith.

''Now tell me,'' said Omondi. ''Why was Candy a part of this early group? The model does not have a role until you start to film, am I right?'' He'd been circling back on our tracks, coming at the Candy–Boyce connection from another angle.

Cliff and Al exchanged glances. Who was going to answer this one? I had asked Lynn the same question and been told Boyce liked having the models around. He considered a beautiful woman one of his fringe benefits when he paid for commercials.

There was a pause.

"I believe it was my idea," Cliff replied. "I thought it would give the trip more of a Hollywood atmosphere."

Candy said, "I didn't realize I was here for atmosphere."

Cliff lit up a cigarette and put out the match with a brisk flick of his wrist. "There's nothing wrong with adding glamour to a junket for the clients, darling."

Candy gave a ladylike snort of dissatisfaction. She reached for Cliff's pack of cigarettes and allowed him to light one for her.

Who was she kidding? Candy had to know why she'd been invited along. Molezzi offered her more coffee, and she brushed him away. Why pretend to be an innocent? She certainly hadn't acted innocent with Boyce. Could something have been going on between them even before the start of this trip? Maybe we'd seen the final chapter of a long story.

I had always wondered how archaeologists pieced together a broken pot when they didn't even know if the shards they'd collected belonged to one pot or to several. It occurred to me now that they didn't put together just a single pot: They had to re-create all the partial pots from a given set of pieces. If they were lucky, at least one of them was more or less whole.

I looked around the group. Would we have to piece together everyone's little secrets? Could we do it by tomorrow night? And if we got that far, would we then know who murdered Lynn?

12

THREE HOURS LATER, we were still at it. Omondi had moved the group outside, to chairs around the campfire. The leaping flames threw our circle into darkness. Faces wavered in and out of view in the flickering light; voices floated on the night air, bodiless. The fire was built African style: long thin logs arranged like spokes on a wheel, not piled one atop another. The logs had burned more than halfway through and the hub was now a bed of glowing coals. My head nodded and I jerked myself awake. I was usually asleep by this hour. I leaned forward and pushed a smoldering log inward so it reached again to the center of the fire. It sizzled and burst into flames. A cluster of sparks floated up briefly and died.

Omondi had taken a quieter role and was letting the darkness and the fire have an effect. People had started to talk more spontaneously. Piece by piece, we'd created a detailed account of everyone's relationships during the trip. As far as I could see, it added up to a thick fog of innuendo, enough to keep us lost for weeks on dead ends. We needed something concrete to serve as a compass. If there was a link between Boyce's heart attack and Lynn's murder, it remained as murky as ever.

I pictured the spear at last night's campfire: haft thrust into the ground, its deadly point quivering against the fire's flames. Who amongst us was capable of taking hold of that shaft and plunging the point into Lynn's throat? Yet I wasn't impressed by Al's theory of a psychokiller, and what reason would a stranger have to attack Lynn? It just didn't fit with Kenya, with life out in the bush.

I sank lower in my chair so I could lean my head against the canvas back and stretched my legs straight out toward the fire. I could identify people around the circle by their feet, which were brightly lit by the flames. Cliff wore soft Italian pumps in pale yellow. It must be his favorite color. Good detective work, Jazz. Madge was in low-heeled espadrilles, a compromise between comfort and propriety. Eleanor was in conservative black heels—of course. Candy wore a wisp of a sandal attached to her foot by two artfully placed straps. I fought my drooping eyelids. The fatigue and anonymity meant to breed confidences were lulling me to sleep.

A lion grunted, probably a kilometer on the other side if the stream. Another grunt, closer to the camp.

"A lion," I said.

Cliff's light voice spoke: "I can't tell you how deflated I am to learn that lions grunt. The MGM roar was so much better." He flicked a cigarette butt into the orange coals. "It almost makes me regret coming to Africa. I have so few illusions left, I hate to lose one."

In the middle distance, a hyena laughed. I wondered if they'd made a kill, and if the lions would steal it. I refrained from disillusioning Cliff further. Hyenas were usually cooperative hunters, more successful than lions; lions often bullied in and stole their kills. When big-game hunters found a circle of hyenas looking on hungrily as lions consumed a carcass, they'd assumed the hyenas waited to steal crumbs from the king of beasts. The truth didn't occur to them because lions are beautiful and hyenas ugly, but once again, life was surprising.

"Is this the palaver?" asked Madge. "I thought we were going to get a chance to tell our ideas." She jiggled an espadrille. "What we know about Lynn."

Omondi's voice came out of the blackness. His gray suit and dark skin made him invisible. "Excellent. Mrs. Hart, do you care to lead the way?"

Suddenly shy, Madge hesitated. "Unless anyone else does?" her voice trailed off.

"What are you? The policeman's assistant?" Al asked her.

"You go first, Al," Madge invited him.

"Hell, no. I don't want nothing to do with this. If you ask me, we're wasting our time. Omondi, you should be out looking for the guy who did this."

Omondi didn't reply. It became obvious he expected someone else to comment. Silence lengthened. I resisted the impulse to speak. Who would the pressure get to first?

The stillness of the night was broken by shrill screams.

"What the hell is that?" asked Al.

"A hyrax," I told him. "It's nothing."

The hyrax's long wail dissolved into a series of piercing shrieks and died away.

"Well, if Al won't say his ideas, I'll speak for myself."

I jumped at the sound of Madge's voice.

"None of us except Cliff, and Jazz, too, I guess, knew Lynn very well. But I always thought she was a very nice girl. Hardworking and cheerful and full of energy. We will all miss her very much. And miss her contribution to the company. A very talented girl."

She leaned forward briefly, and I glimpsed her face. The lines around her large nose and mouth were exaggerated by the flickering light and shadow into a sinister mask. Her words were kindhearted, as usual, but I found myself wondering what Madge was after.

"I've been wracking my brains," Madge continued, "but I just can't come up with any reason one of us would want to kill her. Which makes me wonder if she didn't take her own life. That's all."

"Interesting." Omondi's voice again. "So you think that under her cheerful exterior, she was deeply troubled? A woman in crisis?"

Madge shifted in her seat. "Well, Cliff, what do you say?"

"Frankly, darling, I don't see it. For one thing, if she stabbed herself, why are we looking for a seven-foot spear?"

105

"If you're so clever, why would anyone here murder her?" Madge retorted.

"I was wondering . . ." Candy paused until she got our full attention. "Was there something going on between her and Boyce?"

"What an imaginative thought," said Cliff.

"Well, they were acting awfully palsy yesterday. I just thought that maybe after I wasn't interested, Boyce went after Lynn."

Was that true—not Lynn and Boyce, which I still didn't believe, but that Candy had turned Boyce down, as she kept repeating? Would that explain Boyce's temper tantrum at the pool? Candy was certainly working to direct attention away from herself and Boyce. I massaged my brow, as if that would help my thoughts penetrate further.

"What, and she was so broken up by his heart attack she killed herself?" Cliff said. He held up a hand. Firelight glittered off a silver slave bracelet. "Wait, we've eliminated suicide. Darling, you don't think someone killed her for sleeping with Boyce?"

"Haven't you ever heard of jealousy, Cliff?" Candy arched one foot toward the fire, then the other.

I tried to penetrate the dark to see Eleanor. This was tough on her.

She sniffled. I could hear her rustling for a handkerchief. "Has no one any regard for my feelings?"

Madge said sharply, "Candy, stirring up mud that doesn't even exist is not going to help the inspector. Eleanor, you mustn't let it bother you—"

Al pulled his feet back from the fire. "I don't think Lynn was having an affair with nobody. She knew how to kid around with Boyce. That's all that was. Me, I've been married thirty-three years to the greatest gal in the world. I'm interested in my grandchildren, not messing around with a skirt my daughter's age." He cracked his knuckles. "Cliff here don't like girls, Inspector, you know what I mean? So, nothing doing there."

"Really," Eleanor said. "I don't think I should be listening to this." As if she were a child who shouldn't be exposed to dirty words. "I wish Boyce were here." She began to cry.

"Now you've put your big foot in it," Madge told Al.

"Mrs. Darnell, what you said was true." Omondi's voice was rich and soft. "We have no regard for you. We have regard only for the truth. What we say here that is untrue will disappear. It is nothing. Only the truth will remain. In Swahili, there is a saying"—Omondi's smile glittered in the firelight—" 'The prayer of the chicken hawk does not get him the chicken.' So you see—"

Omondi's soothing tone was wasted. Suddenly, a large bat swooped low over our heads. It was so close, we could see a blur of scalloped wings. Eleanor leaped to her feet with a shriek and covered her hair with both hands.

"Bats are not interested in your hair," I said emphatically. "They eat fruit or bugs. They can catch a mosquito in the dark. They're not going to get caught in your hair by mistake."

She didn't hear me, or didn't believe me. The bat swooped again, six feet above us. Eleanor turned and ran for her tent.

Madge suggested it was bedtime for all of us, and the group disbanded with relief. If any truth had come out, I didn't see it.

Some dark dream awakened me, and I'd learned it was better to get out of bed and break the spell than lie there tossing until the sheets were twisted like ropes. Lynn and Adam were somehow mixed up in the dream, but the images quickly faded. A small wind sighed through the clearing.

I unzipped the mosquito netting and stepped out on my tent veranda. The surrounding leaves sounded like waves and I could feel the goose bumps on my belly. I thought briefly of going back to put on some clothes, and then decided against it. Since I was awake at four in the morning, I might as well have the treat of being naked outdoors. So I pulled one canvas chair up against the tent wall, sank down, and stretched my legs out on a second one. A forgotten towel made a soft pillow for my feet. The awning cast a deep moon shadow where I sat, giving me the illusion I was invisible.

I stroked my skin. It was chilled but still felt warm under my hand. My nipples stood erect, which always pleases me because it makes my breasts look rounder and prettier—even if there was no one else to appreciate it. I almost thought of Adam then, but pushed the memory out of my head before it had formed. I was getting quite good at that, which wasn't surprising after two years' practice.

The clearing looked large and mysterious in the moonlight. Tree shadows reached across the bare earth and melded into the brush by the stream. The bluff was a dense presence except for a single gleam of moonlight reflected from its crest. It couldn't be the same place I'd climbed at midday. That was hard and tangible. Solid. This scene reminded me of a Zen wall hanging I'd once owned. It showed a great blue heron flying. With one sure short stroke of the ink brush, the artist had indicated a mountain and an abyss, so that the heron floated in a tremendous nothingness. I let my mind float.

I felt grateful to my insomnia for this moment of loveliness. Being naked outdoors made my privacy seem absolute. Since Adam, I'd come to crave aloneness. Too much, a small voice piped up, but I let that one pass.

The line of two-person tents extended off to my right, their verandas facing east toward the stream. The sharp shadows in the moonlight made them look like the little square houses from a Monopoly set. Strange to think that in one of them slept a murderer. Maybe.

I leaned back and gazed at the sky. Only a few bright stars managed to compete with the moonlight. Or were they planets? I still hadn't learned the southern constellations. I sat and looked for a long time. It was soothing to gaze upon the cold immensity of space.

I reached over to the pack of cigarettes on the camp table, shook one out, and lit it. I'd resisted earlier, but here I was smoking, as bad as Candy. The match flame was a burst of orange light in the silver and black world. I inhaled deeply and felt a brief dizziness from the strong Kenyan tobacco. One pack couldn't do that much harm, anyway, I lied to myself. I took another deep drag and choked back a cough.

If only we'd never started this trip. I stubbed out my cigarette and looked up toward the bluff. But there was no bluff. A dark shape blocked out the sky. I inhaled sharply.

"Darling, did I scare you?"

"Jesus Christ, Cliff, what are you doing sneaking around camp at four in the morning? Or shouldn't I ask?"

I swung my legs down so Cliff could have the second chair. He sat and reached for my cigarettes.

"Do you mind?"

I shook my head no.

"I saw your cigarette glowing in the dark. Personally, I feel completely safe now that we have our Inspector Omondi on the job. Isn't he magnetic?" He patted the tabletop, looking for the matches. I found them and gave him a light. The flare of the match lit up Cliff's perfect nose, straight brow, and a shock of blond hair.

"He's certainly charming."

"Oh, that's right, you're pretending to be off sex."

"Pretending is sometimes as good as the real thing." I had felt a pull toward Omondi, but I was planning on letting the feeling pass right on by.

"Aren't you a bit chilly?" he asked in his light voice.

I looked down and realized I was a uniform pale shape, obviously naked despite the deep shadow.

"You have me trapped here. If I get up, we'll have two moons."

"It might be blinding."

"Toss me the towel you're sitting on."

He pulled the towel out from beneath him and handed it to me. I slipped it around me like a sarong and tucked the corner in over my breast to hold it in place. So much for privacy.

"I can't see what you're wearing," I said, "but I'm sure it's the perfect thing for dropping by after midnight."

"Now, Jazz, you used to be such a sweet girl. Are two little deaths getting on your nerves?"

I started to reach for another cigarette, then stopped myself. "Is that what brought you here at this hour? To discuss

109

the investigation with me? I'd actually succeeded in forgetting it for a moment. It is four in the morning.''

"Is there some reason you're harping on the time?''

I didn't think Cliff had taken a midnight ramble by himself, and I was curious to know who he'd been visiting. I assumed he was grown-up enough to practice safe sex, but I didn't particularly want him to stir up the staff by propositioning one of the men. Then I realized it was not under my control, and I decided not to worry about it. My crew was experienced; they'd undoubtedly seen it all. They could say no, or yes if they wanted to. Not my business. One of them could have propositioned Cliff, for all I knew.

"Just that it's dangerous to wander around at night,'' I lied. "As I told the group, you're safe in your tent, but there are animals around. Night belongs to the hunters. One time, I got up to pee and surprised a lion wandering through camp.''

"You terrify me. What did you do?''

I could sense, more than see, Cliff push back his hair.

"I peed in my water jug.''

Our laughter sounded loud in the darkness.

"Cliff, can we be serious for a moment?''

"That's something I avoid myself, but you go ahead.''

9"What did you think of Eleanor's hysteria tonight? Do you think Candy could be right? About jealousy? About Lynn and Boyce? It doesn't fit with my image of Lynn, but that could be my own blind spot.''

"Jealousy? Candy is the jealous one. Ever since Boyce called Candy a slut, she's been catty to Eleanor. Have you noticed?''

I nodded. "I actually had noticed, but I didn't know why. I thought it was nerves. I'm surprised Candy took Boyce's stupid insults so hard.''

"That's because you're not a narcissist, darling; you wouldn't understand. Candy craves adoration, and Boyce humiliated her in front of a crowd.''

"But still, the way Eleanor started screaming. I know some people hate bats, but—''

"Are we supposed to love bats now, too? Don't you think

people need something to hate? Why not the bat? That particular specimen was like a flying sewer rat.''

"It was not! Bats aren't even rodents. They're closer to primates. They're beautiful little creatures—''

"You're getting off track. The point isn't the bat. The point is that Eleanor would not bother to notice Boyce flirting with Candy. She wouldn't react to that as a threat. Now, if someone threatened her children, that would be another matter. Eleanor would become as the mother lioness protecting her young.''

"That's another animal cliché that's complete rot. When a young male takes over the troop, he kills the previous male's cubs: The mother lioness doesn't risk her life protecting them. It's more adaptive for her to live and have more young another year. She doesn't even feed her cubs until she's had her fill, for the same reason. She leads the cubs to the kill, but then they have to compete with her and the other adults to get a scrap to eat. In lean years, the cubs starve to death.''

Cliff lit a second cigarette from the glowing nub of his first one and flicked the stub into the night. "How terribly Spartan of them.'' He took a long drag. "I'm not confused that Eleanor is actually a lioness. But she is fiercely maternal.'' He was silent for a moment. "Boyce's death has me thinking about the past.''

"I know what you mean.''

"Can you keep a secret?''

"If it's not related to the case.''

"Not at all. I suspect Madge blabbed this to Candy.''

"It doesn't sound like much of a secret then.'' I reached for the pack and pulled out a cigarette. "Oh, is this the gossip Madge was scolding Candy for telling? About when Madge was sacked as bookkeeper? I wondered if you knew about that.'' I lit up and flicked the match.

"Oh, that was a big blowup over nothing, even at the time. Boyce didn't have to be so insulting about it, but everyone, even Madge, knew she couldn't handle the job anymore. She wasn't interested in accounting, anyway; she was just helping Al get the company started.'' He waved his hand dismissively, making a bright dash in the air with his burning cigarette. "My secret is not about Madge, it's about me and Eleanor."

"Omondi may want to know more about the bookkeeping thing. If he asks me, I'm going to put him on to you."

"What a little traitor you are, darling. I have nothing to tell him—I don't know anything firsthand. Anyway, I don't think there really is much to tell, except that Boyce pushed Madge out, and she's been nursing a grudge ever since." He laughed. "How ominous everything sounds when there's been a murder. Clearly, the two families remained on civil, more than civil, cordial terms. But it's always been a sensitive topic for Madge, and I imagine that's why she screwed Candy's mouth shut tonight." He paused. "Aren't you dying to hear my secret?"

"Of course."

"You know that Madge, Eleanor, and I are all alums of dear Windsor High? The deep dark secret is that Eleanor and I dated in high school. In fact, we were engaged."

I stared at Cliff's shape in the dark. "You?"

"You know what it was like in those days . . . or at least, you've heard. I was trying to act 'normal,' fool myself into thinking I was like everyone else."

"Oh, Cliff, that must have been a small hell."

"Eleanor's not that bad."

"You know I didn't mean—"

"Adolescence *is* hellish, don't you think? Anyway, it turned out well for everyone. I found my true identity, and Eleanor ended up making a brilliant marriage and having four kids, which is all she ever wanted out of life."

"Brilliant? Please, let's not be condescending. Boyce was a horror."

"Darling, it's more condescending to paint her as the victim when she's not." Cliff's cigarette made dots and stakes in the darkness like a visible Morse code. "Your mistake is that you imagine yourself in her place."

"I would never be in her place." Which is why I'm living alone in Africa, but I didn't add that.

"Exactly. But you see, Eleanor loved being Boyce's wife. Considering how dependent she was on him, I think she's doing very well." Cliff puffed on his cigarette. "That bat almost got *me* screaming."

"If she was so dependent, doesn't that argue she would be jealous?"

"Listen to me. She didn't care how many women he ran around with; she didn't compete in the sexual arena, darling. She likes to be pure, up on a pedestal, the virginal mother. She didn't want Boyce's sexual attention." The burning end of Cliff's cigarette made figure eights as he waved his hand. "In case you hadn't noticed, Boyce worshiped her. Eleanor was above reproach. In return, she saw him as he wanted to be seen—masterful." The cigarette described an arc. "She doesn't realize he was a mammoth-sized asshole. She thinks everybody respected him because we all jumped when he said jump." Cliff dropped his cigarette to the ground and crushed it with his foot. "Besides, she's always been more interested in her children and her position than in her husband. As an old-fashioned wife should be, I might add. None of this intimacy crap. Not everybody is a romantic, darling."

I cupped my chin in my hand. "Magnificent, Cliff, but you forgot the canned applause."

"You're not overawed by my acute psychological insight?"

"Eleanor may have been into the sexless mother role or into money or into Boyce's reflected power, but that doesn't mean she would feel fine about Boyce carrying on with one woman after another in front of the whole group. I think his behavior was disgusting."

"Ah, ah, ah . . . you're back on what *you* think, darling. Let's not be so self-centered."

I shut up. I didn't really care about Boyce and Eleanor and Candy. I wanted to solve Lynn's murder, not get caught up in these people's lives. I'd come to Africa to get away from bullshit relationships. I'd been a cultural hermit for two years. Avoiding Americans. Avoiding myself. I shivered. I was afraid. I was afraid if I got involved with people again, all my feelings about Adam would get touched off, would come roaring down on me like an avalanche and bury me forever in white cold rage.

13

THE NEXT DAY at dawn, Molezzi was up before me, ready with a cup of hot tea as soon as I emerged from the tent. The air smelled tangy with eucalyptus from the gum trees that towered around the clearing. A "ke, ke, ke" call made me look up and a two-foot-long hornbill flew overhead on strong wing beats. Its bananalike bill was an effective echo chamber, and I could hear it calling over and over, long after it disappeared from view.

"This is just what I need." I held the thick mug in two hands and sipped the steaming tea. "Thank you."

I'd fallen into a deep dreamless sleep after Cliff left, but there simply hadn't been enough of it. My mouth tasted sour from the cigarettes I'd smoked. I took another sip. There was a fresh towel on the table and he'd filled my basin with hot water. The world had its good points.

Molezzi started away.

"Oh, here." I picked up the cigarette pack from the table and tossed it to him. "Do me a favor and don't give me any more, even if I beg you."

"You want Pall Malls?" he asked.

"No, I don't like to smoke, but sometimes I forget."

"Did you have a good meeting last night?" He slipped the cigarettes into the breast pocket of his white shirt.

"Oh, I don't know, Molezzi. We might have learned one or two useful things, but it all seems pretty confusing. I don't think we're going to get anywhere unless we discover that spear. We'd better find it today, because Mr. Hart says he's going home unless we discover evidence to make him stay.''

Molezzi tried to cheer me up. I checked the camp, then talked briefly to Ibrahima. He sat on a low stool eating a bowl of porridge loaded with milk and butter. A small camp-fire at his feet emitted more smoke than flame. Today his T-shirt read I LOVE PARIS, with a picture of the Eiffel Tower emerging from his navel.

''The camp is looking great,'' I told him. ''Everyone's doing a fine job.'' He nodded his head in dignified acknowl-edgment. ''How is everyone taking this? I hope the men aren't feeling worried?''

No one could quit out here in bush camp, but it wasn't unknown for an entire staff to evaporate overnight when a tour strayed near a town. If word got around that I had bad luck—I didn't bother to complete the thought.

''Everything fine, Jazz. We're working along, making ev-erything nice for everybody.'' He stirred his porridge and took a bite. ''If the man who murdered your friend has strong magic, I'll take you to see my uncle in Nanyuki.'' I'd heard a lot about Ibrahima's uncle, a famous diviner and maker of magic charms. ''He will fix you up. That killer will walk right into the police station, hold out his wrists, and say, 'Lock me up, I am the villain.' '' Ibrahima rested his bowl on his belly. ''I'll talk to him; he won't charge too much.'' Magic could be quite expensive.

I put my arm across his back and gave him a quick hug. ''Ibrahima, can I adopt you as my father?''

''You don't need to adopt me; I am your father.''

I started back to my tent, going over in my mind possible scenarios of what had happened to that spear. Once we found it, if it was the murder weapon, the police would undoubt-edly be able to stop the Harts from leaving the country, since technically it did belong to Al. I wondered if the Masai had searched the area near the stream where I saw the poacher. Maybe I'd check it out myself. I wasn't sure I trusted those particular Masai. Besides, it gave me something to do with myself.

With no trouble I found the pool where I'd been birdwatching. I slowly rotated till I faced the spot where I'd seen the two men, and I pushed through the undergrowth. I threaded my way methodically back and forth until I found a faint trail of broken branches. Maybe the two Masai had come through here.

I knocked against the branch of a whistling thorn, and its resident army of biting ants ran out of the dry hollow spheres the thornbush provided for their lodging. If an antelope chose to nibble on that bush, the ants would do their best to make it change its mind. I watched the ants run up and down the branch angrily, then file back into the pencil-point entrances to their little round houses.

I was breaking my own rules, wandering farther and farther from camp on foot. I pushed my way through the heavy brush and came upon a grassy clearing where a single acacia had managed to escape fire and animals long enough to grow into a small flat-topped tree. There was a large gray boulder embedded in the ground just outside the tree's long shadow. I marched down the center of the clearing, happy to be in the open for a while. There were small yellow wildflowers among the grasses, and the air smelled faintly herbal.

I was thinking how unusual a gray boulder was in this region, when a yellow-billed oxpecker, the tick bird, rose from the boulder with a shrill call of alarm. Striker had taught me the Swahili name for the tick bird. I'd forgotten the Swahili but remembered the translation all too well. "The rhino's policeman."

The "boulder" lifted its head and swung its snout in my direction.

Two heavy horns with wicked points, round funnel ears, wide nostrils, and piggy little eyes. A 25-million-year-old face I'd recognize anywhere. I froze.

So that's why the poacher had been hanging around here. I'd have to alert the park rangers. Right now, the ears were swiveling, searching for sound, and the nostrils flared open.

The rhino was famous for its poor eyesight. If it didn't know I was here, it couldn't charge me. Goddard, the first man to study rhino, used to creep up to them on foot so he could see what plants they chose to eat. The trick, he wrote, was to keep downwind. I hoped I was downwind. I was not about to lick a finger to find out.

The rhino hefted itself to its feet, walked a few steps, lifted its snout, and tested the air again. This time it found me. It lowered its head and shrieked. My heart stopped. Then it charged.

I didn't have time to think. Less than a thousand feet separated us, and the distance was shrinking rapidly. I moaned with fear—a sound I didn't recognize as my own—and ran straight at the rhino. The rhino squealed shrilly. Its lip curled back from yellowed teeth. We raced toward one another.

I prepared to jump aside at the last moment and make for the tree. If the rhino's momentum carried him past me, I might be able to make it before he turned.

They said rhino could turn on a dime.

I knew I wouldn't make it. The tree was too far. My chances of reaching it first were slim. Slim? They were nonexistent. I couldn't outmaneuver a rhino.

When the rhino was within a length of me, it swerved and abruptly stopped. I instantly stopped, too. I gulped air, breathing noisily through my mouth. I had a stitch in my side that cut my breath, and my chest was pumping like a bellows. I grabbed at my side, trying to get the muscle to let go. I looked down at the ground and kept the rhino in my peripheral vision. Staring was a form of animal aggression, and I didn't want to do anything to provoke another threat charge.

The rhino trotted around in a circle, snorting and goring the air. It lowered its ears, rushed a few steps toward me, and again stopped. I held my ground. If I ran, it would certainly run after me, and for all its bulk, the rhino would be faster. Gored or trampled, it would not be good.

The one thing I had going for me was my knowledge. Most animals, even the rhino, don't attack to kill. They use threat displays and mock charges to get their point across to fellow rhinos or other intruders. If really serious, they might land a few blows with their head and chase their opponent as he runs away. Unfortunately, I wasn't built to play this game. Another rhino would be fast enough to run away, and tough enough to sustain a clubbing with that massive horn. I was neither.

Striker said rhinos usually run at the smell of humans. I hoped I lived to tell him it wasn't always so. I wondered if the rhino could see me silhouetted against the sky. Was that why it was riled up? It made a feint toward me, and I flinched, but once again it wheeled away. I had to stop making it nervous.

What signal could I give to turn off its attacking instinct? A dog rolls on its back and exposes its underbelly as a sign of submission. I had to try something. I began to curl over and lower myself to the ground: a slow, smooth curl to make my eighth-grade dance teacher proud. I could hear the rhino snorting, hear its hooves clip clip against the hard earth. I reached the ground in a fetus position and rolled onto my side, feeling horribly exposed.

The rhino screamed again and raced toward me. Its hooves passed not a foot from my head. Dust sprayed all over me. I squeezed my eyes shut and coughed. The rhino wheeled and returned.

It blocked out the sun. There was a stench of rhino shit that cut my breath. I waited for the kidney blow that would dispatch me. Nothing. The rhino was standing over me. I looked through my eyelashes. The rhino lowered its massive head and snorted.

The big horn loomed over me like a strange lesson in perspective. Its base was as wide as the world, its tip a distant point against the sky. Dry mud caked the rhino's upper lip. I could feel the rush of warm air from its nostrils. It put its nose on my hip and breathed in, inhaling my smell.

Then the sun returned. I listened to the hooves clop farther and farther off, then the crashing of brush. I didn't move for a long time.

* * *

I retraced my path to camp, feeling shaken and vulnerable. It was as if I'd stepped outside of time for a moment, faced my own death, and returned. The only outward sign was dust on my clothes, which I brushed off with a few vigorous swipes. It was wonderful to be alive. I wished Striker was here. He'd be fascinated. A good long hug would feel pretty good, too. I didn't want to tell the group I'd been charged: I hoped I could slip back without much comment. Had anyone heard the rhino squealing?

Omondi spotted me as soon as I entered the clearing.

"Ah, I see you are up," he exclaimed gaily. "You and Kakombe are our two early risers. He, too, is out on a walk, I assume. Bird-watching again?" He was cradling a mug of steaming tea in his hands. "But, no, I see you don't have your binoculars."

"I went to check the area I visited yesterday morning, and look for the spear. I wasn't sure if the Masai villagers went that far last night."

"That spear is proving elusive."

"Yes, although I think I know what those two men were doing there yesterday. I stumbled into a rhino."

"Not literally?" Omondi raised his brows.

"Almost. But I've lived to tell the tale."

"I've never seen a rhino," Omondi said.

It was my turn for surprise. Rhino were scarce, but most tourists got at least a glimpse of one. "Does that mean you haven't visited the parks?"

"There is not much homicide out here." Omondi shrugged. "As you know, most Kenyans never see the animals. They can't afford to visit these parks. You need a car. How many black Kenyans do you think have cars?" He thrust out his lower lip, shaking his head. "It is indeed a pity."

"Inspector, any time you like, you tell me, and there's a place for you and your wife on one of my trips. I'd like very much to show you the Kenya I love."

Omondi stared at me, nonplussed.

"It's not a bribe." I laughed.

He took my elbow. "No, I did not have such a thought. I

am deeply touched.'' He put a hand to his heart. ''You have surprised me there.'' He nodded his head gravely. ''I accept your kind offer. It is me alone, no wife. I am a widower.''

''I'm sorry.''

''It has been several years. The grief is quiet now.''

''A girlfriend, then?''

Omondi looked into my eyes. ''No, not yet, no special girlfriend.''

I heard footsteps and turned to see Chris Mbare, my driver, amble over. Not a moment too soon. I didn't like the way the conversation was headed. Chris was pulling on a sweater, his shirt was buttoned crooked, and his round face looked soft with sleep.

''Oh, Chris! You could have slept in. No game drive this morning. Didn't I tell you?''

Chris yawned, showing his gold teeth. ''That's all right, Jazz. You have a lot on your mind. In that case, I'm going back to sleep.''

He left us, and Omondi steered me down to sit on the hollow log at the end of the clearing. He asked me if any new thoughts about Lynn or Boyce had come to me in the night, fragments of a memory, perhaps a dream?

''I think you squeezed every last fact and conjecture out of us last night.''

''Good.'' Omondi touched his fingers together and beat a rapid rhythm with his fingertips. ''This morning, I want to test an idea about how the murder was committed. I think I have figured it out.''

There was a sound of breaking branches close behind us. Something large and fast was crashing through the brush, headed straight toward us.

''The rhino!'' I leapt to my feet and raced for the tents, Omondi a pace behind me. I glanced over my shoulder, expecting to see that massive shape hurtle into the clearing, to hear those staccato hoofbeats gaining on me. Instead, I heard the sound of human panting.

Omondi put a hand on my shoulder. We both turned. Kakombe burst out between the bushes. He was upon us in three

120

strides. His shirt was soaked with sweat and his great chest was heaving with the effort to breathe enough air into his lungs.

"An intruder." He panted. "He got away. The Rover."

I pulled the keys out of my pocket and the three of us ran through camp and up the small rise to where we kept the Land Rover. This changed everything. Was Al right after all about an outside killer?

I leaped onto the running board. There was Chris Mbare, stretched out full-length on the front seat, finishing his morning snooze. I yelled at him to wake up as I flung myself behind the driver's seat, half-sitting on his feet, and with trembling fingers, managed to get the key into the ignition. Mbare pulled himself erect with an exclamation as Kakombe and Omondi leaped into the seat behind us. I twisted the steering wheel hard over and we roared out of camp.

"Go south," Kakombe directed. "I lost him in some thick scrub west of the stream. If we circle round, we may be able to intercept him."

"Good work, Sergeant. Report," Omondi said.

I'd driven cross-country before but never at this speed. I immediately put the far wheels over a log buried in the tall grass. The Land Rover shot forward, one side off the ground. For one awful moment, I was sure we were going to flip, but the Rover fell back onto all four wheels and I kept driving. A bit more dramatic than I enjoy. Chris, proving his sainthood once more, braced himself against the dashboard and muttered reassuringly that I could do it.

Omondi, seemingly unfazed, again asked Kakombe to report.

Kakombe gave us all the details, at a faster tempo than I'd ever heard him speak, although you still wouldn't say his voice sounded excited. He had woken before dawn and was lying in bed waiting for full light, when he heard the drumming wings of a helmeted guinea fowl exploding from cover. What had disturbed it from its sleep? He decided to put on his clothes and circle the camp just to check up on things. He passed behind the tents and heard a faint scratching sound at the end of the clearing. In the vague early light, he crept along—in time to see the bushes beyond the fallen log moving slightly. Thinking it might be an animal, he approached cautiously and followed the faint sounds leading him through the brush. As the sun came up, he was able to distinguish tracks of a barefoot man moving rapidly south. Then they crossed the stream and he lost them. He heard a rhino squealing, but that was way to the west of where he was tracking. He wasted some time circling round, looking for the trail, mad with impatience because he guessed the man might be heading to the kraal due south of us, and wanted to catch him before he did. So he'd decided to run back and get Omondi and the Land Rover.

"Yes," Omondi agreed. "Once the man is in the village, it will be very hard to identify him."

We sped south, following the wide arc of the heavy brush that skirted the stream. On our other side, the plains flowed away from us, dotted at intervals with grazing zebra and gazelle. Blue hills marked the far horizon. Ten miles or so to the right, an escarpment thrust up at an angle, trees bristling along its flanks. Ahead of us, three hyenas sniffed at a spot on the ground, then sloped off into the grass at our approach. The colors of animals, sky, and plants were vibrant in the early-morning light. This was the best time of day to be on a game run. Today, we were after a different sort of game.

Suddenly, the bushes fell behind and our view opened up. Strings of cattle advanced toward us, accompanied by skinny boys armed with thin sticks. I hated these cows at the best of times. They were the Masai version of conspicuous consumption. Thanks to Western science, their range was no longer limited by the tsetse fly, and the bloated herds competed ruthlessly with wild animals for water and food. There was barely any grass left on this side of the hill. It made driving easier, but at the moment, my greatest fear was running into a cow, since they had the unpleasant habit of darting in front of cars.

"We must be near the village," Omondi said.

The Masai herd their cattle into the center of the kraal each night, where they're safe from hyenas and lions, and herd them out again at dawn. I dared glance up from the cropped grass flying under my tires. Yes, there was the brown square of the Masai kraal where the slope flattened out into a broad valley.

"And that's our man," cried Omondi.

A long thin Masai warrior draped carelessly with a single orange cape strode across the large landscape. In the clear light, even the sharp point of his spear was visible. His back was toward us, but he must have heard the Rover, for he turned around and began to sprint toward the kraal.

I gunned the car and we bounced madly downhill. A dust cloud cut straight across our track, but I was too focused on the running man to take much notice. Chris Mbare shouted, "Brake!"

I tromped on the brakes and we squealed and fishtailed our way to a standstill smack in the center of a herd of cattle. The surprised animals milled around us, cutting off a backward escape. We were trapped.

"Damnation!" Omondi thrust his head out the window.

I leaned on the horn. The cattle lowed. A ten-year-old boy ran back and forth, waving his stick and shouting as he stared at us. Kakombe barked at him in what I assumed was Masai. I edged the Land Rover forward, actually pushing against the cattle with my bumper, but this, too, left them unimpressed. Their long curved horns and imposing humps reminded me of Mogul miniatures, but their presence was all too three-dimensional. They kicked up a cloud of dust that choked off both sight and breath. At last, an older boy strode through the thick of them swinging his stick with authority. The cattle grudgingly parted and we drove through. We'd lost critical minutes.

Ahead of us, we saw a thick pile of thorn brush, taller than a man, snaking over the ground. It was the kraal wall. Not fifty yards from the entrance was the running warrior. His long legs were a blur of speed as he dashed for safety. I shifted into third, pressed the accelerator to the floor, and aimed straight at the entrance myself. At the last possible moment, I downshifted and jerked the steering wheel hard over. The car spun sideways and stalled in front of the entrance with a good three feet to spare. Kakombe leapt to the ground, executed a brilliant sprint, and tackled the fleeing Masai. He seized his spear and marched him toward us in handcuffs.

"Very, very good," Omondi said, nodding his head rapidly. "I am most curious to talk to this young man."

A fine acacia stood outside the settlement, raising its flat ceiling of feathery leaves above a woman milking a black and white goat. The goat bleated aggressively, sticking out a pointy muscular tongue. The woman rose to her feet with an exclamation and ran into the kraal.

I stared at the warrior. His long thin ringlets of hair were cinnamon-colored with dust, and there was a light patina of sweat across his high brow. His expression was slightly bored, like a lion faced with a vanfull of tourists. He hadn't said a word.

Omondi filled in the silence with one of his monologues. "The Masai's origins are shrouded in the mists of time, but they are believed to come from the Nile. The short sword they carry at their belts is like the Roman sword. See how their hairdo is like a Roman helmet, their clothing like a toga, their sandals, also Roman. No man is an island. Most fascinating."

"Inspector, I'm pretty sure this is the same fellow who sold Al the spear," I said.

"Yes, I recognize him from the search party last night." Omondi ignored the warrior, looking around us with curiosity. "It is rude to barge in on the village like this. We will wait here for an elder."

Rude? I wondered what kind of reception awaited us.

The first thing that happened was a dozen children ran up and surrounded the car. The little ones were naked; the older ones had shaved heads and wore plain cotton robes that reached mid-thigh. They jostled one another aside to get the best view. An elder wrapped in a blanket pushed his way through them. He stood as tall and erect as any youth, but age had softened his face into thick fleshy waves. In contrast to the warrior's braided locks, he wore grizzled hair cut close to his scalp, but he, too, wore heavy earrings that stretched out his earlobes. He took in the situation in one surprised glance but went through the normal lengthy greeting ritual with Omondi and Kakombe. We clambered out, shook hands, and entered the village.

Mushroom-shaped roofs barely rose above the thorn wall. The kraal was a lovely example of form follows function, not a line wasted. There were about fifteen houses, each one a smooth dome of dried manure.

The first thing I noticed was the barnyard smell. It hit us like a second wall. There were no animals left in the kraal, but the signs that they'd spent the night were everywhere. Two children raced around the corner of a hut throwing dung, and laughing. A woman emerged from a doorway and stared as she jiggled a baby on her hip. She wore a leather sarong, tied over one shoulder. Her exposed breast was flattened and stretched to her waist, sign of many years of child-bearing. She looked sixty but was probably thirty or forty. The simple life is hard on women.

The baby wore only a necklace of magic charms. It took one startled look at us and began to cry. The mother lifted her breast and offered it to the baby, who seized it with both hands and started to suck. The baby's eyes and mouth were rimmed with black. A step closer and I saw the black was a moving mass of flies. There were flies everywhere. I went rigid.

A fly buzzed against my face. Another landed on my arm. I turned to bolt. Two steps, and I caught myself. I'd been in African villages before; I knew about flies. Was I going to run every time something traumatic happened to me? First America struck off my list, then Africa? Soon I'd have no-where to go. I turned and forced myself back, step by step, to Omondi's side.

The elder, draped in a red and white wool blanket, led us to sit on the bare ground next to a hut, where we were joined

125

by three other old men. A circle of ancient women gathered a few feet away. Kakombe remained standing next to his charge. They were the same height, but Kakombe had at least seventy pounds on the Masai.

An animated conversation followed in Swahili. I didn't understand a word, which left the two options of tuning out or smiling and nodding like an idiot as a sign of life and goodwill. I was too busy brushing away the flies to do the smiling routine, but at least I stuck it out. I noticed Omondi also kept swatting away. Five minutes of this and my arm started to ache, but if I stopped for a moment, a cloud of flies would descend to rest on me or crawl around on an investigation of their own. I could see why people eventually gave up and let the flies crawl.

The elders turned to the warrior and began to cross-examine him, with Omondi interjecting questions. Apparently, his name was Meromo ole Something. By now, we were surrounded by every adult and child in the kraal. Several people examined the spear that Kakombe was holding, the one he'd taken from Meromo. Parallel discussions and little arguments broke out among different members of the crowd. People interrupted freely with their own questions and comments. Some of the warriors gesticulated angrily. Others shouted them down. I was starting to get a little nervous: This situation could turn ugly fast.

The chief elder called a regal young woman out of the crowd. She had long legs, smooth gleaming skin, and high round breasts. Her aristocratic appearance was marred somewhat by a fit of mock shyness and the giggles when she glanced at Meromo. The elder talked to her, and Meromo nodded. She crossed the kraal at a fast trot, her bare feet sending up little clouds of dust. She went into a hut at the far end and emerged with a spear. She handed it to Meromo, who held it awkwardly because of his handcuffs and passed it to an elder, who passed it to Omondi, who examined it carefully and passed it back to the elder. Several warriors came forward to look at it closely and comment. A satisfied murmur ran through the group.

"Is that Al's spear?" I whispered to Omondi.

He shook his head sharply. "No, that one is Meromo's spear. He is her favored lover. She keeps his spear in her hut at night. I'll explain later."

What was going on? This was my own fault for not learning Swahili. If this new spear was Meromo's, then whose spear had Meromo carried to our camp this morning? More to the point, what was he doing in our camp at sunrise?

The senior elder spoke and the bored look vanished from Meromo's face. He replied curtly. The elder scowled and began to gesticulate and shout. Meromo pretended not to hear him. A toddler wandered over and crawled into the old man's lap and snuggled into the curve of his body. He subsided and patted the baby, murmuring. Omondi suggested something in a low voice to Kakombe, who addressed the young man in Masai. He shrugged. Omondi spoke again. Meromo shrugged a grudging assent, and Kakombe unlocked the handcuffs. The two of them left the kraal, followed by Meromo's girlfriend, still giggling, and a group of other warriors.

After what seemed to be a protracted expression of thanks, we returned to the Land Rover. We had a new passenger. Meromo sat in the backseat next to Kakombe, who still held the original spear, now poking through the roof. Meromo looked haughty but secretly excited. He, too, was holding a spear, presumably his own. The crowd of children cackled and jumped around him.

Chris Mbare already had the engine going. He brushed a handful of flies away from his head. "All set, Jazz?"

"Don't ask me, I have no idea what's going on," I said to him as I climbed into the middle seat.

Omondi told him we could go and Chris backed slowly out of the crowd. I looked through the windshield in time to glimpse a familiar face at the kraal gate. It was the rhino poacher; he'd kept out of sight during our visit. He had a scowl on his face. I pointed him out to Omondi.

Omondi said, "He is mad because we have his spear."

"His spear?"

"That man has lost all self-respect," cut in Kakombe. "He would rather carry a gun than a spear. He is no Masai."

"Wait a second. I'm totally confused. Would one of you please explain to me what's going on?"

"I am sorry, Jazz." Omondi bowed his head gallantly. "I myself missed some of the discussion that was in Masai. The poacher you saw sold his spear to Al, or rather, had his cousin Meromo sell it for him. Someone used the spear to kill Lynn, as I will demonstrate shortly, and hid it in the camp. During the search party last night, Meromo noticed the spear glinting in its hiding place, but out of consideration to his cousin, he said nothing. This morning, he thought he would pay us a quiet little visit before anyone was awake and recover the spear. He did not want it to be mixed up in white people's mess."

"You believe all this on his word? How do you know he wasn't sneaking in to kill someone else?"

"Oh, you are a tough interrogator, I can see." Omondi laughed. "This is why." He counted on his fingers. "One, Kakombe discovered him as he was leaving camp—and I am sure we will find everyone alive and well on our return. Two, the elders testified that Meromo's spear was the one we saw brought from his girlfriend's hut. The spear he was caught with is his cousin's. Furthermore, he told several of his fellow warriors that he had seen his cousin's spear and was going to fetch it this morning. Lastly, we are about to check out his story about where he found it: If it was there, we will be able to tell."

"What if they were all lying to protect him?"

Omondi shook his head gravely. "If they were lying, we will find out, but I do not believe they were lying. So many witnesses, including the elders of the tribe. You must recognize that murder is a cultural event. No human being has ever existed alone, independent of culture. Man, culture are one, inextricably mixed. This was not a Masai murder. Wouldn't you agree, Sergeant?"

"Yes, sir. To become a warrior is the greatest thing in a man's life," Kakombe's deep bass voice rumbled from the backseat. "As a youth, you must spend long days with the herds. You are not allowed to have a girlfriend. The youths beg and beg for circumcision until the elders give in and say yes."

"And what do they do when they're warriors?" I asked.

"Anything that requires courage; they go on cattle raids, protect the kraal, hunt for skins and feathers. And they have many lovers."

"Many lovers?" Omondi asked, with a wink for me.

"Yes. The warriors share everything. Not cattle, but food and women. A girl chooses three lovers and she may not sleep with anyone else as long as these three are around."

"You seem to know a lot about it," I said.

"I am a Masai." He turned to me and grinned.

Yes, of course. Now that I'd been told, it was obvious that Kakombe was Masai, although his fine cheekbones were hidden under a layer of easier living. His frame was filled out, giving him a clumsy appearance next to the elegance of the nomad beside him. Loincloth and khaki uniform. Long plaits of hair dressed in animal fat and a spongy black crew cut. The old and the new.

The change was inevitable, and undoubtedly laudable in some ways, but it made me sad. First, white settlers had stolen the Masai's best grazing land; now, black farmers were taking the worst. Government programs were teaching the Masai to join the money economy, to trade their cattle, to eat vegetables and cooked meat instead of the milk and raw blood on which they'd subsisted for millennia. The last remnants of our human heritage were disappearing, washed away in a tidal wave of overpopulation, T-shirts, and transistor radios. Although the herder's macho culture didn't appeal to me, I respected their integrity, their right to be themselves. Progress and politics respected nothing.

I looked out at the beautiful morning. I was thankful I hadn't wrecked the Land Rover. We passed a tree full of baboons, backlit by the sun. The babies played tag along the branches, while their elders were still curled on their perches, trying to catch a last little snooze. Farther along, a tawny eagle perched on a big thornbush. A dozen elephants in their baggy pants fed peacefully along a shrubby hillside. A herd of Thomson's gazelles moved from our path and, as always, turned to look curiously at us over their golden shoulders. They have the cutest little ass with two black stripes down each side.

I thought over Kakombe's explanations. It was hard to imagine a Masai attacking a sleeping woman, for rape or murder. On the other hand, at least one Masai had been willing to sell his spear, symbol of his privileged caste.

"Okay, Inspector, you've convinced me that no self-respecting warrior would have killed Lynn. But what about someone who's begun to lose his culture? There are strains on these people that never existed before." I involuntarily glanced at Kakombe, but his face was angled away from me. "And why are you so convinced it was done with a spear? Maybe the murderer used a knife or sword and stole the spear on his way out."

Omondi smiled in a superior way and contented himself with saying, "You'll see."

14

W<small>HEN WE GOT</small> back to camp, I could hear Al's raised voice coming from the dining tent.

"Hell, do what you want, Cliff, but I'm damned if I'm going to be treated like a criminal and have some cop messing through my things. What do they need to search my tent for? Forget it . . . I'm not slowing things down. It's a big waste of time . . . Listen . . ."

We passed out of earshot. Omondi caught me looking at him and shrugged, smiling. "Pity. I had hoped to avoid a confrontation with Mr. Hart."

Madge walked toward us with her arms folded under her big soft bosom. Normally her head would be up, looking and listening, but this morning she stared at the ground, pulled into herself. She stopped still and gaped when she saw us.

What was she scared of? Then I realized how we must look to her. I was covered with red dust from our encounter with the cattle, Omondi bounded through the clearing at his usual speed, Kakombe clenched Al's spear, looking like a giant next to his thin country cousin, and Meromo was striding along, with spear and sword, the loincloth doing little to hide a magnificently muscled body.

Candy, our answer to the Masai cult of beauty, was down near the log, doing calisthenics. She wore a black and white leotard: The top part was a sleeveless undershirt, and the bottom was an elastic triangle that didn't cover an inch of leg below her hipbone. She had her feet wide apart and was bent over at the waist, touching her head to each knee, back and forth and back and forth.

Omondi called out to Madge without pausing. "Our Masai friend is about to show us where the spear was hidden."

"Hey, everybody!" Candy yelled. She crouched at one end of the fallen log, peered inside, and waved us over. "Come here. I want to show you something."

She straightened when we approached, all six feet of her, pulled off her sweatband and ran a hand over her mane of tawny hair so that it flared from her temples. The white leotard top was wet through with sweat and had become semitransparent. As we neared, I could see the dark aureoles of her nipples and the curve of her breasts. Her face was flushed and streaky with sweat, but her mascara and eye shadow were miraculously intact.

She flicked her eyes over us, rested briefly on Meromo, then returned to Omondi. "I found something really weird." Candy smiled at him, a Hollywood smile showing her even teeth.

"What'd you find?" Al asked.

"See for yourself." Candy glanced again at Meromo, who leaned against his spear, cape draped over one shoulder, not paying attention to us. I'm sure the lack of attention puzzled Candy more than his presence in camp.

Omondi squatted and peered into the log's hollow heart. "The spear was removed from here before dawn, by our Masai guest, who noticed it last night." He gave a satisfied grunt. "Just as Meromo told us in the village. This confirms his story." He reached in and pulled out a wad of cloth. "Does anyone recognize this?"

The question was hardly necessary. A body suit of metallic blue fabric dangled from his hand.

"Sure as hell ain't mine." Al laughed. "How in hell did you see it, Candy?"

"It was only a few inches inside," she said defensively. "I noticed something in there out of the corner of my eye when I was doing my stretches, and I don't know, it seemed strange so I looked closer, you know, and all of a sudden I realize it's my leotard. I didn't touch it, Inspector, I figured you'd want to see it just like it was.''

"Very good, my dear girl.''

"Looks like our murderer had a clothes fetish,'' Al joked.

"Hush.'' Madge slapped at his arm. "Let the inspector think.''

Omondi approached the spear Kakombe was carefully holding and without touching it, he examined it minutely, his eyes inches from the wooden shaft. "We will test it for traces of blue fabric. I would guess the murderer used this cloth so as not to leave prints. Pity.'' He looked at Candy. "When did you last see this garment?''

"Let's see.'' Candy picked up her cassette player from the log and swung the headphones like a pendulum. "I wore my flesh-colored one yesterday when I worked out. I wore the blue one the day before, when everyone went on that game run, and I stayed behind to do my routine. I probably left it over the back of a chair afterward.'' She wrinkled her nose delicately. "They get kinda sweaty.''

I looked at Kakombe to see whether he had any ideas to contribute, but he was busy trying to see through Candy's leotard. He had the same deadpan, heavy-lidded look as usual, but he was definitely trying.

Candy wiped her forehead with her sweatband. "Jeez, I'm soaking wet. I had a good workout. Do you mind if I go take a shower, Inspector?''

She looked straight at him. Her eyes were the color of Raphael's skies where they reach the vanishing point, a deep clear blue. I found myself staring at her eyes, a twin to Kakombe staring at her breasts. Each one of us in the group could take a different part of Candy's body and dedicate ourselves to its admiration. There's definitely something hypnotic about extreme beauty.

"Miss Svenson.'' He took her hand and bowed low over it. "You have furthered the investigation with your keen eyesight, and your intelligence in not disturbing the evidence.'' He released her hand. "Of course, you are free to go, with our many thanks.''

133

I felt a flicker of jealousy. I run around like a nincompoop searching for the spear and get attacked by a rhino. Candy stays in camp all morning and finds where the spear was hidden all on her own. Not that it took brilliance on her part. She was bending over the goddamn log all morning, sticking her head between her legs. Now Jazz, I lectured myself, don't be vulgar. This is not a competition. What do you care what Omondi thinks anyway? It was a question I didn't care to dwell on.

"You didn't notice anything when you were working out here yesterday?" I asked Candy. It seemed a bit odd she'd noticed her leotard today but missed the spear, which must have been more obvious.

"No, I didn't," Candy answered. "Maybe it was pushed deeper in yesterday."

Cliff sauntered over, hands in his pockets. He wore a nubby cotton sweater and gray denim pants, pleated at the waist and tapering down to narrow cuffs. His eyes looked puffy from too much drinking. "What have we here? Is Candy starting aerobics classes for the multitudes?"

Omondi threw his head back and laughed. "We are, indeed, a motley crew."

"The Masai did find the spear," Madge told Cliff excitedly. "It was in the log. And Candy found her leotard in there."

Cliff pulled in his chin and gave Candy an appraising look from under raised brows. "Really? How definitely odd."

"The inspector says I'm intelligent," Candy retorted.

"Odder and odder," Cliff said.

"I was just leaving anyway." Candy swung away in a long easy stride.

Kakombe turned to watch her go. Molezzi waited for her at the shower stall, ready with a bucket of hot water and a pile of towels. Meromo pulled a tiny calabash from his belt, shaped like a perfume flask, with an ebony stopper. He poured some snuff onto his palm, sniffed, and sneezed loudly. He said something in Masai to Kakombe.

"Does our friend have a suggestion?" asked Omondi.

Kakombe shook his head. "Only for me. He says, do not be confused by the stampede of the wildebeest."

Al turned to Madge. "Maybe we should go, too. I want to change into some cooler clothes and wash up before lunch."

"Go ahead, honey, I'll be right there."

Al left us. There was the sound of water from the shower stall. Molezzi stood guard with a second bucket, which looked full from the way it dragged his arm down. I wondered how he planned to pour that into the shower reservoir when Candy was in there. I had a moment of sympathy for Candy, which made me like myself better. She didn't get much peace from men. I could see why Madge wanted to mother her. Molezzi grinned when he saw us looking at him.

Omondi turned to his sergeant. "Kakombe, please take this evidence and put it in a separate bag. See what you can do about protecting any fingerprints still left on the spear. Be careful with the point . . . better put a bag around that, too. As you can see, there is blood." He turned to the rest of us. "And now, I will show you how the murder was done."

Madge lay on Lynn's bed.

"You are doing a jolly good job," Omondi encouraged her. "This will take only a moment." He fussed with a pair of jeans. First he threw them on the floor in a heap, then picked them up and flung them on the empty cot.

I stood behind the tent with Meromo and Kakombe, who had returned from stowing away the spear and Candy's leotard. I couldn't see Madge's face, but her whole body looked unhappy and stiff. I admired her self-possession. Omondi slipped out through the hole in the back wall.

"Very good." Omondi spoke in Swahili and Meromo handed over his spear. I heard the sound of footsteps, and Al appeared around the corner of the tent. He was wearing shorts and a red polo shirt. The shirt went with the sunburn on his knees, but the black business socks didn't make it.

"It's going to be a hot one, today. Hey, has anybody seen Madge? I thought she was right behind me. I've been looking all over for her." His brows were pulled together with concern.

I pointed to the tent. "She's in there."

"Mrs. Hart is helping us reenact the crime," Omondi said, gesturing with the spear.

Al's face darkened. "Madge?" He looked into the tent. "What the hell are you doing in there?" He went to the front and pushed through the mosquito netting.

"Al, calm down. I'm perfectly okay. I'm helping the inspector."

"Don't tell me to calm down." Al raised his voice. "I'm not the one who's sneaking off to play cops and robbers. Will you get off that bed?"

"Al, we're busy. You're holding us up." Madge stayed flat on her back.

Meromo grinned and asked a question in Masai. Kakombe lifted a corner of his mouth and looked bored.

"I told you to keep out of this. The inspector can do his job fine without you."

"Stop glaring at me."

"I'm not glaring."

"You are glaring and you're being a bully. Cut it out. I'm a grown woman and you can't tell me what to do. If you want to watch, you can join the others outside."

"Aw, Madge." Al came out of the tent and glared at the rest of us. "Why'd I have to marry such a stubborn dame?" He pointed a finger at Omondi. "Inspector, you're making me mad."

Omondi smiled and clapped Al on the shoulder. The spear waved in his other hand. "My dear fellow, please accept my heartfelt apologies. I know this is a damned nuisance."

Madge raised her voice from inside the tent. "If Al is finished interrupting, maybe we could get on with it? This is kind of hard to do." She paused and added, "I'm glad you're here, Al."

"Okay, baby, I'm right here." Al patted his belly and stood next to me, his legs wide apart.

Omondi advanced toward the tent stealthily, as if creeping up on it in the night. He pretended to slit the canvas with the spear point. Meromo spoke. The spear can cut a rhino's hide, Kakombe translated. Omondi did not enter the tent. He pushed the flapping canvas open and reached in with his spear. He fished inside the tent and pulled the spear back with the blue jeans dangling from its point. He removed the jeans.

"Imagine you hear a noise and turn to see if there's anything there," he said to Madge.

She got onto an elbow and turned toward the back of the tent. Omondi lunged forward with the spear and held it an inch from her throat.

Madge emitted a small but very naturalistic shriek.

"Exactly. The spear was used to hush Lynn's scream. She was dead before she could make a sound."

I stepped forward. My mind surged with ideas. "This explains a lot. Why the pants were outside, why there was no blood on the pants."

"It's crazy," Al said, tucking his hands into his armpits. "No one would kill Lynn to steal a pair of blue jeans." He looked over at Meromo's long expanse of naked leg sticking out of his loincloth.

"Can I get up now?" Madge asked. She sat up.

"Of course, of course," Omondi said. "Thank you so much for your invaluable cooperation."

Omondi returned the spear to Meromo with many thanks and arranged to have him driven back to the kraal. Kakombe and Meromo walked off with the same long slow stride. Meromo flung his cape back over his shoulder, exposing an expanse of gleaming muscled back. Kakombe said something to him and the two of them laughed.

"And now, my dear girl"—Omondi fixed me with his bright eyes—"tell us about Lynn's blue jeans."

My mouth felt dry. How was I supposed to know what the murderer was after?

"Think back," he told me. "When was the last time you saw her wearing them?"

I sat down on the log and looked at the ground. Yes, I remembered noticing what people had thought suitable for mourning when we were standing around the campfire. Candy had worn that slinky black dress that made her look like a Toulouse-Lautrec poster. Eleanor had black ruffles. Lynn had

137

worn a dark suit, because I'd thought of how she was always on the job. She'd worn the blue jeans on the game run.

"Boyce Darnell's pills," I said.

"That's right," Madge turned to Al. "Don't you remember, Al? After Boyce died, when we were standing around the campfire, Lynn said she still had his pills in her jeans."

"She told me she felt weird about throwing them away," I said.

"Tell me more about these pills," said Inspector Omondi.

Madge shrugged. "There's not much to tell. He had a heart condition. The pills were for high blood pressure; he had to take them every day."

"Why did Lynn have them? Was she holding them for him?"

"Yeah, why did Lynn have them?" chimed in Al.

"It was by accident," I said. "When we forded the stream . . . remember how bumpy it was? Boyce's jacket fell on the floor. The pills slipped out and started rolling around. Lynn grabbed them and stuck them in her pants for safekeeping and then . . . well, Boyce collapsed."

"So otherwise, Boyce would have had them in his pocket," Omondi said. "What were the pills in?"

"A standard plastic case from the pharmacy. Amber-colored," Madge said.

"Hmmm." Omondi paced about. "It looks very much like Lynn was murdered only because she woke up when someone was fishing her pants out of the tent. If she'd been killed first, the pants would be bloody. As you said before, Jazz. They are not bloody, therefore they were outside the tent when she was stabbed." He stood still and raised a finger. "Why, we ask ourselves." He paused and looked around his small audience. "Why take an ordinary pair of blue jeans? It must be to get Mr. Darnell's blood-pressure pills. But why?"

I'd known there was a connection between the two deaths. I felt a surge of hope. We were getting somewhere. "Do you think there was something funny about those pills?"

"What do you mean?" Omondi pointed at me as if he were calling on the prize pupil in class.

"Well, why would anyone want those pills? And if they did, why not ask Lynn for them? Stealing them makes sense only if they'd been tampered with. You see? Not one murder, but two."

"You mean Boyce was poisoned?" Al's voice seemed to boom across the clearing.

Omondi snapped his fingers. "Yes, and those pills were the only thing that could give it away. Otherwise, poor Mr. Darnell has a heart condition. No one questioned his death. But if Lynn were to peek inside that pillbox and see something funny." He pantomimed opening something small and peering inside. "The end of a perfect murder."

"Whoever did it must have been desperate to get those pills back." Madge closed her eyes and shuddered.

Omondi nodded. "So the murderer waits till night. Till everyone is asleep." He cocked his head and brought a hand up to his cheek like a pillow. "Then quietly, get the spear that has been left by the fire." He snatched an imaginary spear out of the ground. "No, first, get a cloth to hold it with, so there are no fingerprints." He put a hand to his lips. "This is a cool murderer. Even in this most terrible moment, he remembers fingerprints and takes Miss Svenson's leotard."

Less smart if it was Candy Svenson who did it, and she snatched the first thing that came to hand, but still ashamed of my recent jealousy, I said nothing.

"The killer cuts through the tent wall." Omondi slashed down with his two hands. "Lifts out the pants." He pulled his hands toward his body. "Ah, the pills are in the pocket." He pretended to feel an object between his fingers extract it, and put it in his own pocket. "Safe. But no, Lynn wakes up. She is looking around, perhaps she sees the killer and recognizes who it is."

Madge breathed softly, "Oh, this is awful."

"Lynn says, 'Who is it?' She sounds scared, she's going to scream."

"What is this, a school play?" asked Al.

"Waaa—" Omondi thrust forward with his imaginary spear. Madge and I both jumped. "Lynn will speak no more. Now,

I must hide this spear, quick." He looked right and left. "But where? It is dark. I must be silent. There is a bit of moon. There, at the end of the clearing, yes, a fallen log." He pretended to tiptoe stealthily to the log. "Can it be of use to me?" He bent over and looked inside. "It is hollow. Perfect. I thrust the spear out of sight, along with the cloth, and go quietly back to bed." He wiped his palms together. "It is done."

"That leads us to three questions." I ticked them off on my fingers. "Where is the pillbox now? What was in it? And who wanted Boyce dead?"

"Let us check the log once more," Omondi said. "Perhaps it can tell us the location of the pillbox."

We flocked behind him back to the log. This time he crouched for a long time while he balanced with one hand on the smooth sunbleached wood and studied the dark cavity. "It is too dark. An amber-colored plastic bottle would be easily camouflaged against this rotten heartwood." He stood. "We'll have to open the log with a machete."

"Do you have to, Inspector?" I hated to destroy the log. "Couldn't we try raking it out with something?"

He shook his head. "Sorry, my dear. There is a chance for fingerprints. They can be all too easily rubbed off."

We had a machete in camp that was used to chop firewood to manageable lengths. Ngueye, the strongest man on my staff, began chopping. When Kakombe returned, he took over. The machete bit into the dry wood with a thick cracking sound. Kakombe raised the machete over his shoulder, bringing it down over and over until a ragged gap snaked down the center of the log. His dark skin was flecked with splinters of pale wood. It took a long time. Every now and then he'd pause and he and Omondi would study the hollow, using a flashlight to illuminate the interior. When he was two-thirds of the way down the log, they found the bottle of pills.

15

LUNCH WAS DISMAL. It was hot in the tent and a fly buzzed annoyingly against the ridgepole. Just as we filed in, the airplane returned, reminding us of its departure the night before with the two bodies. Kakombe took everyone's fingerprints at the dining table and went out to the plane. The ink washed off but the mood of suspicion it left was an indelible stain.

"Jazz, you got us booked for a room at the lodge tonight?" Al asked as he pulled back his seat.

I looked up sharply. "No, we're going tomorrow night. Then we take the plane to Nairobi the next morning. I thought you understood when I put you on the later flight home, it meant two more nights here. Remember? You and Eleanor agreed to stay."

"Well, I'm changing my mind."

Madge shook her head slightly and mouthed the words *Don't worry*. Out loud she said, "Be a dear and check if they have any space available for us."

I said fine and left it at that. It wasn't my fight. If it came to a showdown, it would be between Al and Omondi.

Molezzi brought in a platter of sandwiches, a pitcher of iced tea and another of lemonade, and set them out on the side table. I took half a roast-beef sandwich and forced myself to swallow a few bites. I needed the fuel, even if I'd lost my appetite. I should have felt good we'd finally made some progress, but I didn't. Omondi's reenactment of Lynn's murder made it horribly real for me. My theory that Boyce was poisoned would have to be confirmed by the autopsy, of course, but as I ran over it in my mind, it made sense of the facts. It was hard to converse. Each time I looked at someone, I found myself picturing them as a double murderer, and I lost track of the conversation.

I was outraged by the unfairness of Lynn's death. She'd been killed by chance because she'd happened to pick up Boyce's pills, happened to wake up at the wrong moment. It was all bad luck, the mistake of a panicked killer. Killing Lynn had been useless, I thought bitterly, not admitting that the killer still had a chance of getting away with both murders.

Who knew Lynn had the pills? Madge and Al knew she had them from the game run, but that didn't exclude other people from learning about it. When we were around the campfire, Lynn mentioned the pills to me, and to Madge. She'd had them on her mind. Maybe she'd talked about it to Cliff, or even Eleanor: Too bad those pills couldn't help with a heart attack, kind of thing. Someone else might have overheard her.

The killer would have been desperate to recover that pillbox once he found it wasn't on Boyce's body. Which brought me back to the Harts, since they definitely knew not only that Lynn had them but where. It was Al who bought the spear, at the end of the evening. Could he have been planning, even then, to cut his way into Lynn's tent? He was fighting Omondi at every step of the investigation. That telex about the stocks, Madge's comment that Boyce was getting worse, all seemed to imply some trouble at Wild and Free.

Al and Madge were silent, also lost in their own thoughts. Eleanor had received the news of the spear's discovery without much interest. No one told her about the pills or our conclusion that Boyce was murdered. We were all afraid of how she'd react. Omondi got Cliff talking about the advertising business, with Eleanor joining in politely from time to time, and the rest of us bent morosely over our sandwiches.

The fly abandoned the ridgepole, flew toward the light, and trapped itself in the folds of the mosquito netting, where it buzzed insistently.

Halfway through the meal, Candy threw down her fork and burst out; "Everyone is looking at me." We all looked at her then. "You think I did it?" Her voice rose shrilly. "You think I knew where the spear was all along?"

"What are you talking about?" Al asked.

Candy talked over his words. "Just because it was my leotard in with the spear." She pushed her chair back. "It was in front of my tent. Anybody could have taken it. Besides, if I'd put it there, why would I have told everyone where it was?" She looked at us with furious sapphire eyes. "It's not fair to suspect me."

Madge tried to reason with her, but Candy visibly turned up her hysteria and stormed out of the tent. I couldn't tell if it was phony or self-indulgent, but in either case, it didn't lighten the atmosphere of doom.

"The charm of youth," Cliff commented. "When you think you are the star of every drama."

"Don't you think it depends?" Eleanor smiled with tight lips. "My daughters, who are real teenagers, not overage ones, aren't so self-centered, I can assure you of that. I must say I'm getting a little bit tired of Candy's theatrics."

Cliff fell back in his chair. "Darling, I believe that's the first time I've ever heard you murmur a critical thought. Are we witnessing the birth of a new personality?"

"Cliff, now you've embarrassed me. Was that critical? I'm sure I didn't mean anything against Candy. It's just that my girls are so mature, I'm afraid I've developed a small pet peeve about people criticizing teenagers. Inspector Omondi, tell us, do parents here have the same sort of problem with young people that we do in America?"

It was a relief when the meal was over and the group scattered to their tents for a siesta. I stood outside for a moment, trying to decide what to do. The sun dazzled me, especially after the darkness of the dining tent. It was so

bright, it was hard to see. The world was a pointillist painting, dissolved, rather than revealed, by light. The wind had
died and the eucalyptus leaves hung straight down, as if too
hot to move.

The fly, released from the netting, buzzed after me and
landed on my arm. I watched it crawl around the sunbleached
hairs, as if on a desert landscape. It paused, I brought my
hand down in a vicious swat, and watched its little corpse
drop to the ground. Not nice, but satisfying.

I changed into shorts. I was too keyed up to nap and didn't
know what to do with myself. After yesterday's encounter
with the rhino, wandering about on foot was out of the question, but the camp was closing in on me. The Land Rover
was in its usual spot, parked next to the staff and supply van.
That meant Kakombe was back from the plane. I decided to
take a drive. It would be hot, but the movement would create
some breeze.

It didn't turn out that way. I picked up the keys from Chris,
but on my way back from the staff area, I crossed paths with
Kakombe. His skin was charcoal black against the blinding
light as he walked unhurriedly toward me, so that he appeared as a flattened cutout of a giant man. He and Omondi
wanted a ride out to the airplane. I offered to drive them.
Kakombe gave me one of his expressionless looks and said
it was up to the inspector. Omondi acted delighted, and so
we all climbed aboard, and I started it up, following what
was by now a faintly worn track through the grass. I asked
if they'd want me to wait or pick them up later. To my surprise, Omondi invited me to come along.

"Where are we going?"

"You'll see, you'll see."

"I hate flying."

"Don't be so suspicious. We're not abducting you."

"Inspector, am I still a prime suspect?"

We circled the shoulder of a hill and I slammed on the
brakes as a giraffe's knees filled the windshield. The giraffe
stood planted in front of us and chewed its cud, gazing mildly
from under luxuriant black eyelashes. Two babies, perfect

miniatures, stood close by each flank. They were very young, only about eight feet tall, and their heads reached up to her withers. Giraffes only have one calf, but mother-calf bonding is weak, and since they suckle their young for less than two minutes a day, they frequently baby-sit for one another. One of the calves nuzzled between mama's legs, searching for the nipple. She wasn't in the mood, for she moved off slowly, the two babies behind her like ducklings.

"Who said you were ever a prime suspect, my dear girl?"

"Well, I thought . . . because of the blood on my pants. I was wondering if any lab report came back." I slipped into first and started up again.

"It was precisely the blood on your pants that made me believe you were probably innocent. As soon as I examined Lynn's tent, I guessed that we would not find any bloody traces, except for the spear itself. And yes, the lab reports came back: It was not Lynn's blood on your pants."

"That's nice to know."

"My dear Jazz, have you been worrying about this? What do you think—I'm smiling at you and all the time thinking it is you who killed your old friend?"

"You do smile at everybody, and somebody's the murderer."

"Ah, you are not as observant as I thought. I smile, and I smile."

I was uncomfortably aware of a personal reaction to Omondi's words, and also of Kakombe sitting behind us, silently listening. I decided to steer the conversation back to an official tone. I told him my idea of calling Susan Greenburg to find out about Wild and Free stock, and thanked him for letting me participate in the investigation, explaining how important it was to me to find Lynn's murderer.

He brushed my words aside with lavish graciousness. "Let us hear no more of that; there is nothing to thank me for. It is I who am grateful for your help. Protocol is for the capital. Here, I say let us work together to find this killer. That is the African way." He put his arm through the open car window and drummed his fingers on the outside of the door, making a hollow metallic sound. "But do not be offended if I fail to mention your help in my report. Nairobi has different priorities in this case. I am instructed to be very careful, very correct. As I told you, tourism is one of our few cash crops." He laughed. "Isn't that right, Sergeant?"

Kakombe didn't bother to reply.

The airplane stood at the end of the flat stretch of field. I flinched as light bounced off its aluminum skin like a second sun.

"Isn't she a beauty?" asked Omondi. "We are completely up-to-date, you see. The wing tips actually droop to facilitate a short takeoff and landing."

This plane was much bigger than Striker's two-seater, but no small plane is beautiful to me. Terrifying, yes. I followed Omondi inside, wondering what was going on. Where could we be going? Was Omondi going to fly it? It was hardly a 747. I could touch both sides if I stretched out my arms.

There was a strong chemical smell in the air and the trapped heat of the day was stifling. As I squeezed into the aisle, I realized we were going nowhere. Kakombe had set up a miniature crime lab. He had placed a board across the second, and last, row of seats, creating a worktable. The spear leaned against it, its pale surface coated with a fine dark powder, the spear head protected by a plastic bag. In the center of the shelf was the amber pillbox, coated with white powder. Neatly arrayed to one side was a hand lens, a stack of one-inch black squares with clear plastic covers, and the small cards bearing our inky fingerprints.

Omondi picked up one of the black squares. "Hinged tapes for lifting prints," he explained. "One side is adhesive. It picks up the powdered print and preserves it. Quite ingenious. The pillbox, by the way, seems to contain a layer of one kind of pill above another, close enough in appearance to go unnoticed. Unfortunately, the pillbox was wiped clean, but Sergeant Kakombe got some good prints from the spear."

So the pills had been tampered with: We were on the killer's trail and starting to backtrack.

Omondi pushed open a blackout curtain at the rear of the plane. I squeezed over as Kakombe followed, almost in a crouch. He clicked on a battery-powered spotlight. Distorted shadows were flung against the curved walls.

"Quite spacious," Omondi joked. "We have removed the backseats and blocked the windows to make sufficient room for carrying things."

Things like bodies. It wouldn't be so great to have to strap them into seats, especially if rigor mortis had set in. Now I saw where the smell of chemicals was coming from. We were in an improvised darkroom.

A line hung over an array of photographic equipment. From each clothespin swung an enlargement on thick developing paper, like a row of pale bats. Eleven. My God, did that many people handle the spear? I didn't think I'd touched it, but it was the sort of unconscious gesture you did without thinking.

"Sergeant Kakombe has a special fingerprint camera that gives a three-by-two negative. Not bad for a bush lab, eh?" Omondi said. "You see, when we have to move fast, we are fast, indeed. This is the modern sorcery. Are they dry enough to handle?" he asked his sergeant. "Good, then let us take them down; bring along the hand lens and the file of prints and let us get out of this wretchedly hot airplane."

"Yes, sir. Back to the camp?" Kakombe began to unclip the photos as he spoke.

Omondi was already at the door of the plane. "No, I'd prefer to do this in privacy. We don't want to make everyone more nervous than they already are."

"We could spread a tarp out in the shadow of the plane and do it right here," I suggested.

"Good thinking." Omondi flashed me his ready smile. His real smile. "Kakombe, see what you can find back there to sit on."

It was more than an hour later that Omondi threw down the last of the photos. I looked out at the horizon to give my eyes a rest. I'd been squinting at swirls and whorls till they ached.

A line of giraffes stood at the crest of a rise, the way they like to do, all pointed in the same direction but spaced about a hundred feet apart. I wondered why. Maybe it's an extra-safe, and hence relaxing, place for them to hang out, since they can see danger coming from afar. Giraffes aren't very social, in the sense of having herds or family groups, but they're not loners, either. This must be their idea of togetherness, without being too close. Kind of like me.

"That's that," said Omondi, rubbing his eyebrows. "Now, what have we got?"

Kakombe had separated the photos into piles. He picked up the biggest stack in his oversize hand. "From the center of the spear's handle, the only clear prints are mine and Meromo's." He moved it to one side and picked up a single photo. "But just above this area, we have the top half of Cliff's index finger."

That miserable half-print had cost us a lot of time, but in the end we had agreed it could only be Cliff's.

He picked up the next pile. "Lower down on the spear, we have good prints of Madge Hart's third and fourth digits." Two more photos were counted down. "In the last pile," Kakombe rumbled on in his bass voice, "we have clear prints of Al Hart, his right thumb and first two digits.

Omondi tapped his fingers on his chin. "Cliff and the Harts. So that means they are probably innocent."

"What?" My voice came out in a squawk.

Omondi grinned. "Yes, innocent. Otherwise, so much more natural to rub the spear clean."

"I don't know," I said. "You're getting a bit too Machiavellian for me. The person may have touched the spear quite innocently when we were all around the campfire, later got the idea to use it, and picked up the leotard for protection at that point."

"Wouldn't you wipe the spear clean if you'd touched it before?" Omondi asked.

"You're saying you suspect Eleanor and Candy because their prints aren't on the spear?" I thought a moment. "Eleanor might have a motive, but Candy?"

Omondi rose and waved his arms. "Ah, I see you are very down-to-earth. That is good. Very good. But you must have a nose for the dramatic personality. Candy wants attention, all the time, from all the men. She will do anything to get it."

"Still"—I was unconvinced—"she doesn't have to murder to get attention."

Omondi jabbed his index finger in the air for emphasis. "No, but I sense a nervousness in her. I could smell it when she was crying that everyone blames her. I think she has a guilty conscience."

I nodded thoughtfully. "I know what you're getting at. I felt something there too, like . . ." I stiffly folded my legs under me and got to my knees, then stood up. Peering intently at those photos had about done me in.

"Like?" Omondi prompted me.

"Oh, my God." I grabbed Omondi's arm and pointed into the grass in the shadow of the nearby Land Rover. "Is that a—"

Kakombe sprang to his feet. "Simba," he whispered. The word was heavy with threat. I looked down for his gun, but he wasn't wearing one.

I instantly turned back to the lioness. It took a moment to spot her again. She was camouflaged by the tawny grass that reached over her head. All I could see was one golden eye. Then the tail flicked. I must have seen that movement out of the corner of my eye. My mouth went dry and I had a sudden urge to pee.

"There's no great danger," Kakombe said. "She's not hunting."

"Let us not wait for her to crouch for the spring," Omondi said. "We must get into the plane fast." He scooped up the photos and fingerprint cards. "Don't run. Do exactly what I do."

He brought his arms slowly up, extended them to each side, and lifted up on his toes. I suppressed a nervous giggle and followed. Why were we imitating Nureyev at a time like this? Omondi backed toward the entry to the plane, maintaining his balletic pose. I scanned the curtain of grass, ready to yell a warning. I could no longer see the lioness but I knew she was there. Don't make her feel like pouncing, think calm, I directed myself. The dry grass brushed against my legs as I backed toward the plane, afraid to look away, as if one moment of lapsed vigilance would bring the lioness upon me.

The plane was behind me now, suddenly a haven. Kakombe walked toward us, a corner of his mouth lifted in amusement, his back to the lioness. The big brave warrior. I concentrated on lifting my leg the right height to mount the plane backward. It wouldn't do to trip. I made room for Omondi in the doorway. We grinned at each other. Kakombe stood next to the door, calm as ever. He probably enjoyed facing down lions. We peered over him to see what the lioness was up to.

She yawned broadly and began washing her face, licking a huge paw and then drawing it over her nose. We could see the roughness of her pink tongue rasping her fur. The three of us burst out laughing. Omondi began to prance around on his toes, arms held wide.

"What was that for?" I gasped out, laughing so hard my side hurt.

"It's an old trick, to make yourself look as big as possible," explained Omondi. "I learned it from an American who was once mauled by a bear." We burst out laughing again.

"Like something the lioness won't want to pounce on," I said.

"That's it, that's it." Omondi nodded, sputtering.

I bent to look out a window. The lioness had rolled onto her side and was panting in the heat. A slight breeze made the tall grass sigh and sway.

"This is great. How do we get to the Land Rover?" I asked.

"We'll have to scare the lioness away," Omondi began. But before he got any further, we heard a new noise.

16

IT WAS THE staff van lumbering through the grass toward us. The lioness stood up and vanished. I caught a last glimpse of her a hundred yards away, and she was gone. The van pulled up next to the Land Rover where the lioness had been lying a moment before.

Al was at the wheel, with Madge next to him. He cut the engine and they clambered out, looking guilty and truculent at the same time. Al was in the same baggy shorts and dark business socks he'd worn that morning. Madge was wearing a cotton knit dress—the sort that's advertised to travel well— in red and white stripes. A broad white belt accentuated her hourglass figure. They had on their matching pith helmets.

"Hello, hello," called out Omondi.

Al waved. "Hi folks. Hot enough for you, Inspector?" Al took off his pith helmet to wipe sweat from his bald head with a large white handkerchief. He turned to me. "Hope you don't mind us borrowing the van? The key was in the ignition."

"Oh, I'm glad you're here, Mr. Omondi," Madge shouted louder than necessary. "We thought we'd take a little drive and visit the plane. We would have asked Chris Mbare about using the van, but we couldn't find him, either. Everyone is still asleep in camp. This is the hottest day yet, isn't it?"

Why had the Harts driven out here? I cast one nervous glance around for lions as we stepped onto the grass. Kakombe went inside to put away the equipment and the photos.

Madge grabbed Omondi's arm, turning her back on me. "Candy is very worked up over this business with her leotard. She cried in the tent for the longest time after lunch."

Omondi shook his head, his face full of sympathetic concern.

Madge went on: "Cliff and I both tried, and we couldn't do a thing with her. Finally, she sort of passed out from the heat. Maybe after the siesta, you could drop by and tell her she's not a suspect."

"Yes, it is very hard to suspect someone who is crying in their tent."

The irony was lost on Madge, who was usually sharper than that. "You've scared her to death, and I think a few words of reassurance from you would do wonders."

Was Madge playing rescuer, a role she seemed to like? Or was she fishing for some indication of whom Omondi suspected? If Omondi was wary, he hid it under a veneer of charm.

"But Mrs. Hart"—he patted the hand she still had on his arm—"I can hardly do that. At this stage, everyone is a suspect."

"Yes, I know all that," Madge said, "I wasn't suggesting you should lie to her, but right now she thinks she's about to be arrested, which is quite unnecessary." She pulled back her hand, releasing Omondi.

"Mr. Omondi doesn't need your help," Al cut in. He was looking hot and cross.

"Al, I was talking to the inspector." Madge didn't even bother to look at her husband.

"Listen to me for once, would you?" Al was visibly making an effort to control himself. "Just for once in your life."

Madge plowed ahead. "Candy's going to be all right, I'm not really worried about her. It's Eleanor I wanted to talk to you about."

"What's the matter with Eleanor?" Omondi asked.

"I don't think you realize the effect of Boyce's death on

her, because she's not the sort of person to express her feelings openly." Madge crossed her arms under her bosom.

"Aw, for Pete's sake, Madge, Eleanor doesn't want you butting into her business." Al tried one more time.

"Enough, Al. Why don't you look at the plane like you wanted to while I talk to Mr. Omondi, okay?"

Al gave up, knowing an immovable force when he saw one. He climbed into the plane, casting one worried look over his shoulder at his wife.

The tarp was still spread in the shadow of the plane. Omondi invited Madge to sit down with a wave of his arm. She shook her head. "This will only take a minute." But she hesitated.

I was half-intrigued, half-impatient. I didn't think Madge was going to come up with useful information. Had they followed us out here to check what we were doing? I hated feeling so suspicious.

"I say, Mrs. Hart, take all the time you need." Omondi was adept at reverse psychology. He brushed a fly away from his face. Its buzzing sounded loud in the silence. Around us, the immensity of the plain rippled in the heat. A watery mirage hovered above the still grass. High in the sky, I could see black dots: vultures riding the thermals.

"It's this," Madge said. "Eleanor is near her cracking point. She's led a sheltered life since her marriage, and she was very dependent on Boyce. I don't mean financially—she has her own family money—I mean, her whole life revolved around him, and now she's like a lost lamb."

Omondi nodded. "Of course, you are concerned about her."

Now that she was started, Madge went on with conviction. "Eleanor is a conventional person, as you can see when you meet her. Having her husband die on a safari was hard enough." Madge twisted the thick gold band of her wedding ring. She had worn it so many years, it lay in a groove at the base of her finger. "Inspector, she's holding on by sheer willpower. I'm very afraid of what will happen when you tell her Boyce was poisoned. I don't know how much more she can take. Things like this don't happen to people in her world."

"Yes, I understand what you are saying." Omondi nodded vigorously. "A world of respectability."

Madge reached down and yanked a piece of knee-high grass. She absentmindedly tore it into bits as she spoke. "My point is, I think it's irresponsible to tell her out here in the middle of nowhere. Medically irresponsible. We're going home tomorrow; couldn't we break it to her then?"

"Oh, yes, I see your point," Omondi said. The fly returned, and this time he swatted at it aggressively. "Do not worry, once her husband's murder is confirmed, I will break it to Mrs. Darnell as gently as possible; unfortunately, I am experienced in these matters." He looked at his watch. "As for your leaving tomorrow, well, we will have to see about that. Boyce's murder changes the picture, doesn't it?"

Madge's voice turned cold. "Al won't agree to put off our departure again, and I don't blame him. We're not even witnesses. You can't hold us just because we were there when Boyce collapsed. I assure you, we're not staying here forever while you're hunting for the killer."

"Believe me, madame, we are going as fast as we can, and I regret terribly keeping you here, so far from home. I myself must return to Nairobi tomorrow on another case, and we will move you to a hotel. I think that would be a better atmosphere, more civilized and calming." Omondi's gold watch and ring flashed as he gestured. "By the way, Mrs. Hart. Can you tell me if you remember handling the spear Al bought?"

Madge was nonplussed. "I don't understand."

Omondi gestured broadly, flinging his arms out. "Oh, it is nothing. A small item of interest. Did you ever pick up the spear, to see what it felt like?"

"Pick it up?" Madge repeated stupidly.

Al poked his head out of the doorway behind us. "Now you're quiet. Now you don't have anything to say," he flung at her.

154

Madge craned her neck to look at him. "What's gotten into you, Al?"

I squinted my eyes against the sun to peer at Al. It was hard to make out his features. He looked like a gnome from this angle.

"You want to know what's with me? Well, after you prove to Inspector Omondi here that it wasn't Candy and it wasn't Eleanor, they're hardly going to pin it on Jazz or Cliff, are they? Who does that leave, little Miss Know It All? Tell me, who does that leave?"

Inspector Omondi threw back his head and laughed. "Little Miss Know It All. I must remember that. Thank you, Mr. Hart. Both of you save me the great effort of thinking for myself." He tapped his forehead with a finger.

Al came down from the plane looking both irritated and embarrassed.

Madge put an arm around Al's shoulders and gave him a little squeeze. She said, "Okay, Inspector, I get your point. I'm going to stop being a busybody, starting right now."

Al made a derisive sound.

Omondi spread out both hands. "Do not stop on my account. To me, there is room for everybody's thoughts, and I must say my poor head is getting dizzy from so many possibilities. Right now, to speed things up as I promised you, I am going to have our excellent pilot fly me to Masai Mara Lodge. We'll swing by the camp and pick him up. Jazz, you mentioned a phone call you needed to place. Do you want to come?"

I could hear Kakombe inside the plane, dismantling his photo lab.

"Sure, that would be great. How long will we stay?" Gruesome was more accurate than great, given my feelings about small planes, but the call to New York was important. Going by car would be four hours round-trip, out of the question.

"The minimum. We have no time to putter about there. Anyone else? Al? Madge? I can take one more person."

"Hey, that's an idea," Al said. "There's a phone call I'd

155

like to make, too." He hesitated. "I don't know. I don't want to leave Madge here by herself, you know?"

Omondi reassured him that Sergeant Kakombe was staying behind to keep an eye on things at the camp. Madge urged Al to go, then pulled him to one side for some earnest private discussion.

Omondi looked at his gold watch. It had a big face and a wide band, oversize for his slender wrist. In my mind's eye, I saw it as a giant hourglass, and the sand was running out.

I hate small planes. It is an unfortunate disability in Africa, where roads are dreadful and air travel is often the only sensible way to connect two points. There's no need to drive any distance to an airport. Pilots will land anywhere, which is part of my problem. I can't get it out of my head that landing strips should be level, smooth, and paved. The bird's-eye view of the plains, dotted with little toy animals, doesn't have the feeling I love of being immersed in the natural world. I don't care to be above it all. Besides, small planes make me queasy.

Having said all that, I admit that I thoroughly enjoyed the hop to Masai Mara Lodge. Omondi talked nonstop, pointing to animals, trees, animals, rivers, animals, bluffs, animals, water holes, animals, Masai, and animals. He laughed and laughed over a herd of ostrich looking like giant eggs on stilts. He shook his head over elephants in tall brush, at least fifty animals, browsing on a hillside like a slow motion avalanche, leaving a swathe of destruction behind them.

Level with the plane, halfway to the horizon, there was a towering thunderhead. Omondi shouted aloud as a lightning bolt darted with it and dark streaks of rain slanted from its flat bottom to the earth. A line of wildebeest and zebra ran toward the cloud, knowing rain meant fresh pasture. "They smell the rain from afar," he commented. "Rain means life."

I'd rarely met such an enthusiastic person. I studied his profile from the seat behind as he pressed his face close to the window. His skin was dark and smooth, his features soft,

156

his eyes bright. His spongy hair asked to be touched. Omondi was smart, capable, a mature adult, but he wasn't ashamed to be lively and playful. He was an extrovert without the big ego you find in American men like that: It wasn't all me, me, me. I wondered what it would be like to get to know him better; if it were possible. Did he let people in behind his lively exterior? I'd sensed an invitation from him that morning. The real question for me was, would I let anybody in? It had been a long time since I'd even raised the question.

We landed without incident and walked the three hundred yards from the airstrip to Masai Mara Lodge. A waterfall of bougainvillea cascaded over the entrance, and a vervet monkey chattered at us from the roof ridge. Uniformed bellboys unloaded luggage from two zebra-stripped vans parked in front of the entrance. There was no front door; there wasn't even a wall. We looked across a sweep of polished marble, through the cool dim interior, and out a second open wall on the opposite side of the lobby. White-coated waiters moved quietly among small tables, serving drinks in tall frosted glasses to people on a veranda. There was a soft babble of voices.

A young elephant scratched his rear end on a boulder only a hundred feet beyond the bar. We cut our way through a small crowd of dusty, tired-looking tourists who milled around uncertainly on the sidewalk, and entered. The elephant scratched one side of its rear, then shifted position and started on the other side. He waved his trunk in contented curlicues.

A skinny man with stooped shoulders was in front of us at the reception desk. He carried an overnight bag and looked disheveled. His face was red, not from the heat but apparently from shouting at the desk clerk. I got the feeling he'd been yelling for a while.

"Three nights with the baboons—don't tell me you still don't have a room."

The clerk kept his head down and fiddled with his ledger, as if literally letting the man's anger roll off his back.

"An outrage! I reserved a room, not a tent."

The clerk fiddled.

"This is unbelievable." His voice cracked. The man looked close to hysteria.

The clerk spoke in a soft voice without looking up. "I'm sorry, sir. We are overbooked. The luxury tents are the same as a room."

The man's shoulders slumped and he crept away toward the bar, babbling, "Three nights with the baboons. They promised me a room."

"Poor fellow," said Omondi.

"Aw, the guy's a jerk." Al waved a hand in dismissal. "He's just making a stink. A lot of hot air. You notice he never once said, 'Give me a room.' You want something, ask for it, don't complain you're not getting it. I got no time for jokers like that."

"Aren't you blaming the victim?" I asked him.

"That guy loves it. He's going to get a lot of mileage out of this story. I can hear him already. Personally, I'd rather have the stocks."

Had Al really said stocks? I supposed he meant to say room. I glanced at Omondi, but he was turning toward the reception clerk. Had he noticed? Would he recognize a slip of the tongue? I doubted if even an educated African had much exposure to Freud's theories of the unconscious. This phone call to my stockbroker friend might be interesting.

Omondi arranged with the manager to use the telephone. There was a phone booth with a padded seat opposite reception where one could wait in relative comfort for the operator to call back when he'd made the connection to Nairobi, or in my case, to the overseas operator. Getting a call through required both luck and patience.

I left Omondi and Al to make their calls first and went to pick up a paper. I dreaded what I might find. If this case dragged on, we might have a third death on our hands: my little baby safari company. Cliff would probably say there's no such thing as bad publicity, but two murders on your first tour was not likely to inspire confidence. I scanned the front page. Not there. I flipped through the back pages quickly:

There it was, a terse article saying an American woman named Lynn Alexander had died at a campsite outside Masai Mara National Reserve and that the police were conducting an investigation. No mention of Jazz Jasper Safaris—yet. If only we could wrap this up before the reporters got on to it.

I wandered outside, walked in the opposite direction from the pool and cottages, and came upon a line of tents hidden by the main building. A young baboon with a pair of jockey shorts on its head almost careened into my legs. I swerved and he ran off, chased by a playmate. I laughed out loud. The tents had become a baboon playground. A few nursing mothers, the size of large dogs, clutched newborns to their stomachs and looked on benevolently—for baboons. The adults do have mean faces, but I try not to hold it against them.

Nearest the lodge, the tents were intact, but as you went down the line, there were more and more baboons. Three infants used the last tent as a trampoline, while another little fellow swung on a loose guy rope, Tarzan style. As I watched, the tent sagged in the middle, tottered, and collapsed. A juvenile ran squealing from inside dragging a small suitcase. The lid was open and a line of brightly colored sports clothes strewed across the lawn as he ran.

"I told Njombo the tents wouldn't work next to the lodge. These baboons are getting half-tame, and that's no good."

I whirled around. "Striker! What are you doing here?"

17

STRIKER STOOD THERE grinning at me. His laughing eyes met mine and a surge of happiness jolted through me like an electrical connection. I had always known he was an attractive man; for the first time, I felt it, so intensely it cut my breath for a moment. My comfortable little world tilted and threatened to crack up. I literally tottered on my feet as he scooped me into a hug that crushed me against his chest. His own particular spicy smell surrounded me and I could feel his heart beating under my cheek.

"Whoa, Jazz. Steady there." He held me at arms' length and looked at me searchingly. "Are you all right? Little weak in the knees?"

"Oh, I'm fine." I glanced at the lawn as if there'd been a pothole there, not at all ready to admit to either of us that the sight of him had made me wobbly. "Striker, I'm so glad to see you. I was hoping to steal a few days and drop by Mt. Kenya, after this thing was over."

"Has it been horrid?" He joked in a British accent, but his long face furrowed with sympathy.

"Utterly." I smiled. "Unutterably utterly . . ."

"Beastly," he finished. "I'm going to get you talking like a Kenyan yet."

"Surely not," I told him in my best British.

"I'm prepared for it to take a long time. You have to ab-

160

sorb these things slowly and naturally. The longer the better.''

A vervet monkey looked down on us from a jacaranda tree. It watched us intently for a moment, seemed to conclude we had nothing to offer, and returned its attention to a stolen roll.

"Well, the lessons will have to wait for a while, until Lynn's murderer is caught.''

"What are you doing here? Looking for clues at Mara?''

"You may mock, but I am looking for clues. Inspector Omondi needed to fly over to pick something up, and I came along to call a friend in the States. I want to check up on some stuff connected with Boyce Darnell.''

"The guy who died the night before Lynn.''

"Right. We think now he was murdered, too. I'm in line for the phone. I'll tell you all about it over a drink, if you have time.'' We headed back toward the main grounds. "What about you? What are you doing here? I thought you were holed up this week finishing that article on the ivory trade.''

"Yeah, but I wasn't making much headway.'' Striker scratched his temple with a forefinger. "I kept thinking about a killer among your little band. It was distracting, so I figured I might as well drop by instead of worrying about it.''

Drop by from two hundred miles away? I could feel myself tense up. "What is this? Are you playing the Lone Ranger?'' Striker gave me an exasperated look. I knew I was being obnoxious but I couldn't stop. "I'm perfectly capable of taking care of myself. Besides, the police are with us. Your Inspector Omondi does seem pretty good.''

We walked beside a hedge of yellow hibiscus. Two black and yellow butterflies danced a duet above the flowers. The hibiscus dangled their honeyed pistils and velvety anthers to no avail.

Striker linked his arm in mine. "Now don't bristle at me. I know you can take care of yourself. That's one of the things I like about you.'' He paused and looked sideways at me. "Thought you might like to have a friend about.''

I freed my arm in what I hoped was an unobtrusive fashion and stuck my hands in my pockets. The tight feeling in my chest didn't go away. "Oh, I know you like my independence; that's one of the things I like about you, too." So why was I making such a big deal about this? Why not accept his support?

"Then why are you being so weird?" Striker echoed my thoughts.

"I don't know," I said unhappily.

"Oh, forget it. Tell me what's been going on."

We circled round the back of the main lodge. There was a strip of green lawn in front of the veranda bar, and then the rough golden grass of the plains sloped away, dotted with acacia and thornbushes. The young elephant had left his rock. In his place, a Grant's gazelle was scratching the ground with petite black hooves. Its small head was set neatly on a slender curved neck. It glanced around for danger, then nibbled on the bare earth, probably seeking out mineral salts. Up for danger, down to eat, up for danger, down to eat. What a way to live.

We settled ourselves at a table and ordered drinks from a thickset waiter with his hair clipped tight against his scalp. Striker picked up the cardboard coaster, which proclaimed Tusker across a picture of an elephant, and tapped the edge against the table.

I told him about the two deaths and what we'd discovered so far. He listened carefully, asking now and then for details, mostly letting me tell it my way. It reminded me of many hours we'd spent discussing wildlife, figuring things out together, sharing observations and ideas, but all through it, I could feel my tension growing. The more I appreciated his involvement, the more I wanted to contradict everything he said. It was ridiculous.

He tossed the coaster back on the table. "You've certainly make some quick progress. From what you've explained, if we figure out who gave Boyce Darnell some funny medicine, we know who killed Lynn." He laced his fingers behind his head. "Who needed Darnell to die?"

162

"And why choose this time and place?"

He leaned forward, resting an elbow on the table, chin on his fist. "It could be almost anyone. Let's take Eleanor, first. Isn't that the general rule: You're most likely to be struck down by your spouse?"

For some reason, Striker's comment annoyed me. "I was thinking along those lines, too, but Cliff argued me out of it. Eleanor and Boyce did not have a passionate marriage, and I don't think she needed his money."

"How do you know that?"

"According to Madge, she has money of her own. Besides, Boyce was running a successful company for her and bringing home a hefty executive salary, too. His death will make her poorer, not richer."

Striker looked off into the air. He had a long nose with a slight bump in it, which gave him an interesting profile. "Still, as a widow, it's all hers to control. Maybe she fell for someone else and Boyce wouldn't give her a divorce."

"I'm not sure you need to be given a divorce these days. I think people just take one." I looked around the room with irritation. No sign of the waiter. They usually had better service than this. I really wanted that drink. "If she was having an affair, it shouldn't be so hard to discover with a little poking around back home. Still, if you'd met Eleanor: As Cliff says, she has a fetish about purity."

"Maybe she was having a pure affair." Striker shifted in his chair. He seemed awfully restless today. "Moving on, what about Al and Madge? Al bought the spear, and from what you say, he's the only one not cooperating with Omondi. Will he profit from Boyce's death?"

'That's the question that brought me here." I touched my forehead with the back of my hand; it was damp with sweat. The overhead fans looked romantic but all they did was move the hot air around. "I have a friend in New York who's a stockbroker at some big firm. Susan Greenburg. I'm going to give her a call and hope she'll be able to shed some light on that."

I studied Striker's hands—strong and supple—as he played

with the coaster. He spun it on edge like a top. He had a tiny white scar along one finger that I'd never noticed before. I pulled my eyes away.

Striker nodded. "It sounds like something funny was going on with their stocks—"

"Yeah. Why did Boyce hide that telex about the stocks dropping? You could see Al and Madge were upset when Omondi showed it to them, and yet they tried to pretend they weren't."

The waiter finally came with our drinks on a cork-lined tray. Striker relinquished the coaster and the waiter set the gin and tonics in front of us, along with a bowl of peanuts. Striker tossed some in his mouth, then continued. "I would rule out Candy. She was insulted and lost this one job. Big deal. That's not grounds for murder, unless she's pathologically vain, and in that case, you'd think there'd be a trail of corpses behind her by now."

"You haven't seen Candy yet. She's not insulted often. *Au contraire*. Men line up to eat out of her hand."

Striker grabbed my hand as I was lifting a peanut to my lips and nibbled the peanut out of my palm. I pulled my hand back.

"To continue—" I cradled my glass, pressing my hands against its cold slick surface, "I agree Candy's motive seems weak. But Omondi and I both sense something guilty and weird in her reactions. Maybe she feels funny because there was something going on between her and Boyce the first part of the trip. I thought they were sleeping together, though Candy says not. In any case, he was pursuing her, and then he trashed her publicly. She's still young enough to take that sort of mistreatment to heart."

"Maybe, maybe not. Some people are never that young, and some people never outgrow it." The last was a dig at me. He said it with a smile and seemed startled by the narrow-eyed look I threw back at him. I normally laugh easily at my own foibles, but I wasn't feeling my normal self. He mugged back at me and continued. "The strongest thing against her is circumstantial—she had opportunity to tamper with his pills.''

''Not more than anyone else, after they fought.'' I contradicted him with satisfaction.

''You're right, which supports my point that Candy can probably be crossed off. Besides, it's hard to imagine a young girl like that killing Lynn with a spear.''

I sipped from my gin and tonic, appreciating the sharp taste of the quinine. ''Candy is not a sweet young thing. She's more like a young lioness. She might kill for her career, but I really don't see how Boyce threatened that.''

''So we agree.''

I grudgingly nodded.

''Which only leaves Cliff,'' Striker said.

''Oh, I don't see Cliff as the culprit.''

Striker looked surprised. ''That's awfully fast.''

''He wasn't involved enough with either of them to have a motive. As it is, he's lost an old, steady client, and his best young writer.''

''I sense a lack of objectivity here.'' He looked at me over the edge of his glass.

''Cliff is a charming man, but I only met him a week and a half ago. Besides, he's gay.''

''Sounds just like your type then.''

''Striker, let it rest. You're sounding juvenile.''

''I think it's you who's being juvenile with this broken-heart routine. Two years is enough to mourn. You've got to get on with your life.''

''I am getting on marvelously with my life, without the benefit of a boyfriend.'' I felt an intense desire for a cigarette, which I squelched. ''Listen, maybe this friendship idea isn't working out. You make me feel that I'm hurting you all the time by being myself. This is who I am.''

''That's what makes me so mad.'' Striker sounded exasperated. ''I don't believe this is you.'' Silence fell. He looked glumly into his glass, swirled the ice cubes, and took a gulp. ''Let's think about Cliff for a minute at least.''

''Fine. Think about him.''

165

"Losing his best writer doesn't mean anything if he had to do it to avoid a murder charge. He hasn't lost the account with Boyce's death."

"Go on."

"I'm thinking."

"See, there isn't any positive reason to suspect him."

"I guess they'll do a postmortem on Boyce and find out what was in those pills. That should give us something concrete to go on." Striker lifted his glass and the coaster stuck to the wet bottom like a magnet. It fell off and rolled under the next table. "I don't imagine everyone on safari happened to have poison handy."

The lady at the next table put her sneakered foot on the coaster without noticing it. She was busy feeding peanuts to a warthog that begged for handouts at the edge of the terrace. Its long bumpy face was caked with dried mud that had flaked off in patches, making it uglier than usual, but it had an appealing, eager, bright look in its eyes. Two little curled tusks poked out of the bottom of its jaw. It was quite good at catching peanuts.

Striker tossed it a nut. "Animals are much more humane than people. You don't catch them murdering one another."

"You're always romanticizing animals," I said scornfully. "Animals kill for gain, just like people do."

"That's the silliest thing I ever heard. You can't call it murder when an animal hunts."

"I'm not talking about hunting. When a lion or a monkey takes over a new pride or troop, what do you think is the first thing they do?"

"Mate with all the females," he said with a half-smile.

"And right before? They kill all the babies."

"Hogwash."

"No, Striker, they do; you aren't keeping up with the latest animal studies." I knew that was untrue, but I said it anyway. I felt impelled to be obnoxious. "They do it so the females will get pregnant right away from them. That's killing for gain; they want their genes passed on to more offspring."

166

"All right, but that's one small example."

"Infanticide is infanticide. Then you have to admit males do sometimes kill each other in a fight for females or breeding territory."

"I admit nothing. The important point is they usually don't kill each other: They fight ritually, a little shoving back and forth, paw the earth, toss some branches around. Once one has proven he's stronger, the weaker one backs off and is allowed to flee. If only humans were that smart, we'd be a lot better off."

"That's not so different from us. Most of our individual competition is not to the death, either. Besides, it's not as sweet as you're describing it. Those poor lions are covered with scars from fighting off other males. A few years as king and that's it: A strong, fresh younger lion pushes him out of the hunting territory. The poor lion wanders alone for the rest of his life, which isn't long, chased by other lions, trying to get food without lionesses to hunt for him. There's nothing humane about it."

"Are we having a fight to the death?" Striker asked. "You're looking at me with a strange glint in your eye."

"I can't stand it when people who profess to love animals turn around and start criticizing humans. We're not that different; we're all animals."

"Some of us more than others."

I leaned on our little round table, making it rock on its base. "What interests me is that human murders are more irrational than animal ones. Animals kill for self-interest. People get carried away by their emotions and strike out, hurting themselves. We're not protected by instincts the way animals are."

"So you're saying animals are more rational than people."

I nodded. "You might say that."

"How is that different from my saying they're more humane? You've just done it yourself. Hah!"

"Stop gloating," I told him.

"Won't." He crossed his arms.

"You put those words in my mouth."

"You accepted them" he said. "You romanticize animals even more than I do!"

"I was trying to make a serious point, and you're only focused on winning.

"Is that right? The only point I see you making is that I'm a stupid romantic."

"Let's just leave it at stupid."

Striker looked hurt. "Fine. Fine. That's fine." He threw some money down on the table, stood up abruptly, and strode out of the restaurant.

18

Five p.m. in Kenya is nine A.M. in New York, and I caught Susan Greenburg as she started her day on Wall Street. I expected to hear the blaring of car horns rising up from those sunless canyons, but of course, up on the thirtieth floor or wherever she works, all you hear is the quiet hum of air-conditioning and the clacking of computer keyboards. After hearing me out, Susan clacked away at hers for a moment. Then she put me on hold and I listened to the hissing of long-distance telephone wires for a few minutes. Someone had scratched "I love elephants" into the mahogany wall above the telephone. Asshole. Unless the person really did love elephants, in which case, it was more complicated. Couldn't people love without destroying things? I kept my eye on the glass door of the phone booth, hoping Striker would cross my field of vision.

"Jazz, this is your lucky day. As it happens, I know Darnell's stockbroker. Of course, I know half the big guys in this business, but this fella's a particular friend. I had to apply the thumbscrews a little bit, 'cause you're not supposed to sell and tell, but I explained it was life and death. I won't tell you what else I promised. Here's the scoop. Darnell unloaded three-quarters of his stock on the fourteenth, with an order to buy it back February first. Either he knew something would make the stock stay down till then or he didn't care about taking a loss."

"You're saying he manipulated the drop in price?"

"All I can tell you is, when he sold that much stock, the price plunged like an elevator with a snapped cable. It's a good buy now, and it's started to creep up, but not far. Why mess around with a potential stinker when everything else is zooming through the ceiling? February first mean anything to you?"

A middle-aged lady with dyed beige hair and bright pink lipstick put her face up to the glass. I turned my shoulder to her and hunched over the phone. "February first is the last day of this tour. I don't get it. It sounds like Boyce wanted the stock price to be down for the two weeks he'd be away. Why would he do that?"

"I can't help you there, sweetie. If he was avoiding a buyout, he'd want the stock high, not low."

The lady cupped a hand against the glass and peered at me. I shook my head slightly, but she set her pink mouth and folded her arms over her square white pocketbook, as if prepared for a siege. I twisted on the little wooden shelf that passed for a seat, so I wouldn't have to look at her, and tried to gather my thoughts. "Could this whole thing—I mean, making the price go down—be directed at his partner? He's here, too. He owns the next biggest chunk of the company."

"What's his name?"

"Al Hart. He's head of sales and marketing."

"Al Hart? That name is ringing a bell. Hart. Do you want me to call you back or can you hold on?"

"I'd better hold. It's not easy to get a line through to here."

Back to the electronic hum. I could hear one side of someone else's call, but there was too much interference to eavesdrop. The lady with the beige hair glared at me, still hugging her pocketbook to her chest. She filled the doorway; I wouldn't be able to see Striker if he passed two feet away. I opened the door a crack, said, "Would you mind letting me talk in peace?" and closed it again. She spat out some rejoinder I didn't catch, glared a moment longer to prove no one pushed her around, rattled the door handle in a last expression of ill temper, and moved off. Now she would really

170

have something to feel self-righteous about. I rubbed the back of my neck. The tendons were as taut as mooring lines. I breathed deeply and tried to relax, with no appreciable effect.

Susan was back on the line. "I'm a little information machine. Ready for this? Al Hart had been raising some capital for a new venture."

"What's a nuvencha?"

"No, no, a new ven-chur, u-r-e. A new business. You know, like venture capital."

"You mean a high-tech company?"

"Could be anything, high or low. Venture capital is a fancy way of saying other people's money. There was a one-incher in an investment newsletter, said he's starting something in the hair-care field. No public stocks, it's just a gleam in his eye at this point."

"That's interesting." Al was raising money to start a new company. "I wonder if Darnell undercut him by manipulating Wild and Free stocks: make the company look bad just when Hart is trying to impress people."

"It's more than that, baby. Hart has to put in a big chunk of dough himself to prove he's serious, you know what I mean? Borrowing against stocks is a great way to lose everything. They suddenly go down and your ass is hanging out there in the breeze."

"Hold on, you're losing me. Run that by again." I tugged on the telephone cord, released it, and watched it slowly twist itself into a double helix of thick black plastic.

"It's simple. Say Al needed to raise a lot of money fast. He has to put up some collateral, right? So what's he going to use? His house may be fancy-schmancy, but it's not going to raise the dough for him. So he uses his stocks, just like you put a second mortgage on your house. But where a house stays the same value, with stocks, if their value is cut in half, your loan will be called in and before you can shut your legs, you've been royally screwed, pardon my English."

"If the stocks went too low to cover the loan, he'd lose both—stocks and the loans?"

"You got it."

So Boyce was trying to wreck Al's new business and cut him out of Wild and Free at the same time. My mind raced in several directions, like an overexcited dog. "Susan, I owe you one. Thanks a lot. I'll tell you how it comes out."

"Happy to help. *Mazel tov* on your new business. Who knows? I might take a vacation one of these days and have you show me around Africa. Oh, one more thing. If I were you, I'd find out who's inheriting Boyce's share of Wild and Free."

"Wouldn't it be his wife? I mean, there's no reason to think he disinherited her." The lady with the beige hair drifted by, paused irresolutely, and continued out of view.

"Never assume anything when there's money involved. There are different kinds of partnerships. Sometimes it's the partner who inherits."

"Jesus."

"Yeah. I know someone who spent his whole life working for his father for a measly salary, putting up with all the bullshit that goes down in families. He thought it was the family business, you know, like he was working for himself, too, and then the old man dropped dead and the partner walked away with everything. He never got over it. Started drinking; his wife left him. Ruined his life."

"That doesn't seem right, does it?"

"Who said life is fair? Well, got to go now."

"Thanks, Sue. You're a gold mine."

"Tell that to my clients." Sue laughed and we rang off.

I found Omondi in the lobby watching the bustle of people who were returning from their afternoon game runs. In the cool dark of the telephone booth, I'd forgotten it was still daylight. There seemed to be a small stampede to the pool or bar. People came through the main door dressed in khaki, their faces streaked with sweat and Kenya's red dust. Others came from the direction of rooms and cabins, with shining faces and hair wet from the shower. All the tables in the bar were full and a small knot of people waited by the entrance. The gift shop was doing a brisk business in carved wooden animals, sun hats, and film. A distinguished-looking Italian man with a linen jacket draped over his shoulder explained to a companion in accented English that he'd come to Kenya in January every year for the last twelve years. A Swedish family trooped by in shorts and hiking boots. There was a happy vacation mood in the air, which made me feel out of place. I couldn't even return Omondi's big smile. I'd been fixated for thirty-six hours on finding Lynn's killer, but narrowing in on Al made me feel sick in the pit of my stomach. I didn't want the murderer to be anyone I knew.

"At last!" Omondi exclaimed. "You must have had a productive call. I, too, learned some interesting facts. I will tell you later." He clapped me on the shoulder. He had a manila envelope tucked under his arm. "Let us go. Mr. Hart is already outside. It is best to return before the sun goes down."

"What's that?" I hurried my pace as he darted toward the exit.

"This?" Omondi wagged the envelope. "I'm afraid I'm going to make Mr. Hart just a little bit angry. It is something I requested from Nairobi yesterday after he refused to let me look in his tent."

"A search warrant?"

Omondi nodded. "There is also a little notice that no one in the group is free to clear customs while party to a murder investigation. You think the African bureaucracy is slow in everything? See, we can be fast when we need to. They want to get this case cleared up quickly. Quickly and properly."

As if spurred on by his own words, Omondi hastened his pace. We left the lodge, and I could see the police plane sitting on the runway. Damn. I'd wanted another chance to see Striker and apologize for calling him stupid. I couldn't believe I'd acted like such a baby. I hoped to spot him at the last minute, but he was nowhere in sight. I didn't see his plane, either, not that I was sure I'd recognize it. I can barely tell one car from another.

I consoled myself with the thought that disappearing in a temper wasn't exactly the most mature behavior in the world, either, but it wasn't much consolation. Striker and I had reached an awkward point where our mutual attraction was likely to blast us apart if it was thwarted in pulling us together. I didn't want to be pulled or pushed; I wanted things to stay the same. Maybe that wasn't a choice, any more than in my marriage with Adam. Could there be a lesson for me here? If so, I didn't want to hear it.

There was Al, short and round, at the edge of the runway, facing down a marabou stork.

"Ugliest bird I ever saw." Al gestured toward his companion. "Looks like an undertaker with a skin problem."

It was true. The marabou is the size of a child, conservatively feathered in black, with the naked head of all scavengers. Raw pink skin covers the head and neck, and a large fleshy wattle hangs down its chest like a growth. The stork watched us with one eye and then the other and clacked its heavy bill, as if not liking what it saw. Marabous give me the creeps, except when they're aloft. Then they are one of creation's most beautiful miracles of flight.

"Bad-luck birds," Omondi said, and darted forward, flapping his arms. The marabou held its ground for a moment, took a few grudging steps to the side, and clacked its bill.

"There's nothing for you here, go away."

The bird wouldn't go. Finally, we turned our backs on it and mounted the steps to the plane, leaving the stork as the sole witness of our departure. Whose bad luck? I wondered.

19

We were quiet on the return trip. I don't know what the others had on their minds. I was concentrating on not being sick. The queasy feeling in my stomach was not helped by the noisy vibrations of the engine. It was like being caught inside a washing machine, an old-fashioned one with a thick glass window in front, like those at the first laundromat I used—in Manhattan—the year after I graduated from college. My weekly trips there had seemed quite the adventure—not because of the characters who occupied the spoon-shaped plastic seats ranged against the wall opposite the machines, but because it meant I was grown-up, out in the real world, no longer safe in the clean little laundry room in the dorm basement. I could meet anyone there, anything could happen. It was a heady taste of life's possibilities. I shifted on the airplane's narrow cushioned seat. The seat belt, which I'd pulled too tight, dug into my belly. Here I was, living an adventurous life I'd never dreamed of then, and instead of feeling free, I felt more trapped than ever.

Another wave of nausea shook me. I looked over the pilot's shoulder and focused on the horizon; a sailing friend taught me it would prevent seasickness. She was wrong. After all the traveling I'd done, you'd think I'd have developed a stronger stomach. My eyes wandered to the rows of dials, gauges, and whatever else they'd stuck all over the plane's dashboard. Striker would laugh at me for calling it that, but it did look like an overgrown sports car. My head throbbed. At least they could have a curtain decently screening the cockpit.

The sun was an enormous sphere with a flat top and bulging sides that oozed below the earth's edge. There were no clouds to catch and play with its molten orange color. The sun disappeared surprisingly fast, and the sky was left, a gentle spectrum, one shade melding imperceptibly into the next: yellow near the horizon, then a green-blue, a robin's egg blue, dark blue, violet, purple-black. We landed in the soft afterglow, when for a moment the earth seems brighter than the sky. By the time we reached camp, evening had arrived.

Cliff, Candy, Madge, and Eleanor were around the unlit campfire, drinks in hand. The day had cooled off abruptly with the setting sun, one of the advantages of being a mile high. Candy wore a tight suede skirt, a cowl-necked sweater, and high boots in matching suede. The sweater was a sophisticated work, probably one of a kind, done in different textures and shades of cream. I tried to imagine being at a New York party where most of the women were models. Would Candy still stand out? It was hard to picture her blending into any crowd, but she probably did know a circle of people like herself.

"Oh, Jazz, did you get any cigarettes?" Candy asked. "Molezzi ran out of filter tips, and Cliff is tired of sharing."

"Sorry, I didn't think of it. Maybe if you ask Cliff nicely, he'll carry you through the evening. We can get more tomorrow."

"Cliff," Candy wheedled.

"Very well, but you realize you are now indebted to me? I warn you, I always collect." Cliff extended his pack to Candy, who pulled out a cigarette with her long nails. "Did you bring back any clues for us?" Cliff held his lighter for Candy and then lit up himself. He puffed heavily to get it going and squinted at me through the smoke.

My stomach gave a twinge and I looked guiltily at Madge. She didn't notice. She'd bustled over to give Al a sweater and get him settled in a chair with a platter of cheese and crackers.

"Are you sure you don't want to change out of those shorts?" she asked.

"I told you, I'm fine." Al threw a cracker into his mouth.

Omondi answered Cliff. "Much interesting news. Perhaps it is best left for after dinner."

"Oh, what is it, Inspector?" Eleanor twisted her hands. She was wearing a light wool navy dress that looked as though it would itch. Powder and blue eye shadow were not enough to distract from the dark half-moons under her eyes and the strain lines around her mouth. Madge was right, Eleanor should be home in her own bed, in her own house. I felt angry for her; dealing with a natural loss was hard enough.

"No, really, Mrs. Darnell, this is not time for group announcements, but I would like a word with you in private before we eat. Rest assured, the investigation is going very swiftly. This will be our last night at camp."

"Darn right," Al said.

Omondi didn't add aloud that we could move to a hotel tomorrow, now that he had a search warrant for the Harts' tent. We were going to have quite the after-dinner scene when he served it. And when did he plan on announcing that none of them could leave the country? That was a moment I'd prefer to miss.

"That's good news, Inspector. It will be such a relief, won't it, Cliff?" Eleanor opened her eyes wide.

"Look on the bright side, at least there are no gossip columnists out here." Cliff tossed away his butt and immediately shook a fresh cigarette out of his pack. He tapped the end against the cellophane.

"Cliff, cut it. Don't make Eleanor nervous." Madge was back at Eleanor's side.

They were about the same height, but Madge was twice Eleanor in volume, which made her look shorter. She wore a tailored dress in a bold brown and white print, the sort fat women are discouraged from wearing, as if boring clothes will make them look svelte. Actually, Madge still had a figure, that is to say a waist, but she overflowed her clothes in rounded billows above and below. In previous centuries, she would have been the great beauty among us, and Candy would have been pitied as a half-starved freak. Madge looked warm and soft to snuggle up to, like hugging a down comforter. I suddenly realized the money motive, if there was anything to it, could fit Madge as well as Al. They seemed the sort of couple who'd go over big decisions together: Should we start a new business, take out a loan, kill an interfering partner? I shivered and folded my arms around my middle.

"Honey, you should get some warmer clothes on," Madge told me. "As soon as the sun goes down, it's a different season."

I was happy for the excuse to leave. I put on a thick chamois shirt and went to check in with Ibrahima and Molezzi.

Ibrahima was standing over a big enamel pot on the portable stove. He stirred it with a long-handled spoon, then dipped out some meat juice.

"Looks good. Pot roast?"

"Beef stew." He blew on the steaming spoonful and sampled it with extended lips. "Not too bad. Ngueye, get me the black pepper."

Ibrahima wore a SKI KILLINGTON T-shirt with a picture of a skier who seemed to be negotiating Ibrahima's potbelly like a mogul. Ngueye left off peeling potatoes and carrots to fetch the pepper mill, which Ibrahima could have reached in two steps. I guess Ibrahima didn't want to overdo on exercise. Molezzi was polishing glasses on a tray.

"Evening, Jazz. How was your airplane ride?" He sounded wistful and eager.

"Have you ever been in an airplane?"

"No, not yet. My uncle has been to England on one."

"Oh, yeah? What did he say?"

"He liked it very much. He has also been on a metal ship that floated. A big ship, on the ocean. Yet if you throw a little ax into the water, it will sink." He shook his head and sighed. "The world is full of many things." He set one glass down and picked up the next.

"It certainly is." I thought of the everyday marvel of ocean liners. Ever since Miss Marconi taught me the theory of displacement in tenth-grade physics, I had forgotten to wonder at steel floating on water. "One of these trips, I'll get you all up in an airplane for a ride." A burst of laughter and conversation wafted our way from the guest area and reminded me of my charges. "Molezzi, would you please light the campfire and see what people want to drink?"

Ibrahima allotted me a burner to heat up some water, and I took a shower. I dressed slowly. Then I lay on the bed. My body felt too heavy to move. I watched a flying ant crawl across the canvas roof.

"Knock, knock, may I come in?" Omondi's smiling voice called from the tent veranda.

I swung my feet to the floor. "Sure, have a seat." I gestured to the cot opposite me. "I'm hiding in here."

"Ah, I was afraid it might be that. You've been awfully quiet since our trip to the lodge." He sat carefully upon the bed. "Do you want to tell me what's on your mind?"

I made a face. "Not really, but I suppose I should." I fell silent for a moment. "I called a stockbroker friend in New York and she told me a bunch of things, some gossip, some guessing, nothing solid, but very . . . suggestive."

"Suggestive." Omondi nodded rapidly. "I see." He nodded again. "It is rather horrid to be full of suspicion against people you like."

"That's it." Our eyes met. Omondi's were full of sympathetic understanding, and something more, a hint of affection, or maybe of simple human connectedness. As if that were simple. I could feel myself relax, as if held in warm arms. "Horrid is the word. How can I socialize with someone I suspect of murder?"

"I will tell you a technique I use. I examine everyone and suspect no one until the final evidence is in."

"That's fine to say, but what happens when your evidence

179

starts to point in one direction? Isn't the whole point to build a case against someone?"

"The point is to keep an open mind until the case inexorably leads to the killer. Otherwise, you are likely to be led astray by false notions and irrelevancies. When you are in this business a while, you realize that in the course of each case you suspect a lot more innocent people than criminals. That's a lot of wasted suspecting. Better to save your energy and quietly pursue the facts." He smiled encouragingly. "This isn't your job, you know. You can leave it to us."

"Thanks, Inspector. No, I really appreciate it. It's not that I don't have confidence in you." Omondi waved this comment aside as unworthy of being said. "It's that I *am* involved. I don't have a choice about whether to care or not, whether to do my piece or stand aside and count on someone else to do it all for me. I don't mind being upset. It seems inevitable."

"Yes, if you ferret out clues and then get depressed when you seem to be getting somewhere."

To my surprise, I started to cry. It was the combination of everything: the strain of the last two days, my quarrel with Striker, the thought I might be hunting down the Harts, whom I liked. Omondi's sarcastic tone, after his warmth, cracked my shell of self-control.

I tried to choke back my tears and succeeded only in turning them into squeaky sniveling. Omondi shifted to the cot by my side and put his arm around me. I gripped the hand he offered me and burrowed into his neck. He brushed away a strand of hair that had fallen in front of my eyes and the tenderness of the gesture made me cry harder. He kissed my brow, then my eyelids. I twisted to face him and slipped my arm around his shoulder and he kissed me full on the lips. His lips were thick and soft and sensuous. I closed my eyes and gave myself completely to the moment.

Eventually—was it only a minute later?—I broke away. The kiss had changed everything, and I felt disoriented. We looked at each other shyly and I gave him a peck on the lips to say that it was all right, as a promise to continue—but later. He pressed my hand. Already we were establishing the wordless communication of lovers.

"I'm okay now."

Omondi brushed my hair back again. It was an excuse to touch me. I could feel my body yearning toward his in response, but I fought it. We really couldn't jump on each other as dinner was about to be served, everyone wondering what had happened to us.

"Are you surprised?" His voice was soft as a whisper.

"No, not really."

"I could feel the spark there, between the two of us, from our first meeting."

"Yes, I felt it, too." We were constructing a history for ourselves, almost out of thin air, to give a semblance of solidity to this sudden upheaval of feeling. "I like you very much, Inspector."

"I like you very much, Ms. Jazz Jasper."

We smiled and moved apart.

"Perhaps I should tell you what I learned from my stockbroker friend before we go to dinner." The kiss had cured me, where the words of sensible advice had not. I was suddenly eager to tell Omondi my handful of gossip.

Omondi nodded. "Back to business. We are going to be very sensible, I can see."

"Let's see." It took me a moment to collect my thoughts. "Okay. I asked Susan what she knew about Wild and Free stock. First, Boyce Darnell seems to have engineered the drop in stock prices on purpose by dumping a load of his stock on the market. Two—" I counted off on my fingers, forcing myself to concentrate—"Al Hart has been trying to raise money for a new company he's starting. My friend thinks he might have borrowed money against his stocks, meaning that if the price of Wild and Free stocks went down, he'd lose his money . . . the loan, and the stocks." I let my hands fall into my lap. "I'm explaining it badly."

"No, no, go on." He picked up my hand and stroked my fingers one by one with a feather-soft touch. "I am following

181

you. Boyce Darnell made the stock drop so as to ruin Al financially.''

"You got it."

"Very interesting, very intriguing." He dropped my hand, and interlaced his own fingers, bringing them up to tap his chin. "Did Al Hart know? If he didn't know, there's no motive. And if he did know, how would killing Boyce save his loan? You'd think the murder would make the stock go lower."

"This is complete conjecture, but Susan said that some partnerships are set up so that the partner inherits the company. The partner, not the family of the deceased."

Omondi slapped the backs of his fingers against the palm of his other hand, making a quick little rhythm. "That's the best motive we've heard yet." He darted a look at me. "If it's true." He patted my thigh. "We'll check all this out. You have done excellent work, and I can see why you were upset. But don't jump ahead of yourself. The case is not yet closed."

The pats turned into caresses along the top of my thigh. He slipped his arm around me again and I tilted my head back for another kiss.

20

A LION GRUNTED in the night. The peepers hushed as if to allow the lion his solo, then their screechy curtain of sound lowered again. I restrained my impulse to pop out of the dining tent to listen. No one wanted their attention drawn to Africa. This was our third night in camp since Boyce had died, and I knew that everyone was longing to be home.

"Does that lion have a cough?" Madge asked, the most alert to her surroundings, as usual. She swiveled her head to track the sound as the lion grunted again. Round silver earrings framed her face like radar dishes.

"No, that's how they sound. It seems to carry well over long distances; the pride keeps in touch and lets other lions know the territory is occupied." I ate my last mouthful of deep-dish apple pie and put the fork down with regret. Molezzi cleared away the empty plate. "Tell Ibrahima he outdid himself." Molezzi smiled and said he would tell him.

I met Omondi's eyes across the table.

"Great dinner," Madge echoed me. "Nothing like a classic beef stew, when you get the meat tender like that."

At the other end of the long table, Candy and Cliff gossiped about Madison Avenue, effectively blocking out their current circumstances. Who had stolen whose account, the latest rising star, who was drinking too much, who was sleeping with whom. Cliff had put on a pale tweed sports jacket over a yellow-striped shirt, with a lime green scarf at his neck. His sleek blond hair contrasted with Candy's wild mane. Despite the thirty-year age difference, they made a handsome couple. Kakombe watched them through veiled eyes.

Engrossed in their own conversation, Al and Eleanor swapped notes on Al's grandson, Joey, and Eleanor's youngest daughter, Wendy. From overheard remarks, I gathered Eleanor had spaced her four daughters widely apart, making her a historical expert on childhood over the last three decades. I wondered if Wendy had been an unexpected event or a last grasp on to motherhood. Eleanor was reassuring Al that the terrors of modern adolescence were much overrated.

Al took advantage of a pause and turned to Omondi. "Well, Inspector. So what's this interesting news you promised us? You ready to wrap things up here?" He sounded truculent. My stomach tightened.

"Yes, Mr. Hart, after one more piece of business, we will be through with this phase of the investigation." Omondi extracted the search warrant from his inside jacket pocket and handed it to Al. "Regrettably, I must insist on seeing your tent. I'm afraid it is necessary for us to examine everything in the camp before we can move on."

Al read it over twice. I could see his jaw muscles bunch with anger. "This is the living end." He snapped it over to Madge. "Here, look at this."

She took her time reading the legal jargon. "You have no choice, Al. The law's the law." She handed the document back to her husband.

Al tossed it onto the table. "This burns me up." He paused. The rest of us sat silently watching him. "I guess I can't stop you. Shit, look all you want. There's nothing to find. I just don't like the idea of people pawing through my things."

"We'll do our best not to paw, Mr Hart. You are free to watch, if you wish."

"Naw." Al waved him away. "You and Kakombe do your

184

thing. I'm sitting tight right here. Hey, Molezzi, how about a refill? With some whiskey." He held up his coffee cup.

"I appreciate how unpleasant this is for you." Omondi made a tent of his long fingers. "It is all the more important that we have searched everywhere. The murderer might have secreted something small in another person's belongings."

"Something small?" asked Cliff. "So it wasn't a seven-foot spear after all, but a nail file?"

"The autopsy report has come back. As I explained privately to Mrs. Darnell before dinner"—he nodded sympathetically to Eleanor—"our suspicions about foul play have been confirmed. Mr. Darnell's heart attack was set off by amphetamines; they found traces in his blood."

Eleanor looked down and fingered her pearls. Her lips quivered. "I wasn't surprised. I knew it," she said in a tiny voice. "When I heard about Lynn, I just knew." She started to sniffle and hunted around in her pocket for a tissue.

Madge found one in her bag first and handed it to Eleanor. "It's wrinkled but clean."

Eleanor accepted the offering and held it to one nostril.

"What did you find out?" Candy asked. She looked from Omondi to Kakombe, her full lips slightly parted. "You mean it wasn't a heart attack?"

"It was a heart attack." Omondi tapped his fingertips together. "But they found a trace of amphetamines in his blood."

"Amphetamines?" Candy raised her finely arched eyebrows.

"So he was poisoned," Madge said. She leaned heavily back in her chair and glanced at Eleanor. Eleanor was looking down at her lap. She sniffed and patted her nose, crinkling the tissue smaller and smaller.

Cliff cocked his chin. "I can see you thinking, Candy. Rather a thrilling experience."

"It must be, for someone like you who never thinks at all," she retorted clumsily but with feeling.

"You know something, Candy," Omondi said quietly.

"Amphetamines—"

"Yes?" Omondi prompted her.

"My diet pills are amphetamines. At least, I think—"

"Yes," I cut in.

"Perhaps you would be so kind as to show Sergeant Kakombe where you keep these diet pills," Omondi said.

Candy looked at him with her Raphael blue eyes. "I wish I could, Inspector, but I haven't been able to find them for days. Maybe you've noticed, I've been eating like a horse."

"I see. When did you notice they were gone?"

Candy tapped her lips with a finger, thinking. "Gee, I'm not sure. I know I didn't have them yesterday 'cause I really wanted to take one, and I looked everywhere."

"Where did you keep them?"

"In my bag." She indicated an oversize pocketbook, a red cowhide satchel stamped with a fake reptile texture. "They're in a little brass pillbox with a malachite top." She indicated something about an inch high with her thumb and index finger. "I bought it in Nairobi."

"Has anybody seen it?" Omondi looked around the table.

"I guess I saw it earlier in the trip," Madge said. "Didn't you take it out at lunch one day? Where was it? At Treetops?"

"I couldn't tell you." Candy shook her head, sending waves through her mane of tawny hair. "I mean, I don't really pay that much attention. It's like a habit. I just do it, you know?"

I tried to remember. If Candy had been so public about taking diet pills, why would she have called them her secret weapon? I thought I remembered her saying that. She'd puffed out her cheeks, and I had told her she looked more like Mick Jagger than a farm girl. Yeah. She said she had a secret weapon that kept her thin. That's the first I'd known about them. Was Madge making a slip? Thinking something was public knowledge that wasn't? Or, in her motherly way, had she noticed Candy taking a pill at lunch and I hadn't? She might be familiar with diet pills herself.

No one else said they'd noticed Candy's diet pills.

"Would you be so kind as to look through your bag one

186

more time, to be absolutely sure they're not there?'' Omondi asked Candy.

Candy shrugged. "I'll look, but I'm telling you, I looked a hundred times already. I mean, I really wanted those pills. I'm sure I've gained at least a pound." She unhooked the bag from the back of her seat and upended it over the dining table, dumping out the contents in a heap. A lipstick hit the table and rolled to the floor. Molezzi sprang to retrieve it for her. Candy let him drop it into her palm without looking at him.

"Gee, why is that loose? It should be in my makeup case." Candy picked up a printed fabric case, unzipped it, peered inside, pulled open the mouth to display it to Omondi, dropped the lipstick in, and zipped it up again. She put it to one side. "I wouldn't put it in there, anyway." She spread the pile out flat in front of her: a tube of facial creme with a French name; some half-disintegrated yellow credit-card receipts; a maroon address book with gold-edged pages and a little gold pencil; a paper tube of breath mints, half-eaten; a Navaho silver key ring, inlaid with obsidian and turquoise; a checkbook with a calculator attached to the cover; a business date book; a loose luggage key; some postcards from the parks we'd visited; a couple of pens; a black document case with PASSPORT embossed on the front; a pencil flashlight; a cleverly designed wallet with no visible means to open it; some torn ticket stubs from movies or the theater; a square of newspaper that she unfolded to reveal a pair of Masai bead earrings; an imitation crystal perfume atomizer; a packet of tissues in a holder of Japanese rice paper, with a geisha girl simpering under an umbrella; two combs and a brush, although I would have sworn Candy never combed her hair; a small can of hair spray; another leather case, this one holding business cards; and a battered metal pillbox saying Bayer on the cover.

She picked up the last item and opened it. "See, all I have is this thing the aspirins came in. It's not really big enough, and it's all beat up. I've had my eye out for a real pillbox for a while. I hope it turns up. I really liked it—you know how malachite has those swirly patterns. They'd picked a really nice piece with a swirl right off center of the oval."

"Your grasp of the essentials is simply stunning, darling."

"I'm explaining what it looked like," Candy told Cliff, "and besides, we don't know it was my diet pills. I mean, speed is not the most uncommon drug in the world."

Cliff looked slowly around the table. Al and Madge were both leaning back in their chairs, shoulder to shoulder, their round middle-aged faces like a badge of innocence. Eleanor had abandoned her tortured bit of wet tissue and was sitting with hands clasped in front of her, the knuckles showing white. Our eyes met and she gave me a tense little smile.

"You're hardly suggesting that Eleanor or the Harts are on uppers, are you, Candy? As for Jazz, I doubt they're peddling speed much these days in Nairobi. Much more a New York thing, wouldn't you say? And it's tacky to accuse your boss of poisoning his oldest client. Besides, I assure you"—Cliff held out his right hand parallel to the table; there was a slight tremor in the fingers—"I'm quite tense enough without speed. I prefer the conventional drugs: whiskey, nicotine, and caffeine."

"Oh, you know I wouldn't accuse you of anything." Candy held her bag under the edge of the table and swept everything back into it with her arm. "Anyway, you can see, my pillbox isn't here. You can look again in my tent if you want to, Inspector."

Omondi and Kakombe left. The dining tent seemed darker after the flap fell shut behind them. I looked into my coffee cup and remembered our kiss.

"Aren't you going to join your pet cop?" Al said.

I was jolted back to the present and looked at him with alarm. He couldn't know about me and Omondi. Had we given ourselves away already? Kisses don't leave tracks. We'd practically ignored each other all through dinner.

Before I could frame an answer, Madge gave him a pretend cuff on the head that made the flesh of her arm jiggle. "Al, don't be a sore loser," she said. "Omondi is on our side, remember? He's not working just for Jazz."

So Al didn't know anything; he meant that I'd been co-operating in the investigation. She turned to me. "I'll apologize for him. This business of being searched"—she shook her head—"it gives you a hunted feeling, even when you know there's nothing to find. Al's not being his normal sweet self." She gave him a big kiss, squeezing his face between her hands, so that he looked like a basset hound.

"Madge, please!" Cliff raised his shoulders in pretend dismay. "Displays of genuine affection are tasteless, don't you think? I wouldn't even kiss someone like that in private."

Candy reached for Cliff's cigarette pack, sitting by his unused glass of water, put a cigarette between her lips, and turned sideways to point the unlit tip at Molezzi. He leapt to light it as if that was the moment he'd been waiting for all evening. So she did know he existed!

I caught the nasty tone of my thoughts and accused myself of jealousy, but it wasn't that. I enjoyed Candy's beauty. It was something else. She reminded me of the lady who wanted the phone booth while I was making my call: If I stood in her way, she'd be ready to do me in. I wasn't accusing the phone booth lady of being a murderer—except in her heart—and I wasn't accusing Candy, either. Although she might be: If it were a question of character alone, I wouldn't be surprised if she had been the killer. She acted as if other people weren't fully real: We were all walk-on parts, there to serve her needs, from Molezzi to Madge to Cliff. No, I didn't trust Candy.

Now it seemed her pills were the most likely murder weapon. I flashed on the scene by the swimming pool the day before Boyce was killed. Candy had warned Boyce not to mess around with her. Not exactly a major death threat.

Cliff made a joke and Candy threw her head back to laugh, showing an elegant jawline and a flash of white teeth. Candy's beauty set her apart. In a funny way, I was more likely to try and identify with a Masai than with her, another American woman. Yet I'd had my moments of feeling beautiful, and they weren't selfish, they didn't make me into a heartless person. They had to do with feeling wanted, loved, and, yes, with feeling powerful. I nodded to myself. I could see Candy liked power.

Either way, selfish or longing for love, Candy seemed like the most ruthless personality among us. But as soon as I formed that thought, I knew it wasn't true. Cliff admitted—admitted, he boasted—that he lived solely according to his self-interest. I could also imagine the Harts or Eleanor being ruthless in defense of their families. When I'd discussed people's motives with Striker, I'd been completely caught up in my subjective feelings. Hell, I was more interested in disagreeing with whatever Striker said than in thinking things through deeply.

Maybe Candy pissed me off 'cause she reminded me of myself. Isn't that what the psychologists said, that you disliked other people for the things you disliked and denied in yourself? I'd been caught up in my own little world for over two years now, not allowing anyone else in. My backdrop was wide and open as the Serengeti Plain, but was it so different from the safe and lonely bubble Candy inhabited, based on the power of beauty?

I wondered if I would have to understand the murderer from the inside in order to discover his or her identity, and I shivered.

"You're still not dressed warmly enough," Madge exclaimed, "Here, take this." She pulled Al's safari jacket from the back of his chair.

"Will you stop fussing over people?" Al said, grabbing for his jacket.

"C'mon Al, don't be such a pill. You're not wearing it."

I demurred, but Madge insisted, and it didn't seem worth fighting about. I draped the jacket over my shoulders.

"You look like a tent within a tent," Cliff remarked.

"Oh, Cliff, you're so catty." To my surprise, Candy defended me. "Jazz looks great in whatever she wears."

"Meaning I'm usually dressed in a bag." I laughed.

Candy spoke simultaneously. "I think the menswear look still has another season."

190

"Frills next fall," Cliff answered. "Mark my words—you first heard it here."

Footsteps sounded outside and a snatch of Swahili. Everyone fell silent. The tent flap was flung open and Omondi entered, followed by Kakombe, whose huge frame made the tent seem small. The group turned toward them. My chest constricted. What had they found in the Harts' tent?

Omondi held his two empty hands toward us. The pink palms contrasted with his dark sin. "Nothing. We found nothing whatsoever."

"Like I told you, Inspector," Al said.

Omondi spoke directly to Madge. "May I see your handbag, please?"

"Nope. Stop right there." Al pushed back his chair and stood, hands placed aggressively on the table. "Your warrant said tent. You searched the tent. That's it. You're not going through my wife's handbag. It's bad enough you're keeping us in a dangerous situation, without being treated like dirt. You're going to hear about this, Omondi."

For the first time, I saw a spark of anger in Omondi's eyes, but he covered it with a gracious smile. "My dear sir, I am terribly distressed you are feeling ill-treated. I am trying to conduct an effective investigation, with as much respect for everyone's privacy as possible."

Al's forefinger jabbed the table. "I spoke to my lawyer this afternoon and I know my rights." He grabbed Madge's handbag from the side of her chair, took her by the elbow, and marched her out of the tent.

21

THE CAMP WAS quiet. Everyone had long gone to bed. I lay in the crook of Omondi's arm, my head against his shoulder, and stroked his chest, enjoying the feel of hard muscle under silky skin. His fingertips moved softly over my flank, breasts, and belly, as if reliving the highlights of a much-enjoyed journey. Our lovemaking had been passionate and sweet, and surprisingly unexotic.

"You feel wonderful," he murmured into my hair.

"So do you."

"How can it be that you have no boyfriend? It isn't right to be alone."

I didn't feel like going into an explanation about me and Adam, not when I was feeling so good. A deep relaxation glowed through my body. Omondi was right; I'd been celibate too long. I felt an old familiar well-being, a deep physical and emotional comfort that seemed to reach into my very cells.

"What about you? How many girlfriends?"

"Oh, so you think I am a ladies' man? Why, because I told you I would protect us both with condoms? That is merely good sense."

"No"—I smiled—"it's the way you make love . . . as if you can feel what I'm feeling. Also, a little bit of a performance . . . showing off what you know, but in a nice way. I think you love women. Am I right?"

He ran his fingers along my collarbone, to the tip of one

breast, along the curve of my belly, and into the mound of wiry curls, still damp and musky from our lovemaking. "It doesn't seem to bother you."

I got up on an elbow and looked down onto his face. It was a dark oval against my pillow. "Why should it? I'm not looking for a boyfriend. It would be nice if we become friends. That seems ambitious enough."

"Agreed. I would like to be friends. Friends who sometimes spend a beautiful night together."

"Sounds good to me." I lay back on my side and snuggled up against him, entwining my legs with his.

"So you're not looking for a boyfriend? What about Striker?"

"Striker? What are you talking about? How well do you know him?"

"I don't know him, although I would recognize him; we've been introduced. I once solved a small problem for a friend of his, Russ Bartrim."

"Sure, I know Russ. He helps run a safari lodge out beyond Tsavo. So that's the connection. But why are you trying to link me up with Striker?"

"Because you talk about him all the time."

"I do not!"

"Oh, yes, you do. Not by name, but he is often on your lips. I have noticed. 'I have a friend researching elephant poaching and the Hong Kong connection.' 'A friend who lives on Mt. Kenya has followed an elephant herd through a full generation.' 'I have a friend writing a natural-history curriculum for the Kenyan school system.' This is all Striker, is it not?"

"That doesn't mean anything!"

"Ah, little one. You don't want to admit it to yourself, but I know these signs. He is often in your mind. I am not a jealous man; it is as your friend I tell you this. You are half in love with this Striker. Why not admit it?"

I sighed. "Perhaps you're right. But I don't want to admit it. I like being totally independent."

"Independence, is it? Funny, I would guess your independence wouldn't be threatened by love—maybe it is something else."

Lying in the dark, in Omondi's arms, I found myself talking about Adam, about the divorce, about not wanting to try again.

Omondi traced my lips with his finger, then leaned over and kissed me. "You are making things too complicated. Let your heart lead you. It is not a teenager's heart that will lead you to folly. Trust it. What you need is love, not safety. If things with Striker don't work out, you are still whole. Life is long. There is room in it for many things." He paused and the silence lengthened. His soft voice continued: "You may not be in Kenya forever. Wouldn't you regret leaving this love unrealized?"

His words echoed in my mind. I knew he was all wrong but couldn't quite remember the reasons why. "If I wasn't so relaxed, I would argue with you, but right now you could say anything to me and I would agree."

"Really? Let's see."

I awoke a few minutes before the screaming began. I couldn't swear afterward that I'd heard the lion, or what woke me up. All I knew was that I was awake and that Omondi was in my tent, in my bed. We were lying like spoons, his back a smooth curve against my breasts, his ass neatly tucked into the angle of my thighs and belly. His breathing was so soft I could feel it more than hear it. I laid my cheek against his back and savored the warmth of his body. I hadn't felt so peaceful in a long time. It was as if something inside me had melted.

That's when I heard the first scream. I jumped out of bed and pulled on my clothes before my mind registered what was happening. Bumping into me, Omondi whipped into his clothes and grabbed my heavy-duty flashlight. There was a loud crash, the sound of broken glass, and the screaming was replaced by sobs. It was coming from Eleanor's tent.

"Eleanor!" I ran out of the tent.

Despite the moon's clear light, the gum trees engulfed the campsite in their shadows, so that the tents were in darkness. The air was heavy with the smell of eucalyptus. Someone with a flashlight ran toward me, converging on Eleanor's tent. It was Cliff, his body pale in the moonlight. Lights came on in the other tents, voices raised in alarm. If she was hurt . . . I reached the tent door at the same time as Cliff, Omondi right behind me.

"Watch out for the broken glass," Eleanor said tearfully. "I threw my kerosene lamp." She was sitting in bed, the covers pulled up to her shoulders, shaking. The tent stank of kerosene.

"Eleanor, are you okay? What happened?" I picked my way over to her carefully, shards of glass crunching under my sandals, sat on the edge of the bed, and put an arm around her. Her body felt delicate and vulnerable. She clung to me and another outbreak of crying swept over her. Cliff and Omondi crowded in the doorway, faces distorted into masks by the flashlight beams bouncing off the tent wall.

"What happened?" Omondi asked.

Eleanor's face was buried in my shoulder. I shook my head. Others were now milling around in the dark and I could hear them repeating the question.

Candy's voice rose. "Ooh, I'm scared. Was it another murder? This is really getting weird."

"Don't be scared." I could hear Madge's voice. "We're all here with you."

Eleanor's crying subsided into little strangled whimpers. I could feel her tears through my shirt. I stroked her back and echoed Madge's words. "It's okay. I'm right here and you're safe."

She raised a wet swollen face, hiccoughed, and giggled with embarrassment. "Sorry, I got hysterical," she said. "Do you have a tissue?" She hiccoughed again.

I found some on the night table and handed them over. Eleanor gave a good loud honk, wiped her eyes, and smiled weakly.

"Eleanor! Would you please tell us what happened," Cliff almost shouted.

Eleanor looked at him and exclaimed, "Cliff," in a shocked and disapproving voice. The rest of us registered Cliff's lack of clothing. Al burst out laughing.

195

"I know I have knobby knees," Cliff said with dignity, "but the rest isn't that funny. Eleanor, don't you dare say another word until I come back. Give me a second to get my pants on."

Cliff disappeared and was replaced by Madge in a hot-pink bathrobe. "Here, Jazz, let me take over." She pointed her flashlight toward the ground and started to push past Omondi.

He put out a restraining hand. "Better not touch anything in the tent until we know the whole story. If you please."

He moved the beam of his flashlight systematically over the ground. Bits of glass glinted in a pool of kerosene. There was another smear of something wet near the door, too dark to be kerosene. I caught my breath. Blood?

Omondi raised his voice. "Please, everybody will kindly return to their own tent." Madge made a move as if to enter the tent. "That includes you, too, Mrs. Hart. Mrs. Darnell is quite safe now."

"Hey, we have a right to know what's going on," Al protested. "Did somebody attack Eleanor?"

"No, no," protested Eleanor in a quavery voice. "Now I'm not even sure . . . I thought I heard a snuffling sound, and there was a low shape. Was it a lion?" She hiccoughed.

"Your questions can be answered in the morning." Omondi said firmly. He raised his voice a notch. "Please return directly to your tents without trampling up the ground any further. Sorry, Cliff. Good night."

Cliff had just rejoined the group. He swore but cooperatively started everyone back to their tents. I could hear people grumbling, the voices moved off, and in a few minutes, the camp was still. Kakombe was the only person left outside the tent. He was a black bulk except for a startling pair of white boxer shorts.

"Sergeant, why don't you get on some pants and come back with your camera."

"Yes, sir." Kakombe padded away silently on bare feet.

"Should I go, too?" I asked Omondi diffidently.

"No, if you don't mind, I do think we can use your help on this lion business," Omondi replied.

He turned to Eleanor. "Now, if you'd be so good as to tell us exactly what happened. Would you like a whiskey?" he added.

"No, thank you, but I am thirsty." She wiped her nose delicately and tucked the used tissue under her pillow. "Jazz, if you could pour me a little water?"

There was a carafe on the night table with a water glass upended over the open mouth. I carefully poured out half a glass and passed it to her and she gulped it down.

"I'm not exactly sure," she began slowly. "I was sleeping lightly. I'm usually a good sleeper, but the last few nights it's been hard. I lie there in the dark until I don't know if I'm awake or asleep and then suddenly it's morning." She looked from one to the other of us with her wide little-girl eyes. "I think I heard the zipper being opened, but I didn't bother to look. You know that half-asleep state. I thought it was Boyce." She clamped her lips together and struggled to keep back fresh tears.

Omondi nodded without saying anything.

"I must have started dreaming he was still alive. Guess I fell deeper asleep. Maybe I dreamt the whole thing." She struggled down into her covers.

Dreamt it all except for that patch that looked like blood near the tent door.

"Jazz, could I ask you to pass me that other pillow, please?" I handed her the pillow from the other cot. She tucked it behind her, propping herself up more comfortably. "Thank you. The next thing I knew, there was this snuffling sound and a rustling against the mosquito netting."

I watched Omondi inspect the netting and its zipper. Perfectly normal. The lion hadn't clawed it. "Whoever unzipped it, it wasn't a lion," I said. "It was wide open when I got here."

"You mean someone was about to come in and got scared off by the lion?" Eleanor pulled the blanket higher around her chest.

"Or someone opened it so a lion could get inside the tent." Omondi clicked his tongue thoughtfully.

"I don't know." I was dubious. "That's quite a long shot.

People can make snuffling noises, too. Why would a lion come poking around the tent?''

"Why indeed?'' Omondi shone his flashlight once more on the bloody smear near the tent door. "Look here.'' He followed the dark traces to a lump under the hem of the mosquito netting. He pulled up the netting and there on the ground was a small pile of dark cubes. Pieces of beef stew. "Look at this!'' He crouched down to examine the meat more closely. "Someone placed these scraps right inside the entrance. Sergeant, take some photos of this before we remove it, if you please.''

I was startled. I hadn't heard Kakombe return. His flash exploded in the tent. Eleanor and I both cringed and flung up hands to protect our eyes. All I could see for a moment was an expanding circle of orange in a velvet field.

When my vision returned, I said, "It's the same modus operandi, isn't it? Another murder that would seem natural.''

"Well, it's not quite the same,'' Eleanor protested. "I am alive.''

"This worries me.'' Omondi's voice was serious. "The same flavor, perhaps, but the idea was wild. Pardon the pun. It's a gesture of panic. There's nothing more dangerous than a desperate killer.''

"Why me?'' Eleanor asked in a little voice. She huddled into the pillows.

"A good question,'' Omondi said. "Either you are standing in the way of something the murderer wants, that your husband has already died for, or you know something.''

"What could I know? You mean something about Boyce?''

"Yes,'' said Omondi. "The murderer may think you know something that would provide a clue to his or her identity. Wrack your brains, Mrs. Darnell. What could it be?''

22

OMONDI RETURNED TO his own tent for the rest of the night. He joined me early the next morning as I was drinking tea on my tent veranda, blank with fatigue from last night's interrupted sleep. I confess I was musing more about fine lovemaking than the attempt on Eleanor's life. Omondi looked as alert as usual. We smiled like conspirators as we shook hands good morning. He stared at my lips, but a kiss was out of the question; we were too likely to be seen.

"Once more you are up with the birds," he said. "Have you seen your eagles yet?"

I was touched that he remembered. "My eyes are barely open. All I've managed so far is sitting and staring straight in front of me. Can I get you some coffee or tea?"

We walked over to the dining tent, where Molezzi had set up urns of coffee and hot water. We carried out mugs back to my tent. The morning air was tangy with the sharp perfume of the eucalyptus trees. Sun slanted through the canopy of leaves, so that their normal olive color appeared a brilliant spring green. A flock of monkeys chattered noisily in the crowns. Branches dipped and swayed as they moved around. Now and then, there was a brief flash of a brown back or a whip of a tail.

"Don't sit on Al's jacket," I warned Omondi as he was about to sink into my guest chair.

Omondi plucked the jacket from the back of the chair and dropped it on the table. "What's this doing here?"

"Madge forced it on me when we were waiting for you to come back from searching their tent. I had it on last night when we left the dining tent. Don't tell me you didn't notice? I thought you noticed everything."

"Ah, yes, I remember now. I was so distracted by you all evening, and trying not to look at you constantly."

I refolded Al's jacket, keeping busy to mask my embarrassment and pleasure. When I looked up to see why he'd stopped talking, Omondi was staring past me, at the jacket.

"I didn't want it to get wrinkled," I said.

Then I saw what had caught his eye. There was an envelope poking out of the inside breast pocket. Omondi put his mug of tea down and pulled out the envelope. It was addressed in a wobbly schoolboy's script. Omondi read the return address: "Joey Hart."

"That's Al's grandson."

Omondi pulled the letter out of the envelope. "Funny that Joey's letter should contain a telex." I sat up straighter and watched him unfold the thin yellow telex paper. Omondi read it intently and passed it over to me. "I would guess Al didn't want us to see this."

It was from Al's investment counselor, informing Al that Wild and Free stock had fallen precipitously and asking for permission to start selling Al's stock to cover his loans.

"It confirms what your stockbroker friend passed on to you yesterday."

"I wonder when he picked this up." I handed it back to Omondi. This discovery made my talk with Susan all the more relevant, but I couldn't feel happy about it. "We passed through Nairobi for one night on our way down from the mountains and people did pick up mail."

He saw my serious face. "You are thinking this is one more link in a chain of motives, but you must remain objective." He put the letter back in the envelope and tucked it into his own pocket. "Al might have gotten it as late as yesterday, when we flew over to Mara. It won't be hard to trace.''

After breakfast, Omondi packed his things and flew off to Nairobi. I hoped the case wouldn't stall while he attended his trial or whatever it was he had to do. Omondi assured us we were top priority, but then why was he being called away just as we were getting somewhere? We had to find out when Al had received that telex, who inherited Boyce's share of Wild and Free, if the amphetamines in Boyce's blood matched Candy's prescription diet pills.

"I will continue to work on the case from Nairobi. Sergeant Kakombe will stay behind to keep guard," he had announced before he left. He looked handsome in his gray tropical suit, eyes lively despite the gravity of his announcement. "He will make sure no harm comes to Mrs. Darnell, or to anyone. Please, do not be fearful. In the light of morning's reflection, it seems to me that last night's episode was meant as a warning.''

The others seemed to take this conclusion at face value. I wondered whether Omondi believed it himself, or was merely trying to soothe us? We'd found lion spoor by the stream not far from camp, but there were no tracks near Eleanor's tent. It occurred to me that the meat was planted as part of a plan to kill Eleanor, maybe drag her body out of the tent and make it look like a lion's work. Following Omondi's lead, I kept my thoughts to myself. We couldn't know what was in the killer's mind.

Meanwhile, we were released from the campsite. I stayed behind with the staff to take down the camp, sending the others ahead to Masai Mara Lodge with Chris Mbare. He'd see everyone into their rooms. The way the plane flights worked out, we'd overnight at the lodge and fly back to Nairobi the next morning. Al insisted I keep their reservations on the night flight to New York, even though Omondi served him official notice they were not free to leave the country. Al's smirking "We'll see about that" left me uneasy.

Molezzi and I moved methodically through the tents, bundling up dirty linen into pillowcases, folding the light-wool blankets and packing them into a trunk. I wasn't in the mood to chat, and after a few efforts at conversation, Molezzi tactfully let me be.

Eleanor's empty tent smelled faintly of face powder and a floral perfume. She'd been the first at breakfast, not characteristic for her. She was tense but calm. She didn't look as if she'd slept any more that night; the skin under her eyes was beginning to look bruised. Still, she'd taken the time to do a careful makeup job. I noticed she stayed close to Madge all morning. Despite Omondi's calm words, she must be terrified.

Molezzi tossed me one end of the blanket to fold. I hoped Chris Mbare wouldn't have any trouble at the reception desk. I'd confirmed the reservations that morning, but you never knew. I remembered the baboon man yelling at the clerk, which led to thoughts of Striker. I concentrated on getting the corners of the blanket lined up evenly in a neat rectangle. What if Striker was at Mara? What if Omondi said something to him about us—no, he wouldn't. And I was not going to blurt any confessions to Striker. I placed the blanket in the waiting trunk outside. Our relationship had to be resolved on its own terms. If only Adam had told me he was unhappy in our marriage, instead of hitting me with a pregnant coed. Grad student. Big difference. We moved on to the next tent.

"This is good, Molezzi. When we're through with the sheets and blankets, I want to pile all the mattresses outside. Let me finish this tent while you get a straw mat to place them on so they don't get dirty. Ask Ibrahima where they are if you can't find a clean one." Molezzi agreed, with his little cat's smile, and ambled off.

Striker must be home by now. I yanked the covers from a carefully made bed. If he hadn't returned to Mt. Kenya, he wouldn't hang around the lodge; he'd have come here.

I found myself half-listening for the sound of an airplane. It was very quiet: a snatch of conversation in Swahili from the staff area, unintelligible to me, the ever-present drone of cicadas and grasshoppers, a breath of wind that made the leaves whisper. The sun had reached the line of tents and soon it would heat up under the canvas.

Everyone had seemed relieved to be returning to the lodge, as if a more public place could dilute suspicion and fear. After last night, it was a good thing we were leaving camp. No one would have agreed to stay another night. I folded the blanket in two and raised it under my chin so it hung smoothly, then folded it again.

The group had set off in the Land Rover almost cheerfully. Al had passed off the hidden telex with a shrug and his, by-now-standard, comments about Omondi wasting time and messing about in his private business. Madge had squeezed his arm and said nothing. I could tell Al was disturbed only because he'd packed up all his cameras. It was the first time he'd gone on a drive without his garland of equipment.

Molezzi came back with the mat and we passed through the tents again, a two-person mattress-moving team. The work went fast and was soothingly mindless. I enjoyed the opportunity to use my muscles; the stretching made my back feel good. It was getting hot. I stripped down to my T-shirt. Even Molezzi was sweating. We struck the tents and piled them near the mattresses. Six tents. The seventh tent, the one Lynn had slept in, and the mattress from her bed, were in the plane to Nairobi.

Chris Mbare returned by early afternoon. He'd left the Land Rover at Mara and was in the small truck I'd leased for a year. It was once khaki, though between the mud and the dents, you could hardly tell it had ever been painted. It almost looked like a motorized rock, worthy of the Flintstones. I was glad to see Chris's smiling round face and hear that everyone got a room, and that Kakombe was following Eleanor around like a moving mountain.

It was hot work loading the folded tents and cots, the trunks of linen, china, and kitchen equipment into the truck, and even with all of us, it took a good few hours. This must be why Seven Seas used those permanent camps, where the tents actually had indoor plumbing. It wasn't practical to set up and strike a full luxury camp. The thing to do—if I got enough work to justify it—would be to leave a permanent camp here. That probably meant hiring two men to stay on as guards when the camp wasn't in use. Expensive—unless I could rent the camp to other tours when I wasn't using it. Hmmm. Would that be a nice side business, or would I be giving away one of my only specialties? I'd have to talk it over with Striker.

I sighed. What was I going to do about Striker? I remembered my first sight of him yesterday, that one moment of joy when he'd taken me by surprise, which I'd tried to blot out by being an asshole. I stared sightlessly across the campsite. What would I do if our friendship was wrecked? I'd relied on him all along, I reflected bitterly. I'd pretended to need no one, fooling only myself. I'd been able to live like a semihermit because I knew there was one person, not too far away, who sensed what I was going through and who cared, without interfering. And I'd done the same for him—caring without demands and obligations.

Striker thought he was in love with me under these circumstances, but how would he act if I gave in and we got seriously involved? It was so easy to love someone you couldn't have. Would he find me as entrancing as if I was available? I wasn't ready to find out. I didn't want to back away from our special friendship, either. I felt heartsick over the whole mess.

We'd finished packing and were having a drink in the shade before hitting the road when I heard the distant hum of an approaching plane. I ran to the edge of the trees where I could see the sky toward Masai Mara. A small plane, starting to bank. If that was Striker, I still didn't know what I was going to do. Could I risk telling him the truth?

23

I TURNED TO Chris Mbare. "Looks like it's coming in. Would you drive me over to the landing strip? It may be Dan Striker, you know, my American friend."

We took the staff van. Heat waves shimmered above the grass. A plume of dust rose ahead of us in the still air. As we got closer, I saw it was an elephant taking a dust bath. She kicked at the hard earth with the edge of her toes, sucked the loosened dirt into her trunk, and then expelled it with a noisy snort over her back. She seemed to be enjoying herself, a fat lady with a powder puff after her bath.

Another large female stood nearby with a little calf no higher than her belly. Two human-looking breasts hung between her front legs. She touched the calf reassuringly with her trunk. The baby leaned against the mother's pillar of a leg and studied us with innocent curiosity. The other adult, the baby's aunt and coparent, was less pleased with our presence. Interrupting her dust bath, she pulled up to her full height and trotted toward us, holding her ears out to their enormous width and writhing her trunk. Chris trod on the gas and as we spurted past her, she trumpeted derisively at our backs.

By the time we got to the landing field, the plane was down. I recognized its high-spirited profile, nose high and tail low.

"It *is* Striker's plane." I could hear the happiness in my voice and glanced self-consciously at Chris.

"Will you fly back with him? Ngueye is a good driver, you know. He could take the van and I'll take the truck."

"Let me check with Striker first and see what he had in mind. He may be heading home and not want to turn around." It was a silly thing to say to an African. It wouldn't seem natural to Chris that someone would be in too big a hurry to help a friend. It wouldn't seem natural to Striker, either, for that matter. I was trying to save face in case he had stronger reasons for not flying me over.

Striker wore a leather cap over his dark hair, aviator glasses, and an open-collared shirt that revealed a muscled chest. He gave us his big open smile, with a bear hug for me and a strong handshake for Chris. When I explained we'd dismantled the camp, he immediately suggested I send the staff on their way with the vehicles and that he'd get me to Masai Mara Lodge. So Chris drove off, and left Striker and me facing each other under the immense Serengeti sky.

The silence lengthened. Striker's eyes were hard to see behind his sunglasses.

I was the first to speak. "I'm sorry. I acted like a jerk."

"I did, too. Storming out of there."

"I was contradicting everything you said, just to be disagreeable. I've never once thought you were stupid . . . I think you're brilliant."

"Thank you."

"Things are looking worse and worse for the Harts."

"Forget the Harts." Striker folded his arms across his chest. "Let's talk about us. It wasn't being called stupid that bothered me, it's that you said it to hurt me. Why are you so angry at me? Did I do something? What's going on, Jazz? I don't want us to mess up what we have."

"I don't either." I looked down and fiddled around with my watch strap. "You're very important to me."

He pulled me to him and kissed me. I tried to pull back but he gripped me tighter. I felt borne aloft, as if in an eagle's talons. Striker's kiss was harsh, wild, full of raw emotion, soaring and free. I gave in to it, to him, was overwhelmed by my own response, resisted again. He released me and I stared at him with my lip trembling like a five-year-old about to cry.

"Do you know how I feel about you?" he asked.

"Don't, don't."

"You're driving me crazy." His voice was pained.

I exploded into sobs—hunched over, noisy, blubbering, shuddering sobs. Striker held me and I cried, holding nothing back.

"It's okay. It's okay." His voice echoed basso profondo in the cave of his chest under my ear, soothing as the waves inside a seashell. "Let it all out."

I pulled away. "I've cried more in the last week than I have in the last two years. I'm tired of crying."

"You've needed to cry."

"Oh, piss off. You sound like a leftover from the sixties."

"Don't start being an asshole again."

"Well, you better not kiss me again. I don't want to be kissed."

"I know you're scared, Jazz. So am I." He gave me a straight, deep look and a half smile. "Let's risk it together."

"Gobbledygook."

"It's not and you know it. We both know it. You're a bloody fool to turn your back on this."

"I'm not turning my back . . . more like my side."

"It's time to face forward."

I couldn't take the next step with Striker even if I wanted to; Omondi rose up like a wall. I was safe behind my Omondi wall of friendly sex with no entangling emotions. Safe and alone.

"Your timing is terrible." I threw the words at him. "You sense my vulnerability right now and you're moving in for the kill."

"My God but you're an aggravating person. An argument for every occasion."

"I'm stubborn. It's one of my chief virtues."

"More like a regrettable habit."

We smiled at each other. Striker lifted my left arm and looked at my ribs. "Now how much of this side do I get? Or is it the other side?" He touched my side. "Not too skinny, not too fat. Do I get some flank, too?" He moved to grab my hip, but I skipped aside.

"C'mon Striker. No kissing, no grabbing."

He shifted back to a serious face. "I'll back off, for now, but you know you're going to have to decide soon. This can't continue."

"I know that." I let out a noisy sigh. "I know that, Striker, I'm really sorry. I guess that right now I need to be desired, not had."

"Goddamn it." He pulled off his cap and threw it on the ground. "Had!" He fought visibly for control over his temper, and lost. "You think I want to have you?" he shouted. "What are you talking about? I don't want to have you, I want to love you."

Suddenly I could feel a wave of heat rise into my face. The top of my head seemed to expand and be held in a vise at the same time. "Love! Love!" I took a wild kick at his hat and missed. "Words are cheap. Adam told me he loved me ten times a day, but he loved his goddamn cock more. I've had it with love, do you hear me? It means nothing. Nothing! You, you—" I sputtered, unable to connect with a thought, but that didn't stop me from yelling. "You want to love me? I don't believe you! You've been a bachelor for twenty years, after a brief fling at marriage. Why should I believe you want a real relationship? You're so busy analyzing me and my fears and my running away and my clinging to an old grief. What about you? What have you been doing for twenty years, buried out in the middle of nowhere? You love pursuing me all over Kenya—all that proves is that you love pursuit. So just leave me alone, okay? Just goddamn leave me alone."

We stared each other down, jaws clenched and eyes bright with rage. I wanted to hit him. Striker picked up his hat, jammed it on his head, and got into his airplane. I walked rapidly away as he started the engine. The air from the propeller buffeted my hair and clothes. I put my hands over my ears. He taxied to the end of the field. I turned to watch. Great. What was I going to do now, walk to Mara?

The plane turned and started toward me down the length of the field. The propellers whirred, picking up speed, becoming an invisible blur. The sun bounced off the windscreen, so that Striker was invisible, too. Goddamn everything to hell. The engine whined, then slowed to a dull roar. I could see the propeller again. Instead of picking up speed, the plane taxied slower and slower. Striker pulled up next to me.

He looked down at me and scratched the side of his brow with one finger. "All right, so what do you say to a cup of tea? I packed a hamper and a thermos." He coaxed me with an endearing look. "Are you willing to drink tea with the enemy?"

The lava receded back to wherever it came from. My chest relaxed and my breathing returned to normal. I touched the hair on the crown of my head. "Whew. I'm afraid I blew my top there, for a moment." I gave an embarrassed little laugh. "Tea sounds great. Did you bring crumpets and scones?"

"Never had a crumpet in my life."

"Me, either."

"Maybe we're more alike than we realized."

"Maybe you're right."

It was a beginning.

24

STRIKER DROPPED ME at Masai Mara Lodge, refueled, and set off for home. As I headed for the lodge, the weight of the investigation came back down upon me, slowing my steps, slumping my shoulders.

There was the usual line of zebra-striped vans in front of the entrance, empty and waiting to take groups out for their evening game viewing. The drivers were gathered on the sidewalk, exchanging tips about where to see lion and cheetah, the two favorites, and generally socializing. I greeted the few of them I knew by name.

As soon as I entered the lobby, Madge came up at a trot, waving her arms. Her brown eyes were wide with excitement and alarm.

"Jazz, thank God you're here. You wouldn't believe what happened."

My heart pounded in alarm. "What? Is everyone okay?"

"Yes. Sorry to scare you." She put a hand to her ample chest. "They got my pocketbook."

Muggers at Masai Mara Lodge?

"Al's chasing them; they ran around the corner of the lodge. I thought I'd cut through here in case they come round the front."

"Madge! Who got your pocketbook? Will you tell me what's going on?"

"I'm telling you. The baboons. The little so-and-so's stole

my purse, right off the terrace wall. I put it down for one split second and—gone. C'mon, let's see if we can find them.''

We headed outside, passed under the cascade of purple bougainvillea, and around toward the luxury tents. We burst through a flock of superb starlings that flew up like chips of sapphire all around us.

''We were having drinks''—Madge panted—''and I put my purse down right next to me. Whew.'' She stopped for a moment, breathing deeply. ''I can't take this pace. I don't like Al running around in this heat, either.''

We rounded the lodge. The luxury tents were there, lined up neatly in a row. One tent had the flaps tied back and I could see a woman lying on her cot inside, peacefully reading a novel. No sign of Al or the baboon troop.

''Let's try the other direction.''

We walked briskly toward the pool. Sounds of splashing and children's laughter rose above the hibiscus hedge. The lawn in front was empty except for Al. He had an open purse dangling from his arm as he bent over and searched in the grass.

A big adolescent baboon sat on its haunches and watched him intently from a dozen feet away. Its fur was thick and luxurious, brown with gold highlights, and its interested expression was almost human. It looked like a cross between a person and a dog.

''Al!'' Madge waved. ''Look who's here. We went the other way first.'' We reached his side. ''You got it!'' She gave him a big kiss and took the bag. ''Did they leave me anything, the little thieves?''

''Look at this mess.'' Al gestured across the lawn. ''Your stuff is all over the place.''

Madge was inspecting her purse. ''You got my wallet back. That's the most important.''

''The money is nothing. What about your passport? We're supposed to be getting out of here tomorrow.''

''Hold your horses, Al. Give me a minute here.'' She unzipped a little pocket in the lining and pulled out the square

211

blue booklet. "See how good I am? I keep it safe in this side pocket." She slipped the passport back inside. "Okay, so let's see what we can find here. Did you see them open it?"

The three of us tacked back and forth over the closely mown lawn and gathered up a trail of lipsticks, matches, her sunglass case. Piece by piece, we gathered everything in sight and deposited it in Madge's bag.

"I think that's it," Madge announced.

"Hey, what's this?" Al held up something small between thumb and forefinger.

Madge and I went up for a closer look. It was a white pill.

"Give it here." Madge held out her palm and Al dropped his find into it. "That's one of Boyce's pills."

"Or one of Candy's," I said quietly.

Madge gave me a startled look.

"What the hell is it doing here?" Al said.

"I don't know. It looks like it was in my purse. I don't like this." Madge closed her fist on the pill.

Al started searching quickly around the same spot. "Look, here's another one."

"And another." I pounced on a pill lodged among the short blades of grass and handed it to Madge.

"It sure looks like these were in my purse."

"See, this is what comes of carrying a purse so crammed full of junk, you don't even know what's in there," Al said.

"Look, Al, don't blame me. I haven't used my purse since we got to camp. This bag was sitting in the tent for days. You think I should have gone rummaging through it looking for Candy's missing pillbox?"

Al handed Madge a few more pills. "This stinks. I smell a frame-up."

"You mean someone's trying to pin the murder on us?" Madge looked scared.

"We should give these to Kakombe." I wondered what the Harts would have done with the pills if I hadn't been here.

"I guess you're right—they'll want to test them," Madge said. "Kakombe's hanging around outside Eleanor's door.

She's been in bed ever since we got here. I tell you, Jazz, I'm really worried about her. I'm afraid she could crack up any second." Madge shook her head. "This business about amphetamines in Boyce's blood is the last straw. I think she's more upset about that than someone being after her."

"Which is just as well." Al continued to scan the lawn for pills. "Don't you start putting ideas in her head about how she should be scared, you hear me? Eleanor's being guarded. Nothing is going to happen to her."

We were getting closer and closer to the baboon, who studied us, as if hoping we were about to produce something good to eat.

"He's got something." Al pointed to the baboon.

I looked carefully. Sure enough, the baboon's right paw was tightly clenched around a small chunky object. A patch of yellow metal glinted between his fingers.

"What is it?" Madge started towards the baboon.

I grabbed her arm. "Careful, you'll chase him away. Let's get a bribe."

I left the two of them to keep an eye on the baboon and ran back to the lodge. I sped through the empty dining hall and through the swinging doors into the kitchen. Enormous aluminum pots stood on a black kitchen range. There was a row of half-eaten cakes on a counter, not yet put away from high tea. A man in cook's white with a muffin-shaped hat sat on a stool drinking a cup of tea and digging into a wedge of yellow cake with white frosting. It took me a few minutes and a handsome tip to wrangle a bunch of bananas out of him. When I raced back, everyone was where I'd left them. Al and Madge stood side by side watching the baboon watch them.

"Okay, Al, stand back." I gently tossed one banana to the baboon. He shifted his prize from the right paw to the left, scuttled forward, and took the banana. His beady eyes were fixed on the bunch of bananas in my hand. I handed a second banana to him, at arm's length, holding it way over to the left. My ploy worked. He dropped the metal object and grabbed the second banana with his left paw. I then held

213

out a third banana while slowly backing away. He followed, clutching a banana in each hand. Al moved in and picked up what the baboon had dropped. I jettisoned the remaining bananas. The baboon managed to scoop them all up, held them against his chest with one arm, and loped off to hide in the tall grass and eat his booty.

I turned back to Al and Madge, who stood with heads bent, and examined the metal object. "I bet you already know what it is," Al told me.

"Candy's missing pillbox?"

"Hole in one." Al held up the little brass and malachite box. "Pretty little thing, ain't it?"

"Oh, Al, you shouldn't be touching it," Madge exclaimed in dismay. "What about fingerprints? Here, put it in this." She held out a tissue.

Al obligingly dropped it in the tissue. "I can tell you one thing. The one guy's prints that aren't on that thing is the murderer's, and you better believe it. That thing was planted in your purse."

"I hope Inspector Omondi believes me," Madge said. "Al, maybe we should call our lawyer again. Between hiding that telex about the loan, and now this . . ."

"Maybe you're right, chiquita. Why don't you give Jazz this stuff. She can give it to what's his face, Kombe. Let's go in and discuss this in private."

I found Kakombe tilted back in a chair outside Eleanor's door, his long legs stretched out in front of him. He didn't bother to stand up, even when I handed over my tissue-wrapped package and explained the situation to him. He nodded and without opening it, tucked it into his shirt pocket.

"I will take care of this." He gave me his usual flat gaze.

There didn't seem to be anywhere to go with that, so I turned and left.

When I got back to my room, I found a note slipped under my door from the management. Inspector Omondi had called and left a number where I could reach him. I looked longingly at the shower, turned, and headed back to the lobby. Getting cleaned up would have to wait. The phone was being used, and I asked them to page me at the bar when it was free and the operator could get a line through to Nairobi.

Cliff and Candy were at one of the little round tables. Cliff was in his white suit with a butter yellow silk shirt. Candy was in a sun dress that showed off her tanned and muscled shoulders, left nothing to doubt about the shape of her breasts and belly, and then flared out into a free-flowing skirt that tumbled about her calves. I joined them and ordered a fresh orange juice.

"Jazz, we need your wildlife expertise." Cliff draped an arm over the back of my chair. I could smell alcohol on his breath, and pulled back. "Did you ever read Tolkein?"

"Sure. Hobbits, little people with hairy feet."

"Remember Gollum—a slimy kind of creature with pads at the end of his fingers who lived in a sunless cave?"

"Is this about wildlife or about your room?"

"My room has a window and a charming view of the garden, but I do seem to have several roommates."

"Geckos."

"No, Gollum."

"You can call them Gollum if you want to, but most people call them geckos. They're a type of salamander, with sticky round toes. Climb on walls. Fast-moving."

"Ah, yes, exactly. If you want to see a half dozen or so, step into my shower."

"Look at it this way, Cliff. They eat bugs."

"Gross," Candy said. "Listen, Jazz, are we just hanging around the lodge till tomorrow morning or what?"

Cliff asked, "What are you proposing, darling?"

"I was wondering if we could do an evening game run. I mean, since we're here. I mean, we don't all have to act like we're in mourning."

"You certainly don't have to worry about that." Cliff lifted his glass to his lips and drained the last drops. He signaled the waiter for a refill.

Candy bristled. "You're no one to talk. All you've done in the last three days is drink and make wisecracks."

"That's all I ever do." Cliff grinned at her.

"Seriously." Candy opened her Raphael eyes at me. "We haven't seen a cheetah yet, and I was kinda hoping to see one. They're my favorite animal."

"You look like a cheetah," I told her, and was rewarded with a pleased smile. "I'd be happy to take you out for a run, say around five? I have to make a call first." I looked at my watch. "You might want to change, and we can meet in the lobby. Cliff, you interested?"

"No, thanks, I'm comfortable right here." He lifted his fresh drink to us in a silent toast.

The operator told me to stand by while she put the call through. I held the phone more tightly than necessary, feeling nervous and excited at the prospect of hearing Omondi's voice.

"Hello? Miss Jasper?"

It was Omondi, but something was wrong. His voice had lost its timbre.

"Hi, Inspector Omondi? What's the matter?"

"I am at headquarters." Was that the reason for the Miss Jasper? "I have already told Sergeant Kakombe, but I also wanted to tell you myself."

Ah, was there a reason for Kakombe's silent treatment? Had they found something important? Maybe Omondi had told Kakombe to keep quiet because he wanted to tell me the news himself.

"Sorry, I missed that. What did you say?" I asked.

"The investigation is over."

I sat up straighter. "Over? You know who did it?" My mouth went dry.

"No, my dear. I'm afraid we'll never know who did it."

"Why not? What are you talking about?"

He didn't say anything.

"You had all those leads . . . we have the picture of what happened. We can work on the hard evidence." I stared at the wall, too intent to be irritated by the "I love elephants" graffiti. "I have some important news for you. I think the diet pills turned up. I—"

"Yes, I smell the tracks also, my dear Miss Jasper. But the dogs have been called off." His voice sounded weary and very far away over the hissing of the long-distance line.

"Called off?" My voice sounded unpleasantly shrill, not like my own voice at all.

"Two unfortunate accidents," Omondi quoted in an officious voice. "Please offer these important visitors our apologies and every assistance with the remainder of their trip."

"You can't do that!"

"If there's no crime, there's no investigation."

"Wait a second. Cutting through the back wall of a tent and killing someone is not an accident. We have the tent and the spear. There's proof that Boyce's pills were tampered with, that he had amphetamines in his blood. Somebody unzipped Eleanor's tent and left meat inside. These are not accidents. You can't dismiss them like that."

"Miss Jasper, calm yourself. I agree with you, but I can't conduct the investigation against the express orders of my superiors. I am very sorry."

"This is not going to go over well with the group. This is not how we do things in America."

"Think again. It was someone in the group who pulled these strings. And I can't think of anyone besides you who's going to make a fuss about it. The case is closed."

I clenched my jaw and stared at the wall two feet in front of my eyes. Omondi was right. Eleanor would be relieved to be spared the scandal. Al had been uncooperative all along, and now he and Madge were worried they'd be accused themselves. Cliff wasn't a fighter. Candy could care less. They'd make comments about African corruption, but no one would do anything. They'd all be secretly relieved.

"Can you at least tell me what you found so far?" I asked.

"Yes, I don't see why not. Al didn't pick up that telex until after Boyce and Lynn were dead, so he probably didn't know about the stock manipulation. More to the point, Boyce's children inherit the company, not the Harts. That leaves them without a known motive. As for means, the top layer of pills in Boyce's pillbox was diet medicine and

217

matches up with the amphetamines in his blood. So we have confirmation of the murder weapon.''

Great, but as far as suspects, the case was wide open again. Without the financial motive, finding the pills on the Harts seemed much less suspicious. As Al said, it could easily be a frame-up. Or maybe we hadn't dug deeply enough yet. We couldn't stop now.

''Are you still there?'' Omondi asked.

''I'm still here. Still alive and sniffing. They can call you off, Inspector, but they can't call me off. I'm going to find that killer.''

25

SERGEANT KAKOMBE WATCHED me approach across the lawn from his post in front of Eleanor's cottage without a sign of recognition. His arms were crossed over his chest and he'd tilted the chair so it could rock on its two back legs. The picture of relaxation.

"Sergeant, I just spoke to Inspector Omondi."

He waited for me to continue.

"I assume you've been told the case is closed."

An infinitesimal nod.

I stopped and tried to match his flat stare. He held my gaze without blinking. "Look, Sergeant, I'm upset enough about this as it is, I really don't need a silent treatment from you, okay?"

Kakombe let the chair legs back down to earth. "What do you wish to know, Miss?" he asked coldly.

"Nothing. Nothing. I'm just trying to talk with you." Something clicked. "Listen, if you think I tried to kill this investigation, you're wrong. Lynn was my old friend. I want to see the murderer caught—whoever it is. And I'm not stopping, either."

Kakombe closed his eyes and nodded in acknowledgment. "You are a fighter."

"What are you still doing here?" I glanced at the closed curtains of Eleanor's room.

"A police car will pick me up in the morning. While I am here, the inspector suggested I continue to keep watch."

So Omondi had the decency to be that responsible, at least. Not that it was his fault the investigation was squelched. I wondered who pulled the strings. Al and Madge were calling their lawyer at this very minute; they couldn't have moved that fast. I remembered Al's important call yesterday when he'd come to the lodge with me and Omondi. Shit. And I'd felt so guilty for even suspecting him.

Just then the curtain flicked aside and Madge's face looked out. She looked as surprised as I did. The curtain fell back and the door opened. "I thought I heard voices. Are you looking for me?"

Behind her, I could hear Eleanor's voice saying to invite me in. I stepped into the room. It took a moment for my eyes to adjust after the sunlight outside, even though Eleanor had the lamp on by her bed. She was lying fully clothed on top of the covers. From their rumpled look, she'd been there a while. A magazine lay open on the bed beside her. It was a small room with two twin beds and the usual assortment of hotel furniture. The three of us plus her luggage took up all the available space.

"Hi, I'm sorry to be such a hermit," Eleanor began.

"Oh, that's all right, Eleanor. We understand. You don't have to explain." I leaned against the dresser by the door. "I came by because I have some news."

Eleanor studied her hands. "I'm almost afraid to hear it." She riffled the corner of her magazine.

"Well, I don't know whether you'll think it's good or bad. I spoke to Inspector Omondi on the phone just now. He informed me that the investigation of the two deaths has been called off."

"Called off?" Madge advanced a step toward me.

"They're officially declaring them accidental deaths."

Eleanor stared, gape-mouthed. "What?" she exclaimed.

Her hand moved in a startled reaction and the magazine slipped to the floor with a noise. Madge picked it up and put it on the nightstand, her back momentarily toward me. I wondered what emotions were flitting across her face.

I rested my hands on my hips. "Apparently someone—someone in this group—got to the higher-ups and exerted pressure to close the file and let us go home."

Eleanor addressed Madge. "What do you think? Of course, I want justice done, but—"

"Yes." Madge nodded. "You wonder if they're capable of finding the right person. I think this is just as well. It's not as if staying here can bring Boyce back."

"No, he's gone. And that poor young girl." Eleanor's eyes filled with tears, but she kept herself under control. "I can hardly believe it. We can go home."

Omondi had been right about their reactions. Given the circumstances, I was hardly in a position to defend the competency of the local police, but it made me mad to hear him patronized. There had been nothing incapable about his conduct of the investigation. On the contrary, he'd been outstanding. That was the story of Africa: individual talent, official corruption. Though much less in Kenya than elsewhere. Oh, shit. No point fuming. Too bad I'd handed all those pills over to Kakombe.

Madge sank onto the edge of the bed near Eleanor and reached for her hand. "Now you can start putting this nightmare behind you."

"I really am, Madge. I'm not going to think about it. As far as the children have to know, their father simply died of a heart attack."

"Excuse me, I don't know if either of you is interested, but Candy asked for an evening game run; she needs some distraction." I looked at my watch. "I told her I'd take her out around five."

"What time is it now?" Madge asked.

"Almost four-thirty."

She patted Eleanor's hand. "If you have the energy, it might be good for you to get out, get some fresh air?"

"I don't know," Eleanor said doubtfully.

"Well, if you want to," I told them, "meet us at the lobby

entrance, under the bougainvillea. It'll be a shorty, an hour at most.''

Ahead and behind us, a procession of vans crossed under the hotel's arched gateway and scattered in different directions off the park's main road. Two lions were draped over a rock outcropping next to the entrance, like a living advertisement for the lodge. We passed them and entered another world. The plains rolled away to a distant escarpment. We turned down a smaller dirt road. The only sounds were wind and bird song. The tall grass stood out sharply in the slanting evening light, its color and texture changing as it swayed in the breeze.

"If only they could capture that subtle green-gold in fabric.'' Candy sighed. "What a fabulous color.''

Madge looked out the open side of the Rover appreciatively. "What can be simpler than grass? Yet it can't be done.''

"Subtlety isn't your image, is it, Candy?'' Cliff asked in his light voice. To my surprise, he'd emerged from the bar at the last minute and decided to join us.

Candy ignored the barb.

"Cliff, you're losing your sense of humor,'' Madge told him. "Lately it's been all acid and no honey.''

"That's enough.'' Al patted her, reining her in. "One more day, and we'll all be getting back to normal.''

"Al, you make a wonderful Sir Galahad, but I resist being rescued,'' Cliff said. "Madge is quite right. I've been an absolute cat, lately. I'll try and recapture my usual sweet disposition.''

"Hey,'' Al broke in, "talking of cats—look straight ahead.''

Mbare slowed the Land Rover and came to a full stop. The track we had chosen was blocked by three male lions. They were stretched flat on their sides across the middle of the dirt road, napping. Two of them didn't move, although we'd stopped within a few feet of them. The third one wearily raised himself partway onto his elbows, looked away from

222

us, and yawned enormously. His pink tongue lightly touched long white teeth in a perfect question mark.

"Too bad Eleanor didn't come. She would have loved this." Madge looked at Al. "Did you get that on film?"

"Hold on a minute." Al was busy switching lens. "We're too close, I have to take off my tele-extender. All I need is the regular zoom lens. I'm going to get every whisker on that lion's face."

The lion who had yawned lay back down without a glance in our direction.

"Aw, shit." Al was finally ready. "Jazz, can you get him to sit up again?"

I twisted in my seat to face the other passengers. "I don't believe in bothering the animals any more than we are already. We're not in any rush. Let's give it a few minutes."

We waited. I enjoyed studying the lions' muscled bodies and the details of their coats. "You can tell these are young lions by their faces and manes," I started to lecture.

"No scars!" Madge said.

"Right. Within a few years, they'll all be battle-scarred, and their manes won't be so full and magnificent."

One of the lions raised his head a few inches and gave us an indifferent stare.

"He looks right through you." Candy sounded slightly dismayed.

"Don't like feeling invisible?" Cliff asked.

"I guess since we're not food and we're not a threat, we're no more worthy of attention than a rock," Madge said.

"As long as we're in a vehicle, they don't perceive us," I told them. "If you were on foot, you'd get a reaction. Either fight or flight."

"It's amazing how close they let us get to them. Isn't this fantastic, honey?" Madge smiled at Al, who took his photo and leaned back with a satisfied look.

Mbare backed away from the lions and plunged into the long grass. For the next half hour, we charged cross-country, now on dirt roads, now pushing through grass that reached up to the windows. Twice, we forded narrow streams at high speed that carried us rocking over the boulders.

Every few minutes, new animals appeared before our eyes, not paying us the slightest attention. Birds of all sizes, shapes, and colors burst up from the grass. We saw four species of eagles, a secretary bird with a snake in its hooked beak, a crested crane looking like a Japanese print come to life. Gazelle, wildebeest, topi, bushbuck, impala, tommies, and zebra grazed in scattered groups. We even saw the elusive dik-dik, an antelope no taller than my knee. It stared at me with its enormous liquid eyes before disappearing into the grass. Three different species of antelope mated in front of us; babies suckled at their mother's teats or were pushed away; zebras engaged in noisy horseplay. We passed a fallen tree where a troop of vervet monkeys played tag. We paused to watch a lone elephant at a big mud puddle, sucking up water in his trunk and shooting it over his back. Nearby several giraffes were bent over the tops of acacia trees, munching them down to size. The Serengeti would be a forest if the animals didn't eat the trees.

It was a terrific game run, even if it was all ordinary stuff. I could tell everyone was having a great time, including me. I let myself forget all about recent events and be absorbed into the present moment. That's the magic of this place, I told myself. It puts all our human affairs into a different perspective. We are not the whole world, thank God.

"Hey, Jazz, how about a cheetah?" Candy called out, ruining my illusion of universal contentment.

I looked at Mbare and he shrugged.

"Let me get on the roof," I suggested. "I'll be able to spot farther from there." I swung around the edge of the bucket seat and hoisted myself through the sunroof, letting my legs dangle into the cab.

Cliff and Candy started to talk about work, a jarring note for me, but probably the truest sign that they were enjoying themselves, feeling more normal.

"We could do it like this, with you perched on the roof and the camera in a second van off to the side." Cliff stood

224

up and poked his head out of the sunroof next to me. "The thing is to get you with wildlife in the same frame. If we just cut back and forth, you might as well be posing in the studio." He paused. "What we really need is some action."

As if on cue, we turned a bend in the track and were on top of a big Cape buffalo. It staggered to its feet, obviously interrupted in the enjoyment of a nice mushy mud wallow. Gobs of mud stuck to its flanks and fell with a plop. Massive curved horns weighed down its brow. It raised its muzzle and sniffed the air, eyes round with alarm.

"Cape buffalo. Mean-tempered animals. We're perfectly safe in the car. As I explained about the lions, it doesn't really know we're here."

"I want to stand, too." Candy crowded in next to Cliff and I shifted over slightly on my rooftop perch.

The buffalo stood its ground and glowered. Mbare honked the horn. The buffalo took a step toward us. Mbare leaned out and banged hard against the side of the Land Rover to encourage the buffalo to move along. The buffalo stopped.

"This is a great shot," Al exclaimed. "Madge, hold on to my belt, would you? I want to get him face-to-face."

It seemed to happen all at once. The buffalo started to trot toward us. Suddenly Cliff lurched heavily against me and knocked me off balance.

"Candy!" he exclaimed with annoyance.

At the same time, not before—of this I was sure—Mbare threw the Land Rover into reverse. I lost it. My legs flipped up over my head, I bounced once onto the hood of the Rover as it backed up under me, and landed on the ground with a thud that knocked me half senseless. I lay there, not knowing what had happened. My immediate concern was trying to breathe and get some wind back in my lungs. They didn't seem to be working properly.

I could hear Candy scream. By the kindness of fate, I'd fallen to one side. The buffalo picked up speed and charged the moving vehicle. There was the sound of broken glass and of metal tearing. I was still flattened. All I could see was the sky, complete with vulture.

Mbare threw the Land Rover into forward and lurched to a stop right next to me. He leaped out of the driver's seat. The buffalo crashed into the back of the van, taking out the spare tire, as the others told us later. The tire was a lifesaver. While the buffalo shook loose the strange black object dangling from its horns, gored it through, and left it for dead, Mbare hoisted me into the Rover, climbed in himself, and got us the hell out of there.

My body had gone cold and I shivered with delayed fear.

"She's in shock," Madge said, and enveloped me in a pillowy hug. I tried to extricate myself. I didn't want to be hugged by Madge just then.

Cliff was almost as white-faced as I was. "Candy, you almost got her killed."

"*I* almost got her killed? What are you talking about? You knocked into her."

"You tromped on my instep."

"I couldn't help it. Madge bumped into me."

Madge retorted angrily, "I was just bending over to get a good grip on Al's belt. I didn't bump you that hard." She caught herself. "Come on, let's not squabble like children. No one's to blame. It was an accident. Thank goodness, Jazz is all right."

An accident: I looked at the three of them and wondered.

26

THE PROPELLERS ROARED to life, filling the plane with noise and vibration. I breathed shallowly, nauseated by the smell of gasoline, and looked out the window to distract myself. I wasn't looking forward to today: the bustle of Nairobi, the hassles of getting everyone settled into the Grand Palace Hotel, a fancy dinner, and out to the airport for their midnight flight home.

All I'd had for breakfast was tea and a roll, which was now sitting in my stomach like a hard lump. A herd of Cape buffalo grazed in a straggling line next to the runway. Those heavy horns almost joining in the middle of their low foreheads no longer reminded me of a barbershop quartet. Even munching on grass, they looked dangerous. It matched my mood.

Cliff tilted his head to look past me from his seat on the aisle. "Ah, your friend from last night came by to send us off."

The plane began to taxi down the asphalt runway. I checked my seat belt, although I knew I'd already locked it. I could still feel the spot on my back where I'd bounced off the Rover. Thank God nothing had broken.

"I loved the way Chris Mbare scooped you into the Land Rover. When I go home, I shall tell everyone, Tarzan lives. I won't add he's round-faced and black and only five foot five." Cliff smoothed the fabric of his pants. "Hopeless. I don't know what possessed me to buy linen. The look on the hanger is so marvelously crisp; half an hour of wear and you look like you're wearing wrinkled pajamas. And I pride myself on being a realist.''

''A cynic, Cliff. You pride yourself on being a cynic. A realist is different.''

As the plane swung round at the end of the runway, I had a glimpse of the luxury tents. The baboons were in residence, along with a knot of tourists excitedly gesturing and taking pictures. That was where Striker had found me, before our stupid quarrel. Our last meeting together had been good. What an unbelievable kiss. I basked in the warm sundrenched memory and for once didn't worry about the future. We had a date for drinks at the Grand Palace tonight. Soon this murder craziness would be over.

We picked up speed. The pavement was a blur outside the window, the nose of the plane lifted, we were aloft. Below, I caught one last glimpse of the lodge next to its water hole, in the middle of a golden plain. More and more animals came into view as we climbed. I saw a herd of elephants, a row of giraffe standing on a ridge, antelope by the hundred. For a moment, I was elated at all the splendor. I hoped I could pick up a client quickly and get back out here.

A tall black stewardess came by and offered us drinks. Her hair cascaded from the crown of her head in an elaborate beaded coiffure of tiny braids. Cliff ordered a gin and tonic. Hoping to placate my stomach, I asked for plain tonic. The stewardess efficiently doled out two glasses, ice, a miniature bottle of gin, two bottles of Schweppes, and peanuts in shiny foil packages. She moved on down the aisle, dispensing smiles and refreshments.

I tried to open the peanuts, but the foil wouldn't tear. ''This is pathetic. I couldn't fight my way out of a paper bag.''

''Wait a second, I'll help you. I'm just getting the cap off this tonic.'' As he spoke, I gave a last tug at the foil, which ripped wide open with a metallic sound. Peanuts flew everywhere, joined by a sudden explosion of tonic. We looked at the mess and started to laugh.

"A bottle of this tonic in the bag with you, and you could dynamite your way out." Cliff dabbed at the tonic dripping down his cheek.

We munched and drank in silence for a while. It was now or never.

"Did Al or Madge tell you about finding Candy's pillbox in Madge's handbag?"

"Yes. Or rather, the baboon found it. Smart fellow." Cliff pushed the button on his armrest and reclined his seat.

"I handed it over to Sergeant Kakombe before learning the case was closed."

"You're burnt up about that, aren't you? Are you suspecting me?"

"Should I?"

"Jazz, believe me, I'm deeply saddened by Lynn's death. Lynn was my protégé." He took a hefty swallow from his drink. "I discovered her, I nurtured her talent. I liked her. Her murder shocks and angers me." The *no smoking* light blinked off and Cliff immediately lit a cigarette. "You might think I've shown that in a funny way, but, you know me, I don't care for sincerity." He shook out the match and poked it into the tiny ashtray in the armrest.

Do you believe someone who admits he's insincere? I looked at Cliff's manicured nails, his hand lying gracefully on his linen pant leg. "You don't seem to care whether I suspect you or not."

"*Au contraire*, if you excluded me, I would feel terribly ineffectual." He took a long drag on his cigarette and let the smoke flow out his nostrils. "I suspect everyone of anything as a general policy."

My head swam. I checked to make sure there was an airsickness bag in the seat pocket, gripped the armrests, and closed my eyes. A black swirling dizziness engulfed me. I opened my eyes and tried focusing on the horizon again. I took a small sip of tonic. My mouth tasted like old shoe leather; it even made the tonic taste funny. I pushed my glass away.

Al stood up in the aisle. "Drinks are on me," he said. "I want to offer a toast to Eleanor." He held his glass high. "What she's been put through . . . it's been terrible. Come through it like a champ. Here's to Eleanor." He drank. "We're all thankful to be heading home." He didn't look in my direction.

"Doesn't anybody but me care there's a murderer loose in this airplane?" I muttered to Cliff.

"People don't like to think of unpleasant things. They'd rather pretend it was all a mistake. It makes life easier. Sneer all you like, by the time you get to our age, you value pretense a lot more. Besides, we don't *know* it was one of us."

I grabbed a magazine out of the pouch in front of me and flipped through the pages savagely without looking at them. Lynn's death was not a little unpleasantness to be blown away like a bad smell. I thrust the magazine back in its pouch. "I made a promise to myself, which takes effect immediately. I'm going to find the killer before we leave Nairobi. I'll present the police with a case so sewn up, they can't ignore it even if they want to." I hit my fist against the armrest. "I mean it."

Cliff lifted an eyebrow. "How do you propose to do that?"

"That's the part I still have to figure out." And with that, I reclined the seat back, folded my arms, closed my eyes, and began to think. It didn't occur to me until later that it was stupid to make a resolution like that out loud.

"Sorry I'm late!" Candy rushed up to me in the lobby of the Grand Palace. Heads swiveled from every direction. It was hard not to notice Candy, especially in her cavewoman outfit. Supple suede, soft as silk, fell in careful tatters that showed glimpses of a long slim thigh as she moved. She pretended not to notice the stir she caused.

I smiled at her. "That's okay, Candy; I enjoyed people-watching while I waited." It had taken her forty-five minutes to freshen up after lunch and meet me downstairs, but there was no point in getting annoyed. "I forget how many people there are in the world after two weeks in the bush. Isn't Cliff coming?"

"No, he said he's had it with carved animals and khaki. I think he's more interested in the bar than in shopping."

Cliff's defection suited me. Candy was my quarry this afternoon. I'd decided to trust my instincts about Candy. There was something in her behavior since Boyce's death that seemed out of character—too much tension, a hint of guilt. Omondi had commented on it, too. The physical clues kept connecting back to her, but it wasn't that which guided me. When I asked myself why now, why here, my sense was that things had started to go wrong that afternoon by the swimming pool when Boyce fired Candy. It wasn't much to go on, but it was all I had. One broken twig to track a killer down a week-old trail.

"We hardly had time to visit the market when we arrived," Candy continued as we moved toward the door, "and I definitely want some of those big straw shoulder bags. They're selling in the States for a fortune right now."

The street was blinding for a moment. I almost felt dizzy. "Oh, they're exporting them to the States? That's great. Do you remember seeing the peasant women with those bags?"

Candy shook her head.

"We passed some on the road, in the highlands, between Nanyuki and Nakuru. After visiting Mountain Lodge." She still shook her head. "Anyway, they put the straps across their foreheads and let the bag hang behind, across their upper backs. Those straw bags can hold much more weight than you'd think. Let's cross here."

Across the street, an old-fashioned bank in white and gold stucco asserted itself with two-story columns, next to a row of dingy one-story shops. Their open doorways promised shadowy coolness and dusty merchandise. Without a pause, Candy darted into a jewelry store and I followed. The owner smiled unctuously and hurried over to us. He took one look at her suede tatters, sized up Candy as the serious shopper, and concentrated on her. One by one, necklaces, earrings,

231

and bracelets were lovingly placed on a bit of velvet for her inspection. Candy dismissed most of his offerings but returned to some strings of malachite beads. They bargained amicably and agreed on a modest sum.

"Jazz, you should get one," she whispered when the man's back was turned. "They're easily worth triple the price, more if you get them restrung."

I tried on the beads, too. The stones were cool and heavy around my neck. The green looked nice with my tan. "I like them," I announced with satisfaction. "I knew it was a good idea to go shopping with you, Candy."

Candy got another five dollars knocked off the price since we were buying two necklaces, and swept me triumphantly out of the shop. "No more of these little stores," she announced. "Let's get over to the main market."

The sidewalks were crowded with Kenyans. The women wore light cotton dresses in pastel colors, the men dark trousers and white short-sleeved shirts.

"If one more little floral print walks by," Candy said, "I'm going to scream." She almost stepped on a woman ahead of her. "Jeez, people walk so slowly here. You can hardly tell you're in a city. I hope they have some good African fabrics in the market. Hot colors, with a lot of pattern to it. I did a commercial for Club Med in Nigeria last year. The women there dress fantastically."

"Is that where you learned to bargain?"

"There, and in Morocco. Look who's here."

Al and Madge walked down the street toward us, laden with packages. They were busy talking and looking at the shop windows. Madge spotted us and stopped to chat.

"I couldn't resist another safari outfit. You can never have too many, right, Al?" He shrugged philosophically with a half smile, enjoying the role of the indulgent husband. "Get a load of this hat. It's even more authentic than the one I got at Masai Mara." Al obligingly handed over a large package, and she wrestled out a white dome helmet and tried it on. It fit low on her forehead and her nose jutted out majestically below.

A small silence fell into Madge's expectant pause. I tried to change the subject. "Eleanor didn't come with you? Is she staying in her room till we leave?"

Madge lost her smile. "Yes, she's not in the greatest shape, despite the brave face she puts on things."

The crowd eddied around our small group in the middle of the sidewalk. 1 shifted from foot to foot, impatient to get going. I'd had enough of poor Eleanor's terrible ordeal and wonderful bravery; what about Boyce, what about Lynn? They weren't around to be admired or pitied.

"You know," Candy confided to Madge, "I've felt weird ever since you told me about Eleanor."

"Told what?" Al asked.

"Oh, nothing, nothing," Madge brushed him off. "Just girl talk, right, Candy?" She was jostled by a passerby. "Let's not stand here gossiping all day. I have a lot more presents to buy." She put the hat back in its bag and bustled Al off.

I felt a heightened alertness, like a dog raising its ears and sniffing the breeze. What had Madge told Candy? Was this the missing piece I needed to find?

"Weird about what?"

"Oh, nothing." Candy watched Madge disappear into the crowd. "I shouldn't have said anything."

"On to the central market?" I knew better than to push on her directly, or she'd clam up. I didn't have time for any false moves.

Candy pointed down the block. "You can practically see the front of the building. It's only a couple more blocks."

Was she forgetting I lived here? One more example of how other people weren't that real to her. We chatted about clothes as we walked the short distance. That is, Candy chatted and I listened. My interest in clothes peaked when I was sixteen years old. It was all the fault of my big feet and insufficient masochism. You couldn't dress properly for the ball if you wouldn't wear little glass slippers. Though I'd heard recently women were wearing running shoes in New York on the way to work. The day they could wear comfortable shoes *in* the office, I'd know equality had arrived. We passed through a tunnellike passage full of stalls that sold carved animals and bead necklaces to tourists.

"Junk." Candy dismissed it all with barely a glance and swept me past the blandishments of the shopkeepers into the central market.

It was an enormous vaulted room with a balcony running around all four walls. My first impression, as always when I entered the market, was an intoxicating wash of sound and color and scent. Most of the ground floor was an explosive display of tropical fruits and flowers. I stood and stared, feasting my eyes on the luscious shapes and colors.

Candy didn't pause. "Come on, the basket sellers are on the far side." She pulled off her sunglasses and perched them on her head.

I dutifully tagged after her, feeling like a little girl on a shopping expedition with her mother. The sensory overload was beginning to make me dizzy. I wasn't used to the city yet. And my stomach definitely felt weird. Usually, as soon as I got off the plane, I was fine. Don't let me get sick now, I prayed.

The basket sellers had taken the two-story back wall of the market to display their wares. Soft round baskets with leather shoulder straps hung from floor to ceiling. They were straw with multicolored stripes.

"I'm going to load up on these," Candy whispered to me. We approached the counter. "I love those big ones." She pointed. "They can double as a beach bag, or you wear it for an everyday, sporty look."

A large woman ambled over to us. "Yes, Miss. Can I help you?" she asked in her soft African English. "Lovely baskets."

Under Candy's orchestration, a great number of baskets were pulled down, admired, compared, and haggled over. I was feeling decidedly queasy by this time. I tried to ignore the signals from my stomach. Finally, we shuffled away, loaded down with a nest of bags hanging from each shoulder.

We exited through the back wall and found ourselves in an alley of potters. Stall after stall displayed identical earthenware pots. Some were large enough to hold a child. They were a pale pink color, washed out by the strong sun. I was feeling sicker, but I didn't want to leave until I'd heard about Madge's girl talk with Candy. What could she have said to make Candy feel sorry for Eleanor? Could this have any bearing on the murders? A broken twig, a disturbed leaf. It could be nothing.

I hefted a small pot. "I wish these weren't so heavy," I exclaimed.

"Primitive art is the greatest. *Vogue* did a big spread on it this fall. I guess you must have missed it." Candy pulled down her sunglasses. Their big square lenses were shaded from dark to light like a Siamese cat. "These pots go great with my dress."

"I was thinking of a gift for Eleanor. She could ship it back," I commented, determined to work her back into the conversation. "Probably too earthy for her?"

"Oh, Eleanor is not as angelic as she makes everyone think." Candy picked up a pot and turned it over to look at the bottom. "These are awfully heavy."

"You've got to admit Eleanor has a special quality. She could walk through a mud hole and not get her shoes dirty." I reached for a round one from a stack taller than I was, trying to appear only half-interested in the conversation.

Candy tapped one of the large amphora. It gave out a dull ring. "You'd be surprised," she countered. "Did you know that Eleanor . . ."

The shopkeeper, a small dark-skinned man with pocked cheeks, came bustling over. "Very nice, very nice, Miss. Good price. You want big pot? Tell me what you want to pay. I give you good price."

I cursed inwardly. "Could you reach that top one down for me?" I asked, hoping to keep him busy. He was too short to reach it, and disappeared into his lean-to, promising to find another like it.

I turned to Candy with studied casualness. "What were you in the middle of saying?"

Candy looked blank. "I don't remember. Do you like this one?" She held out a lopsided bowl.

"I love that wavy line on the side. So you think Eleanor would like these? Should we buy her a little present? I feel bad that I made things harder for her."

"Oh, don't feel bad, Jazz. Nobody blames you." She put the bowl down next to its brothers. "I feel kinda bad myself cause I snitched on Eleanor, you know, to Boyce. I was so mad at him. Could you believe it, saying I look like a call girl because I wouldn't sleep with him." She cast an appreciative look down at herself, flexing her foot in its elegant wisp of a sandal so that her leg was stretched to its full, magnificent length. Her thought was obvious: Women as beautiful as she didn't need to be call girls. "He was such an unbelievable jerk. But then I felt guilty, you know, that he died disgusted with her." She picked up a wide-mouthed jar and frowned at it. "Everybody saying how much he'd adored her and everything." She put it down and showed her teeth in a little satisfied smile, despite her professed guilt.

Snitched what? I wanted to scream. My head started to pound and I fought a wave of dizziness. "Maybe he didn't say anything to Eleanor, so what's the difference."

"Are you kidding?" The little smile grew broader. "When I told him Eleanor had slept with her first boyfriend . . . and actually had to get an abortion in high school? I thought he was going to drop dead right then and there."

"Madge told you that?"

Candy nodded. "We were talking about what a creep Boyce was, then we started to talk about Eleanor, and Madge was saying Boyce wouldn't be so quick to call names if he knew the truth about her. We had a good laugh over it. You should have seen his face when I told him. I thought he was going to have a fit."

"I can imagine."

"It would have been bad enough, but knowing the man made it much worse."

"What do you mean, knowing the man?" I asked, holding my voice low and steady. I couldn't believe Candy had kept this to herself. If only she'd told Omondi right away; how could she be so blind, so irresponsible? I fought my temper, hoping nothing showed. I felt as still and alert as when I'd stood face-to-face with an uncertain rhino.

"Can you believe it?" she said. "It was someone in our group."

I was chillingly aware that I had no authority to make Candy say one word more than she wanted to. "Well, Boyce might still have gone to his grave without confronting Eleanor," I said, returning to a successful angle.

"Boyce? Don't make me laugh. He started calling, like right away, to check up on my story somehow. I think Madge saw him coming out of the phone booth all shook up. He said if it was true, he was going to divorce Eleanor and cite Cliff in court." Candy smiled with amusement.

"Cliff?"

"Yeah, so you can see why Boyce went berserk. His wife getting pregnant by a gay before he married her." Candy laughed. "I got my revenge on him all right!"

"But Candy! What was he going to do to Cliff?" I tried to sound naïve. My head whirled with the implications. I pictured Cliff wandering about the camp in the middle of the night. I again felt the sharp pain of his shoulder lurching into me, knocking me out off the van roof into the path of the buffalo. I pictured Cliff sitting calmly next to me on the plane that morning, saying he wanted me to suspect him. God, the man was cool.

Candy swung her baskets more comfortably over one hip. "Jesus, you should have heard him threaten Cliff." She giggled. "But I figured, what can he do to Cliff? He couldn't cite him in court." She looked into the stall for the pot seller. "I hate slow service. I have a lot to do before we leave." She turned back to me. "I mean, there's no law that your wife has to be a virgin when you marry her. If he spread it around his wife slept with a queer, he'd be making a fool of himself. There was nothing he could do except bluster."

"He could try and ruin Cliff's business," I pointed out. I

put a hand to my forehead. It was cold and sweaty, not a good sign.

"Oh. I didn't think of that," Candy said in an unconcerned voice. "Well, there's no use worrying about it now, since the guy's dead. He can't hurt anyone anymore."

Exactly, I thought. A wave of sorrow and dismay overtook me. Cliff. It mixed with the heat of the sun, the smell of dust and sweat, and the knot in my gut. He once told me he'd decided long ago to fall in love only with himself. And I'd thought him so amusing. I was revolted by the thought of our laughing talk on the plane this morning.

I remembered something else and my stomach tightened with fear. I swore that I would find the killer. Then I'd sat there with my eyes closed and my drink on the folding tray in front of me. How careless could I get? I reached out to steady myself on a waist-high chair. Cliff could easily have slipped something in my drink.

"Candy, why didn't you tell Omondi any of this?"

"Well, I did feel a little weird keeping it secret, but Madge would have murdered me if I'd blabbed."

"That was more important than finding a killer?"

Candy gave me a pitying look. "You've got a lot to learn about making it in the business world. Talking about Cliff and Eleanor could have done me a lot of harm." She ran her fingers lightly across the rim of a pot. "I figure this way, Cliff owes me one. Not that he did anything, but the police would have jumped on him. You know how they love to go after gays. I explained the setup to Cliff and he agreed there was no point mentioning it." Candy smiled. "The whole thing has worked out great for me. Cliff could do my career a lot of good."

As if from a great distance, I could hear her saying, "You look green. Are you all right?" A burst of stars obscured my vision, then turned to darkness. The last thing I knew, I was falling, pots were falling with me, and in the distance, Candy was screaming.

27

I swam up into consciousness. There was a bustle of noise and movement; even with my eyes closed, I could sense the commotion. I peered through my lashes. Candy was crouched over me, looking scared. Beyond her, I glimpsed a crowd. An enormous housewife elbowed aside an elderly man for a better view and exchanged a joke with him in Swahili.

Above the excited babble, I could hear the pot vendor's voice. "Eee-ee! You must pay. You break. You must pay. Verr-ry expensive pots."

I sat up slowly to survey the damage. Cracked pots lay like broken pumpkins all around me. It looked as if I'd taken out about a dozen jars.

"Twenty of my best pots!" the man cried. His face was twisted in mock agony.

"The price of this pottery seems to go up when it's broken," Candy retorted.

I put a hand to my forehead as another wave of nausea swept over me. "My head is feeling like a cracked pot. I'm afraid I'm going to be sick."

Candy turned on the stall keeper. "We must have a taxi immediately," she ordered. "My friend is very ill."

The man pushed his face up to hers. "You pay for my pots!"

To my relief, a stocky policeman pushed his way through

the crowd at that moment. He took in the situation at a glance. "My brother, calm yourself," he addressed the shopkeeper. "These ladies are not thieves, to break your pots and run."

He turned to the crowd. "You have seen it all. Now go about your business." A gaggle of children had appeared from out of nowhere and, ignoring the policeman, jostled for a view. "Go on." The children reluctantly backed off a few feet. He pointed to a nine-year-old boy in T-shirt and scruffy shorts. "You, go get a taxi on Kenyatta Boulevard," he barked. "Tell him a white lady has fallen down and needs to go to—" He turned to Candy.

"The Grand Palace," I filled in. I couldn't afford to go home and baby myself. Whatever Cliff had slipped me on the plane was obviously not fatal; I'd been as sick as this before from *turista*. I thought of calling Omondi but decided to put it off. I needed to corroborate Candy's story. If the police could ignore all the existing evidence, they would certainly ignore Candy's hearsay about a motive. There was no point in calling Omondi. He wouldn't be able to do anything; he'd feel guilty or badgered; I'd be angry. I had to present him with a case his superiors couldn't ignore.

"The Grand Palace Hotel. Do you have that?" the policeman asked. The little boy nodded with a bright grin, turned, and ran. "Very well, now the rest of you, move off."

By the time the taxi pulled up at the end of the alley, the policeman had arranged a reasonable payment for the broken pots, helped me to my feet, and lent a supporting arm to make sure I didn't crash over again. The three of us slowly made our way to the taxi.

I wasn't thinking straight, but I knew the first step was to check out what Candy had told me. I couldn't do that lying at home with a washcloth over my head. I didn't want to act on gossip, either. I hoped Madge was back from shopping. She wouldn't want to tell me Eleanor's secrets, but I'd find a way to convince her. I'd like to get that piece corroborated, though what she told Candy wasn't as crucial as knowing Boyce's reaction. I'd have to talk to Eleanor, too. That would be tricky. And then what? Confront Cliff with his motive?

He was far too cool to be bullied into a confession. My mind stalled at that point. I'd think of something when I got there.

Candy tried ineffectively to brush the dust off my skirt, laden as she was with her bulky straw bags. "You are a mess," she said, wrinkling her nose at the acrid smell of dust.

I sneezed. "It's hopeless, Candy. Forget it for now. I just hope we get to the hotel before I'm sick all over the place." My stomach was like a hard rock. "I must have *turista*."

"Not bad timing." Candy tried to cheer me up. "At least you left it for the last afternoon of the trip. You can nap for the rest of the day and at midnight we fly out. I don't think anyone's in the mood for a farewell dinner, anyway. Pretty lucky—we got the shopping done."

I put my hand to my brow. Should I strangle Candy now or later? Nothing to do this afternoon but nap? I had a murderer to catch between now and midnight. My head swam and I tottered on my feet.

"Not much farther," the policeman encouraged me. He tightened his grip on my arm.

I looked at Candy speculatively.

"You're looking funny," Candy said. "Would you like some water or something?"

I stopped staring. "No, it's just that you gave me a good idea, Candy."

I had the glimmerings of a plan. A farewell dinner. I'd invite Omondi, too. We needed to shock Cliff enough to break his self-control. What if Eleanor pretended to collapse. No, to have a heart attack. Omondi could declare her dead and we'd accuse Cliff of poisoning her. She was the one person who knew Boyce was going to ruin you, Omondi would thunder, and that's why you killed her. Cliff would cry out, Not Eleanor, I killed the others but not her.

I made a strange sound, half laugh, half groan. This is what I called a good idea? I'd have to do better than this. My stomach gave a lurch and I clutched it with both hands.

"Are you all right?"

"Just get me to the hotel."

I awoke in the late afternoon, too groggy at first to even wonder where I was. I was stretched out on the thick mattress and burrowed my head deeper into the pillow. The room was dim. Lines of light around the closed draperies told me it was still daylight.

"Are you awake?" Cliff's voice spoke above me.

I rolled over and looked at him in bleary confusion. "What are you doing here?" I mumbled. My mouth tasted terrible.

"It's my room." Cliff put a hand on my forehead. His hand felt cool, heavy, enormous. "Candy paged me in the bar and we brought you up here. Still feverish. You've been sleeping like a bear for hours."

I pulled myself into a sitting position and looked around me. The Grand Palace was always a world unto itself, but after a week in a tent, it seemed like another planet. The room looked huge and colorless. Heavy drapes muffled the light, closed windows and air-conditioning walled out the sounds of the outer world. The furniture seemed over-stuffed, as if designed to lure you in and never let go. People spent their whole lives in rooms like this, slowly turning heavy and gray themselves, unaware they were suffering from sensory deprivation. And they call this civilization.

I moved my legs under the covers. I was dressed; they'd only slipped off my shoes. I remembered fainting in the market. A few flashes of the trip back to the hotel: the cop's strong arm helping me to the taxi, a short bumpy ride, hanging on to a strap, a confused whirl of people in the lobby.

I sank back on my pillows. "God, I guess I blacked out. I don't even remember getting here. And there's something . . ." I brushed my hair away from my face with the back of my hand. Something important. I'd wanted to talk with Madge, or was it Eleanor? Well, it would come back. "I hope I didn't get sick in the taxi. Or the lobby." I grimaced at the thought.

Cliff had walked into the bathroom. "I can't hear you with the water running," he yelled back. He came into the room, "Now, what were you saying? You haven't shut up for a minute." He handed me the glass. "You've even been mumbling in your sleep."

"I don't think I have a fever, I'm just broiling with all these covers on." I flung back the wool blankets. "My stomach isn't funny anymore. I feel fine."

"Darling, stop right there. The hotel doctor came by and said you probably received a mild concussion when you fell out of the van. He left these pills for you to take." Cliff's open palm descended in front of my face with a fat pill on it. "They'll make you a little sleepy. He's going to come by again around six."

"Concussion! That's ridiculous. I don't have a concussion. He doesn't know what he's talking about!"

Cliff pushed the glass of water at me. He looked down sternly. "Doctor's orders. Now, let me see you take it, like a good little patient."

"Why are you bossing me around? Being sick doesn't make me a half-wit."

He loomed over me. "This case had been too much of a strain for you. I'm sure you'll be glad to see the last of us."

I bent my head back to meet his cool blue eyes, and my mind clicked into focus. It was like a fog bank peeling back to reveal an onrushing locomotive. I remembered what Candy had told me in the market. Cliff and Eleanor. Cliff and Boyce. Cliff next to me on the plane when I swore I'd catch the murderer. Whatever he'd slipped into my tonic hadn't been strong enough. He wouldn't make that mistake a second time. My heart started to pound so hard, I was afraid it would show. My hand trembled as I reached up dutifully and took the pill.

"You're looking pale and shaky. The best thing you can do is stay in bed."

I bent over the glass, palmed the pill, pretended to swallow it, and gulped down the water.

"That's a good girl." He walked over to the wall and pulled on the drawstring until the heavy drapes swung open. I tucked the pill out of sight under the mattress: Two could use the same idea. Sunlight streamed through gauzy curtains.

243

"Cliff, could I bother you for another glass of water?" I held out my empty glass to him. As soon as he disappeared into the bathroom, I jumped out of bed, picked up my shoes, and raced for the door. I didn't bother to close it behind me.

28

I RAN DOWN the hallway without stopping to put on my shoes, and made for the staircase. The thought of hanging around in front of the elevator was not appealing. As I plunged into the staircase, I could hear Cliff call my name angrily. A door slammed. What would he do now?

I whirled down four flights, the staircase widened, and there was the lobby below me. I paused on the last landing to let my breathing slow down. Tourists from every corner of the globe filled the high-ceilinged room with their voices. Couples in safari outfits and evening clothes lounged on the overstuffed sofas and crisscrossed the room. There were enough palm trees to start a small coconut plantation. A big fountain, tucked into the curve of the staircase, created a wall of background noise, reminding me of the stream by the camp. In the middle of the lobby, an outsize bouquet of wild banana blossoms stood on a central pedestal, like a flock of scarlet macaws about to take off.

"Jazz! Just who I wanted to see." Eleanor was at the foot of the stairs. She waved and started to climb up.

"Don't bother, I'll come down." I hurried down the last flight of stairs.

"Why are you carrying your shoes?"

I looked at the running shoes dangling from my hand. "Let me put them on," I said, ignoring the question. I sat down on the last step, slipped them on, and tied the laces.

"I wanted to talk to you, too." I glanced around the crowded lobby. "It would be nice to be somewhere quiet, where we won't be interrupted." Or found.

"You wanted to talk to me?" She looked around the crowded lobby. "How about my room? We can talk while I pack. I've amassed so many extra bundles, I don't know how I'll fit them all in."

"Sure, that's fine."

We walked over to the bank of elevators with their brass and mahogany doors. One was standing open and empty and we walked right in. "What floor?"

"I'm on three."

I pressed the button and the doors closed with a smooth whoosh.

"So you went out, after all," I commented.

"Oh, I didn't go far." She smiled thinly.

Now that I could see Eleanor at close hand, I noticed how tense she seemed. She wore a navy shirtwaist; maybe navy was not her color. Her skin looked unhealthy, sallow. She was holding herself very stiffly. Her free hand kept fluttering up to the pearls around her neck. There was also a faint hint of whiskey in the air.

"I saw Candy," Eleanor said. "She told me you fainted in the market, in the middle of buying me a present. I was on my way up to see how you were. I feel so badly you stayed out in that heat for my sake. You really shouldn't have. Everyone's been so kind."

The elevator stopped at three and Eleanor led me to her room. She fumbled at the lock.

"Please, have a seat." She gestured toward the armchair arranged on each side of a low cocktail table. There was a bottle of scotch, some soda, an ice bucket, and one used glass on the table. She walked over to the dresser and checked herself in the mirror. "I look ghastly." She pulled at a wayward strand of her lacquered hair. "Can I offer you a drink?"

"No thanks, I think I better not." I put a hand to my stomach. "I'm feeling better, but I don't want to tempt fate."

There was a half-packed suitcase on the bed, with the lid

up and clothes scattered about. "You don't mind if I pack while we talk, do you?" she asked.

"No, go right ahead." I paused, wondering how to begin.

Eleanor went to the closet and came back with a dress on a hanger. She tossed the hanger on the floor and carefully arranged the dress on the stack already in the case, then went to fetch another one. "I always bring too much. I didn't wear half these dresses." She fetched her pocketbook and transferred a small brown paper parcel to the suitcase. "One last present for Wendy. I couldn't resist."

There was a loud knock on the door. We both started nervously.

"Who could that be?" Eleanor sounded annoyed.

"Listen, if it's Cliff, do me a favor and say you haven't seen me."

Eleanor cast me a questioning look.

"I'll explain later."

She stood behind the door and opened it a crack. "Hello, Cliff."

I knew it. I was safe with Eleanor, but I couldn't help feeling scared, and I didn't want to see him. Things were speeding up now. If I could get Eleanor to open up—if she knew anything—then I'd call Omondi. He might be willing to help me, off the record.

I couldn't hear what Cliff said.

"Sorry, I'm not dressed," Eleanor said through the crack. "I just stepped out of the shower. . . . Oh, that's okay. . . . No, I haven't seen her. . . . How strange. Do you think it's the concussion? Maybe she went home. Wait a little while and try her apartment. . . . Who'll help us to the airport, then?"

She got rid of him, locked the door, and returned to her packing. "What was that all about?" she asked.

"The explanation is kind of roundabout. I hardly know how to say this." I poured myself a glass of soda, then sat playing with it. "I get the feeling you're happy with the way things have been left dangling."

Eleanor bent over the suitcase and all I could see was the

top of her stiff blond hair over the upright lid. "I'd hardly use the word happy," she said.

"Sorry, poor word choice. I meant that you don't mind the investigation being called off."

"No, I don't, dear. Do you think you could pour me a drink, too?"

"Sorry." She was even harder to approach than I'd expected. I sloshed a small amount of scotch into a glass, filled it with ice to make it look like more, and topped it up with soda.

She took a long gulp and returned to the bed, resting the drink on the night table and going back to packing. "You probably think I'm terrible."

"No, I don't. I can understand, but I think you're wrong. It seems easier to sweep it all under the rug." How undiplomatic could I get? Had I forgotten completely how to deal with people? I searched for the right words. "I can see why you want to stop the tragedy right here and now. Trying to find out who did it seems like you're prolonging the agony. And you ask yourself, For what?"

Eleanor fetched a long dress from the closet and folded it neatly on top of the others.

"Maybe you think you know who did it, and you don't want that person to be caught . . . you don't want it all to come out," I continued.

That got her attention. She looked up sharply. "What do you mean?"

"Candy told me what she did."

Eleanor took another gulp from her drink and replaced it carefully. "I don't know what you're talking about."

She sounded phony as hell. She was lying. This was my first break: Boyce did confront her. I hoped I could get her to confirm that he'd threatened Cliff. I'd been so afraid we'd have only Candy's word for it.

Eleanor picked up a pair of shoes, put them in a plastic bag, and tucked them in the side of the case. I waited for her to speak but she didn't say anything. Her hands moved swiftly, almost angrily, arranging clothes in the suitcase.

I spoke rapidly. "Maybe you don't realize what got Boyce started; it seems Madge told Candy about all that ancient history between you and Cliff, thinking it would make Candy feel better, you know, after Boyce called her a slut. I can hardly believe Madge'd be so stupid."

"Madge always hated Boyce."

I nodded to myself. Yes, Madge must have gotten her own satisfying revenge from telling tales that made Boyce look small.

The moment had arrived for me to take the plunge. "Anyway, Candy says Boyce went crazy and threatened to drag you and Cliff into court. Is that true?"

"What if it is?" Eleanor's voice went up. "What business is it of yours, Jazz? Can't you keep your nose out of this?"

"No, I'm sorry, I can't." I looked down into my drink and watched the bubbles come to the surface and disappear in tiny explosions. "I can't let it drop. I'm not setting myself up as the big arbiter of justice. Whoever it was killed Lynn, too, and I can't let that go."

"Well, I'm afraid you're going to have to." Eleanor's voice went hard and I looked up.

Right into the nose of a dainty little handgun.

29

A RED, ROARING, rushing pounding of adrenaline surged through my body. Above the din in my veins, my mind was calm. I was mesmerized by the gun, couldn't take my eyes off it. So that's what a real gun looked like. How could people in robberies be fooled by toy guns? No one would mistake this gun for a toy. It was a serious tool made of thick gleaming steel. Maybe those people didn't get to see the gun this close.

"How do you like my gift for Wendy?" Eleanor's voice was new, sharp-edged and cold. "I was afraid it would be hard to buy a gun in Nairobi, but the service in this hotel is marvelous. It's a simple question of whom to bribe."

I put my drink down on the table. My coordination was off and the glass clinked loudly against the top.

"Put your hands up."

I obeyed, despite a sense of unreality. Had I wandered into a late-night movie? I'd missed a key scene. What was going on? Was she trying to protect Cliff? They couldn't still be involved. Nothing made sense. Although my mind felt detached and calm, the roaring in my veins made it hard to think straight. Or maybe I was scared to admit the facts in front of me. I lifted my eyes from the gun to Eleanor's face. A mask of hate and fear distorted her features into something monstrous. Or mad. In that moment, I recognized the truth. Eleanor was the killer. Not Cliff. Eleanor. A bolt of terror stabbed through my icy detachment, but I barricaded myself against it. Don't panic: The words repeated in my brain, over and over, in time to the pounding of my heart.

I forced myself to speak calmly, firmly. My tongue felt swollen in a mouth gone totally dry. "What are you doing? Put that gun away before it goes off by mistake."

"I tried to talk you out of it, but you wouldn't listen."

She was convincing herself she had to kill me. Unfortunately, there was a certain crazy logic in her decision. If not for me trying to reopen the case, she'd be home free. She'd almost gotten away with two murders. But how did she think she could get away with killing me? She wasn't thinking beyond the immediate release from my breath hot on her trail. I'd been only a step behind her.

"I'm listening!" I shouted. "We're still talking!"

I eyed the distance between us. The problem was the furniture. I sat, blocked by the cocktail table. Eleanor stood, protected by the bed. There was no way I could jump her.

"Oh, no we're not, young lady. The discussion session is over." She smiled at her little joke. A terrible smile, so stiff her lips could barely pull back over her teeth. The smile of a hyena before it bites into its victim's genitals.

In an instant, Eleanor was going to kill me.

"You killed Boyce to keep that old scandal quiet," I said.

"That's wicked nonsense!" Eleanor's voice was shrill. The gun wobbled in her hand, then steadied. It was pointed at my stomach. "I couldn't care less about scandal. I did it to protect my children."

"Your children? Do you think they want a murderess as a mother?" As long as we talked, I was still alive. Should I try to jump her, furniture blockade and all? I didn't want to get shot in the stomach. She'd probably miss. What if she didn't, at this close range? I had to get us out of the room.

"They'll never know. You're the only one who cares what happened. I heard you talking to that police sergeant outside my room. You said you wouldn't give up. I'm going to make you give up, with a bullet."

Again, the terrible smile. She was enjoying herself.

251

"You won't be able to get away with this. Killing me in cold blood will make everything worse."

"I killed him in a perfectly natural way, so that the children would never know," she spoke as if to herself. "And now you're going to tell them." She raised the gun.

"Go ahead!"

That caught her attention.

"Shoot me and you'll be caught immediately. The kids will find out everything."

Eleanor's eyes shifted right and left. "I'll have to take you outside. That's much better. There's that big park behind the hotel that you told us was full of robbers. Nobody goes there." Her hand fluttered up incongruously and fingered her pearls. "I've got to get you out of here."

I felt a short burst of triumph. I'd delayed her, and we would have to go through the crowded hotel and the streets. There should be a chance to break free. But what if I couldn't? I had a sinking feeling in my guts. Once she had me alone behind some bush, there'd be no help, no one to break in the door and rush me to the hospital. I'd be finished. There was only one way: I had to escape before we reached the park.

"Get up and turn around."

I slowly got to my feet and faced the wall. The wallpaper was pale gray with a woven texture. A conventional painting in a gilt frame showed Mt. Kilimanjaro, pink with dawn—or was it sunset?—while an elephant raised its trunk in the foreground. Was this my last view of the mountain?

"Put your hands behind your back. I'm going to come over and tie your hands. If you try to grab the gun, I'll shoot you dead."

I thought of Lynn, lying in her own blood. Eleanor had killed two people already. I put my wrists together. As long as my legs were free, I had a chance. She looped a cloth belt around my wrists and tied it tightly, pinching my skin. It was awkward but effective. Then she draped her raincoat over my shoulders.

"Turn around. That doesn't look too bad at all. No one would know. And now for me." She draped a blue cardigan over her gun hand. "Sweet little sweater, isn't it?" She stepped back. "Open the door and walk slowly into the hall. Don't forget I'm right behind you. Believe me, I'll shoot to kill."

I walked to the door and turned. "You'll have to live with this for the rest of your life." It sounded like a line from a grade-B movie. Eleanor wasn't impressed, either.

"You think that scares me? I've already lived with worse. I don't mean Lynn or Boyce, either. I killed my only son. Robert, my first child."

"You mean your abortion? In high school?"

"Madge doesn't know everything. Even Cliff didn't know. I never had an abortion. Abortion is murder."

The incongruity didn't seem to strike Eleanor. I let it pass. This wasn't the time to launch into a prochoice speech.

"So you had the baby?"

"Yes, I had the baby." Eleanor's eyes went dark. "Robert. I held him in my arms. You don't have children, do you?" She stared at me with hatred, as if not having children was a capital offense. "Cliff had offered to marry me, but my parents thought I could do better. They told the school I was depressed and sent me off to a "health spa" to hide my big belly. Sure, I got depressed. They made me give Robert away."

"That's very sad." I wondered if there was a way to reach her. She seemed beyond reason, but the more I understood her, the better my chances were of getting out alive. "But giving a baby up for adoption isn't murder."

"Five years later, after I married Boyce and we had Margaret, I tried to find him. It was illegal, but with money you can do anything. I hired a private investigator."

"And you found him?"

"The people who adopted him were a lovely middle-class couple. Except the father was a drunk. They think he fell asleep with a cigarette, watching TV." Her voice was mechanical. "The house burned down. All they found were charred bones."

"Awful." The funny thing is, I really meant it.

253

"My son burned to death. I had to live with that and pretend nothing was wrong; it almost killed me. If only I hadn't given him away." She shrugged. "I feel bad about Boyce, but I had to do it. He was going to take Wendy from me."

"He couldn't have done that."

Eleanor gave a dry mirthless laugh. "You didn't really know Boyce. He got whatever he wanted. When Candy told him about my first baby, all of a sudden I was shoddy goods. He only wanted the best. That was one of his little sayings. He was going to divorce me and take the children." She looked fiercely at me. "I'd sworn I would never give up a child of mine again. Never. That's why you have to go."

"And what about Lynn? She didn't do anything to you."

She flushed with anger. "It's all Boyce's fault. Why did he have to drop his pills in the van? It was all so perfect."

"You took Candy's diet pills and topped off his pillbox with them, was that it?"

Eleanor smirked.

Whether I got out of this alive or not, I wanted to know the whole story. It had become my story too, now. I ignored the pain in my bound wrists. "You planned to remove the diet pills from his pillbox when you went to sit with the body . . . was that your plan? You expected to find the pills in his pocket, where he usually kept them."

"Yes." Eleanor blinked her pale blue eyes. "I had it all planned out. No one would have ever known. Then Lynn picked up his pillbox. I was afraid she'd look inside and realize something was wrong."

"So she had to go, too."

"Luckily, I heard Lynn saying she had them when we were standing around the campfire. I got Boyce's pillbox from her pants that night and hid it with the spear. When the police arrived, I still had Candy's pillbox. I needed to get rid of it quickly, so I stuck it in Madge's purse. She didn't even notice it." Eleanor smiled stiffly. "It all worked out beautifully, and this will too."

Beautifully? Suddenly, any trace of fear was gone. I was filled with anger. How dare she? How dare she be so complacent about murdering Lynn? How dare she threaten my life? Who did she think she was, to take human life? The words burst out of me before I knew what I was saying. "May you burn in hell forever, you lousy bitch."

Another one of her terrible smiles. "That's enough. Open the door. Slowly. And no funny business. Remember I have the gun trained on your spine."

I turned to do her bidding, fighting to get control of my anger. I had to stay calm enough to think. One small error of judgment and I'd be dead. "I can't open it without my hands."

"Step back, that's right, in the middle of the room where I can see you."

I looked around for a possible weapon, something, anything I could use. The bed was strewn with clothes, the suitcase half-packed. The room key sat on the dresser. It was ridiculous: What could I do, take a nightgown in my teeth and use it as a shield?

She opened the door while keeping the gun trained on me Then she stepped out into the corridor. "Come on."

I joined her in the hall. She stayed out of reach, not trusting me, even with my hands tied. My mind clicked back into its icy calm and I got an idea. I guessed Eleanor was far too bourgeois to leave the door open, and I was right. She reached to pull it shut with her eyes on me.

"Do you have the keys?" I asked in an everyday tone of voice.

Her eyes flickered automatically toward the inside of the room. That moment of inattention was my chance and I went for it. I crouched and ran for the head of the stairs, only a few yards down the hall. There was an explosion of sound. She'd fired at me! I burst forward, rounded the corner, and flung myself down the stairs.

A bit too precipitously. With my hands tied behind me, my balance was off. I lost my footing, slipped, and missed a stair. The raincoat fell off my shoulders. I landed on it, tangled my feet, and began a free-fall. Without my arms, there was no way for me to grab hold, to protect myself. The

255

best I could do was curl my shoulder and try not to land on my head. I felt like I was being kicked on every part of my body. I figured I'd stop when I hit the landing, but once again, I was wrong. I'd picked up so much momentum, I kept going.

It probably saved my life. It's hard to shoot a human landslide. I bounced off the wall, slammed into the mahogany balustrade, and down the next flight of stairs. I landed in an awkward heap at the bottom, with one leg curled under me. I fought my way up to my feet. My left leg immediately buckled and I fell heavily on my side. I got to my knees.

"Stand up and then hold it, or I'll kill you. I mean it." Eleanor stood at the landing above me, pointing her little blue cardigan at me.

I put all my weight on my good leg and managed to stand. There was the sound of running footsteps on the floor above me.

"Is everything all right?" A man's voice sounded alarmed. He could see Eleanor on the middle landing, but not me. "Was that a shot?"

"I thought that was a shot!" Eleanor glanced up at the man, then looked down at me as she answered. She braced her gun arm, pretending to cup her elbow. "It sounded so close."

"You didn't see anyone?"

"Not a soul. How scary! I think it came from upstairs. There's a penthouse on the roof."

"What's that raincoat doing on the stairs?"

I was tempted to call out but thought better of it. I could see the gun peeping out at me below the folds of baby-blue Orlon. I didn't want to find out if she'd shoot me in front of a witness. She seemed desperate enough to shoot the man, as well.

"Oh," Eleanor said, "that must have slipped from my shoulders." She picked up the raincoat, one eye on me through the banister. So I balanced on one leg, listening as Eleanor told the man she'd call security, as his footsteps moved off down the hall.

256

Eleanor walked down the stairs and draped the coat over my tied arms again. "Get going. As you can see, I'm quite prepared to shoot you, so don't think of talking to anyone. If I see your mouth open, I'll pull the trigger."

My mouth felt too dry to ever open again, so I merely nodded.

"You heard me. Move."

I'd read in psychology books that masochists are thinly disguised sadists. All those years of sweetness and submission peeled away before my eyes as Eleanor grew into her new role as tyrant, savoring the power of life and death over me. I moved.

Three flights of stairs. I had no choice but to walk on my injured ankle. The pain was intense; I clenched my jaw to keep from crying out. Knowing the pain was coming, I could slowly shift onto that foot. At least it didn't buckle beneath me again. I hoped for a chance to trip Eleanor, but she stayed a few stairs above me and the chance never came.

The sound of people in the lobby grew louder. We turned onto a broad landing and there was the enormous room below us. Giant chandeliers glittered above the forest of dark palms. Women's evening dresses, red, royal blue, and emerald green, struck brilliant notes among the khaki of safari outfits. Someone must have told a funny joke, because a small group of people burst into guffaws of laughter. I scouted vainly for an ally, for anything I could turn to an advantage.

The fountain was directly below us, tucked into the curved sweep of the final flight of stairs, and the roar of its artificial waterfall reminded me poignantly of my beloved stream in the Serengeti. I could see silvery coins glimmering in its depths. I took a closer look as another crazy idea began to form in my mind. The fountain's pool looked to be four or five feet deep.

I moved toward the stairs.

"No." Eleanor sharply reined me in. "It's too crowded. There must be a back stair. Keep going down the hall."

I remembered the back stair. I visualized the route we would take: down the narrow uncarpeted cement staircase,

257

out into the ill-lit parking lot, and directly into the park across the street. At this hour, the park would be deserted.

I cast one last look over the lobby, hoping for I knew not what, when a familiar form came through the revolving doors and walked over toward the bar with long relaxed strides. Striker. I'd forgotten our plan to meet here before dinner. My heart began to pound so hard, my whole body shook.

"Move."

I measured the height of the banister. Could I get over it with no arms and one good leg? I'd have to fall over, head-first. The coins gleamed at the bottom of the pool. I could end up a paraplegic if this went wrong.

"You'd better believe me. I'll shoot you right here and now if you don't get going." Eleanor's voice was unrecognizable. A gloating megalomania distorted it into a monstrous imitation of Boyce's voice.

I gave a mighty bound with my one strong leg and threw myself over the banister headfirst. There were screams and a gunshot. I curled myself into a cannonball as I hurtled downward. God bless the architect who designed this hotel on a grand scale: The pool stretched below me like a safety net. I hit the water with a tremendous splash and went straight to the bottom. I struck hard enough to hurt, but the water cushioned me and nothing broke. I started to stand and felt a blow to my shoulder that knocked me back into the water. The lobby was in chaos.

Above the pandemonium, I heard Striker's voice calling out my name in an indescribable yell that seemed to thunder off the walls. A trumpeting bull elephant had nothing on him.

I dove and did the frog kick toward the waterfall. When I surfaced for breath, Striker had reached the foot of the stairs and started up them three at a time. He didn't look at me; his eyes were focused on Eleanor; he yelled something at her I couldn't catch. If she shot him, I didn't want to live.

Eleanor had only one idea. She ignored Striker as she bent over the railing, pointed the gun straight down at my face, and pulled the trigger. Her hand jerked and the shot hit the water behind me.

I was fast running out of blood and strength. Dark clouds spread out from my shoulder into the clear water. I gulped air and flattened myself against the marble back of the waterfall, praying I'd be less visible among the foam of the falls. It was a bad mistake. The waterfall pounded onto my wounded shoulder like a club. I blacked out for a second but managed to thrust myself away, back into the center of the pool, an easier target.

I looked up in time to see Striker reach the landing, in time to see Eleanor put the gun into her mouth. I closed my eyes but there was no way to block out the thunderclap of a single shot.

30

I LAY BACK against the pillows, looked at the familiar prints of van Eyck and Rembrandt on the walls, and tried to ignore the throbbing in my shoulder. It was only a flesh wound, the doctor had cheerfully told me. I never wanted to find out what bullet-smashed bone felt like. I was too weak to do more than lie in bed and look in front of me.

It was peaceful in the bedroom. Outside, children laughed and called, busy with some game. From the row of cottages behind the apartment building came the bleat of a goat and the smell of wood smoke. There was a mouth-watering aroma of chicken roasting on a fire.

I could hear people moving about in my kitchen: running water, the low rumble of Striker's laughter, the higher giggle of my neighbor Khady Camera, clattering dishes, the sound of a wooden spoon knocking the sides of a bowl. Khady was teaching Striker how to make Senegalese peanut stew.

Khady poked her head through the doorway to tell me Ibrahima and Molezzi had come by while I was asleep and would return later. Her face was sculptural, all smooth planes and triangles, with high cheekbones, narrow chin, and almond eyes. Even her blue-black skin reminded me of an ebony mask. "Want some tea?" she added.

I smiled at her. "Thanks, I'm fine for now. When are you going to take a rest? Moussa must be wondering if you've left him."

Khady laughed. "Moussa is at the soccer match. Don't worry about him. Peanut stew is his favorite, so he will be very happy." She pointed a long index finger at me. "I can see you want to get rid of me and have Striker for yourself. You are right to worry." She grinned. "If you don't watch out, I will steal him from you and have two husbands."

I tried to tell her how much I appreciated her help, but she laughed off my thanks with typical earthy graciousness. "What's mine is yours. Except for Moussa."

Khady took a joking farewell of Striker, and I could hear the door close behind her. Striker came into the bedroom.

"Sleeping Beauty awakes."

"Now don't start getting princely ideas."

He smiled. "Sorry, my mistake. The wicked witch awakes."

I smiled back. "That's more like it. At least witches fly."

"I'm not sure I would call it flying, but you did take a flying leap."

"You know, it was the sight of you coming through the revolving door that gave me the courage to jump."

Striker perched on the edge of the bed, lifted my good hand, and kissed my fingers one by one. "I often have that effect on women." His lips caressed my wrist.

I laid my head back on the pillow, the better to enjoy what he was doing. "I had the most wonderful dream when they gave me the anesthetic."

"Tell me," he murmured into the curve of my neck.

"I dreamt I was flying on the back of an eagle. We soared over the Serengeti. It was dawn, and the sun lay in long shafts of light over the grass."

Striker's lips moved over my face, a fluttering of butter-flies, until he came to my lips, and the softness gave way to fierceness. It was as amazing as our first kiss, a soaring, piercing, sweet swirl of emotion and lust.

Suddenly I shrieked.

Striker jumped back. "Your arm! Did I hurt you? I was trying not to touch it."

"Actually, you got my foot. Right shoulder, left foot. I'm completely booby trapped."

"So what's new? I'll just work my way around the sore parts."

We talked, and kissed, and talked. We dreamt up future trips and projects. We came up with a great idea for a special-interest tour that would visit scientists in the field and give people a more in-depth look at animal behavior. And a cross-cultural tour, visiting villages and farms, a chance to talk with regular Kenyans. Cliff would be back next month with Candy and the film crew. We hatched a plot to interest him in also doing some public-service commercials to explain how elephants create the African bush habitat by their vora-cious appetite for trees. If only people understood that once the elephants are wiped out by ivory poaching, we'll lose all the plains animals—"the works" as Al would say—I was sure the public outcry would reach around the globe.

I got so excited, I wanted to jump out of bed and start writing the proposals, but Striker restrained me. He set off for the market, leaving me weak and frustrated in bed. I comforted myself with the thought that my long emotional convalescence seemed to be over. Physical healing is com-paratively fast.

A while later, there was a sound of two African voices from my living room: Khady and a man. Not Ibrahima. It was Omondi.

"Hello," I called.

Khady came in first. "Striker not back yet? Here's some fresh orange juice Astou made for you." Astou was her teen-aged daughter, a giggling, lively girl with an unending stream of male visitors.

"That's so sweet of her." I took the heavy glass and gulped at it gratefully. "This is wonderful."

"Guess who's here? The inspector. Can he come in?"

"Sure. Hand me that robe, would you?" I sat up a little higher in bed and Khady helped me slip one arm into the cotton robe and drape the other side over my sling. "I won-dered if he would visit."

Omondi bounded into the room with his quick steps, shaking his head and smiling broadly. "Ah, my dear. You doubted if I would come to see you?" He held his hands out, palms up. "Have you forgotten? We agreed to be friends." He glanced back at the living room, where Khady had discreetly retired. "I will remember always."

"Me, too." I smiled at him.

"I am relieved you are smiling. You're not terribly angry with me for dropping the case? I cannot tell you what I felt when I heard you'd been shot. It was as if I myself had received a bullet." He put a hand over his heart. "I rushed immediately to the hospital. I was there when they wheeled you out of the operating room."

"You were? I guess I was too drugged to know what was going on."

Omondi pulled over the wooden chair from the corner so he could sit right by me. He picked up my hand in his dark elegant one.

I looked at him seriously. "Of course I was mad when the investigation was closed, but not at you. I knew you were pretty frustrated yourself."

Omondi closed his eyes and nodded. He looked at me with his sharp eyes. "I feared you wouldn't let it drop."

"Do you know who squelched the case? How did Eleanor manage to bribe somebody?"

"It wasn't her. Al Hart fixed it. He feels bad about it now, of course. He told me he was worried he'd be accused of the murder, after we found the telexes about Wild and Free, but mostly he was in a big hurry to get home and rescue his new company. He used some business contacts; it was all done from high up, as personal favors. Even the police commissioner could do nothing. Tourism is crucial to our survival— but let's not get into that. Al sees now that it was dangerous to put business ahead of a murder investigation. Tell me, how did you uncover Eleanor?"

I smiled crookedly and shook my head. "When she pulled out a gun and said she was going to kill me, I figured it had to be her."

263

"You do not mean it?"

"I'm afraid so. The one thing I did right was latch on to Candy."

"After the Harts," he teased.

I nodded. "I'll admit I thought it was them, until you explored the financial motive. Then I went back to your advice, not to get stuck on the first solution that comes to mind."

"I'm glad to see you listen to me."

"When I asked myself, Why now? Why was Boyce killed now? My mind kept going back to the big scene when Boyce fired Candy. It was the only unusual event on the trip."

Omondi leaned forward. "How was Candy the missing piece?"

I told him the whole tragic story of Eleanor and Cliff's baby, and how Candy used Madge's gossip to revenge herself on Boyce—with fatal consequences.

Omondi leaned back and tapped his fingers together rapidly. "Ah, yes. I see how it falls into place. So it was Eleanor who put the meat in her own tent, unzipped the front, and pretended to hear an intruder. How did you get Candy to tell you all this?"

"Something she said to Madge pointed me in the right direction. The tricky part was coaxing Candy to talk." I gave a short laugh. "Except I jumped to the wrong conclusion: that it was Cliff. I thought he'd pushed me out of the van on our last game run—I'll have to tell you about that sometime—and even that he'd slipped something into my drink on the plane that was making me sick."

"That's why detectives always work in pairs. It is too easy to let your imagination run wild when you can't talk it over with someone."

"Speaking of talking things over . . . I want to thank you for our talk, that last night. You know, about life being long, and trusting my heart?"

"You and Striker?"

I nodded.

"When I heard he was the first one to reach you and Eleanor, I guessed." Omondi's eyes sparkled with pleasure. "I am a very wise cupid, am I not? My grandfather was a great sorcerer. Of good magic only. He was famous for his love potions. He became very wealthy."

"Is he still alive?"

"No." Omondi shook his head. "I'm afraid he was his own best customer. Eight wives." He grinned. "He died happy." Omondi pushed back the chair and got to his feet. "Well, my dear, I'm very, very happy to see you looking so well."

"Yes, except for feeling like a herd of wildebeest ran over me, I'm in great shape."

Omondi turned at the door. "By the way, we'll need an official deposition from you. Will you be fit enough by tomorrow? I could come by with a stenographer."

"Of course, that's fine." I watched Omondi leave, smiling ruefully to myself, but I long ago gave up the fantasy you can have everything. My eyelids grew heavy and I slipped sideways into sleep.

When I awoke, my arm was throbbing, the sun was across my feet, and the prints were in shadow. A blue bowl holding a pyramid of oranges sat on my nightstand.

I turned. Striker was sitting by my bed, reading a book. He'd put Billie Holiday on the record player. Her joyful and melancholy voice flowed over us, filling the room with its complex beauty.

Striker put aside his book. "That was a good long sleep. Anything I can bring you?"

I took his hand and pulled him in for a kiss.